CEDARWOOD CABIN

JADE WILKES

CONTENTS

Editor: Hannah G. Scheffer-Wentz, English Proper Editing Services
Formatting & Cover Design: Disturbed Valkyrie Designs

CEDARWOOD CABIN

AUTHOR'S NOTE

Please review all the content/trigger warnings on my website before reading this book. This book delves into the theme of Stockholm syndrome and takes a dark turn. It is a standalone book with no cliffhanger. Please note that if you are uncomfortable with dub-con, this book may not be suitable for you. Your mental well-being is important.

The paperback/hardback both feature an extra bonus chapter.

Content Warnings: Please visit www.jadewilkesauthor.com/contentwarning for the complete list of 65+ content warnings.

PLAYLIST

Life That Never Happened - Cameron Eve, Curt Phfeiffer
Man! I Feel Like A Women - Shania Twain
Black Velvet - Alannah Myles
All These Lies - Cameron Eve, Billy Douglas
The Living Years - Mike + The Mechanics
Stop And Stare - OneRepublic
Regulate - Warren G, Nate Dogg
Gimmie More - Britney Spears
I Feel Like I'm Drowning - Two Feet
Lord Give Me A Sign - DMX
Dreams - Fleetwood Mac
Everywhere - Fleetwood Mac
Jigga What / Faint - JAY-Z, Linkin Park
Left Outside Alone - Anastacia
Bells In Santa Fe - Halsey
Nazareath - Sleep Token

Picture lockdown...Imagine being stuck in a cabin with two biker men for three weeks. The possibilities are endless.

ONE

FLORA

The curtains are open just a fraction to let enough light shine in. I sweat as I lay in bed, my body feeling clammy against the sheets. I slowly raise my head from my pillow and take a deep breath. Images of my mother flash in my head and my heart starts thumping wildly. I picture her weak body, the sound of the medical machines, and the smell of the antiseptic-filled hospital. I try not to panic, but the images refuse to leave my mind. I grip the bedcover frantically, trying to calm myself down. I look around the room at the light purple walls with photographs of my mother and father, the bedside table with clutter, and my makeup desk with hardly any makeup displayed.

It was just a nightmare. Calm down.

I don't want a panic attack, so I try to calm myself down by continuing to breathe deeply.

The mirror on the closet door catches my attention. I stare at myself; my long, dark, wavy hair tangled from sleep. The freckles across my face stand out against my pale skin. My eyes always manage to catch people's attention. They are different colors: one deep green and the other rich blue. I see a younger version of my mother looking back at me and I feel a lump form in my stomach.

I know it's painful for my father to be around me. I must constantly remind him of my mother, of what he lost: his greatest love. I know he tries to mask it with a brave smile.

I hear noises coming from the kitchen. My father is up, probably sipping his morning coffee—a ritual he never skips.

I reach over to the nightstand and grab my phone, the mattress making a creaking noise under my weight. I unlock the screen to see no notifications, but I'm not surprised. My social life has been non-existent since I moved from England to Washington with my father four months ago.

Not like it was bustling before—I lived a pretty secluded life. My mother homeschooled me and my only friend was the girl who lived next door, Holland. Since moving, we have drifted apart and hardly ever contacted each other anymore.

My only living family members are my father and auntie, who lives in England. My auntie likes to send letters and care packages, but she feels more like a distant relative than a close family member.

I swipe through my phone and check the local news. The headlines are boring reports of Covid cases rising, a new bakery opening, and a piece about local bikers wreaking havoc. I let out a sigh as nothing interests me, placing my phone back down on the side table. A sense of loneliness washes over me as I get out of bed with another deep breath, rubbing my eyes before making my way to the door. The floorboards creak underneath me as I descend the stairs.

Halfway down, I look over the stairs banister and see my father standing in the kitchen, pouring himself a cup of coffee.

"Morning," I hear him greet. I watch him as he places a bowl on the table. I continue down the stairs, smelling freshly brewed coffee.

My father glances up at me. “Breakfast,” he announces.

His smile has always been a comfort for me. I sit down at the table and look into the bowl.

“Porridge...Oh, wait. Over here, it's called oatmeal.” My father corrects himself.

I rub my eyes, pick up the spoon, and dig in.

“How did you sleep?” he asks.

“Had another nightmare, so not great.”

We eat in silence for a few moments, the only sound between us is the spoons against the bowls.

“I think it’s best you tell your therapist about the recurring dreams,” he suggests, resting one of his hands on the table.

“I will...” I reply, looking down at the oatmeal.

My father swallows a mouthful of oatmeal, making a gulp sound.

“When is your next appointment?”

“It’s actually later today.”

Dread fills me. I’ve been having therapy since the death of my mother. My therapist is a stern, older British lady. After moving from England, my father insisted I continue my therapy with her, so now we have our sessions over video call.

My father reaches over the table and places his hand over mine. “It’s tough, Flora. I know. However, you’ve made good progress.”

I appreciate his support and give him a nod. I glance at the clock, seeing how many hours I have left before my appointment.

“I’m trying.”

I give him a reluctant smile, trying to ease any concerns he has.

“Just one step at a time,” he says softly, squeezing my hand.

We finish our breakfast in awkward silence. My father has always shown me support—I can never fault him for that.

I look at him as he eats his oatmeal. After losing my mother, you can tell the last four years have taken a toll on him. His dark brown hair and beard are now streaked with gray. Wrinkles bunch at the side of his eyes.

I have one of his eye coloring and one of my mother's. My blue eye is from him and the green eye is from her. People used to joke about how I stole one of their eyes. I used to see the comments as light-hearted, but now they feel like a reminder of how everything has changed.

As if reading my mind, he mumbles, “You look so much like her.”

I give him an awkward smile, not knowing how to respond.

Before standing up from the table, he pats my hand. “We’re in this together, remember?”

He starts clearing the table, picking up the bowls and cups.

“You got anything planned for today?” he queries.

My mind wanders to painting. “I’m just gonna do some painting, then I have my appointment later.”

My father nods. “Okay. Are you looking forward to our hike tomorrow?”

A smile spreads across my face. “Yeah, I am,” I say with more joy.

I love hiking; it is one of my favorite hobbies. We used to do it often with my mother, so my father and I have decided to carry on the tradition. I always seem to find peace whenever I hike in a forest, like all my miseries would just dissolve away. Actually, everything within the forest is a sanctuary—from the singing of the birds to the odor of the trees.

“I’m glad,” my father says, his eyes lighting up. “Fresh air will do you good.”

A figure in the kitchen window catches my eye, startling me slightly. My father looks up to see what caught my attention.

My father opens the back door and his work colleague, Marty, stands as he waves.

"Hey, Marty. What are you doing here?" my father asks.

"Can I get a lift to work? My car has decided to act up," Marty replies as he steps into the house.

"Sure, I just need to get dressed. I'll be five minutes," my father says, rushing to his bedroom.

I take a moment and observe Marty as he leans against the kitchen counter, folding his arms. He is only a couple of years younger than my father. There is a rugged handsomeness about him that I can't put my finger on.

He catches me looking at him and smiles. "Good morning."

"Good morning," I reply. "Would you like a glass of water?"

Marty grins and mockingly repeats my British accent, "*Water.*" He chuckles. "Sorry, it's the way you say water. It's cute," he says as he smirks. "But no, thank you."

I chuckle under my breath and roll my eyes at his joke. "Well, I'll never get used to how Americans say it."

Marty shakes his head and laughs. "One of those things. How are you finding Washington?"

I feel a bit more at ease. "The forests are beautiful and the town is quiet. It's different. I miss home sometimes, though."

"Change is tough, but you'll find your footing here. I bet you get told this all the time, but you look like the double of your mother."

Since moving to Washington, I have heard that a lot from the locals. My mother was born here, but moved to England with her father when she was eighteen. She always wanted to move back.

I can tell Marty has a hint of nostalgia in his eyes as he smiles. "I'm not sure if your father told you, but I went to school with your mother. She was so sweet."

"She was a lovely lady. My mother always spoke fondly of

Washington. Feels odd, but comforting to live where she grew up," I reply.

"I can understand why it would feel odd. It's like you're walking in her footsteps. You might discover part of her life you never knew."

"My mother made it sound beautiful growing up here. Being here helps me feel closer to her."

We hear my father walking around his bedroom as we fall silent. My father makes an appearance, dressed in his uniform. "Okay. Let's hit the road."

Marty straightens up, unfolds his arms, and gives him a nod.

"Have a nice day, Flora," Marty says, throwing a wink in my direction.

"You too, Marty," I reply, watching them head out the door.

As soon as the door shuts, the house quiets. My thoughts feel lighter after speaking with Marty.

THE SUN FILTERS THROUGH THE KITCHEN WINDOW, CASTING A SOFT, orange glow over everything in its path. I throw on an oversized linen shirt with loosely fitted jeans. To avoid my hair getting in my face, I tie it up into a messy bun.

I set the table with my watercolors with my blank paper staring back at me.

Since my mother's death, my paintings have all been monochromatic. I just haven't been able to paint with colors anymore. My father encourages me, but I still paint in black and white.

I dip my brush into the black paint and feel a sense of calm wash over me as I start painting trees.

As I paint, the image of a forest starts to appear. I've always found solace when painting nature.

I watch the clock to ensure I don't miss my appointment with my therapist. I let my feelings pour into the painting as it slowly comes into form. I paint small trees that are dark with white beams shining centermost through them. I step back and assess my work before adding final touches. The ticking of the clock catches my attention. I gather the painting supplies and clean up the table. I retrieve my laptop from the living room and place it on the kitchen table, ready for my appointment.

Realizing I have only two minutes, I sigh and mentally prepare myself. I feel my phone vibrate on the table. Glancing over, I see a text message from my father, reminding me that I have my therapist appointment and wishing me luck.

I open my laptop and feel both nervous and uptight. I take a deep breath before pressing the link to join the appointment. I adjust the camera and ensure my audio is in place. My therapist joins the appointment and I greet her with a fake smile.

"Confirm your name and age, please," my therapist says in her stern, British accent.

I want to sigh, but suppress it and reply, "Flora Lockley, twenty."

As my therapist writes notes, I observe her. She is a typical, older British lady with white hair that's neatly trimmed into a pixie cut. Her glasses nearly cover the deep wrinkles on her face.

She adjusts her glasses and pushes them down her nose. Due to the different time zones, it's evening in England. The room is dark, with just a lamp shining in the room.

"So, Flora, how have you been since our last session?" she asks, probing.

I take a deep breath before answering, "Challenging, but I've been painting a lot."

She adjusts her glasses. "Painting and artwork can be a powerful outlet," she observes.

"It helps me process," I agree. "However, I keep having nightmares recently."

She writes down notes while listening as I describe the images that trouble my sleep.

"I see...Grief can manifest in different ways. It's common for people to have nightmares after a loss. Have you found peace or relief at any moment?"

I hesitate, but my hiking trip with my father comes to mind.

"Yes, in small ways."

"It's about finding things that can bring you relief, Flora. You must remember to allow yourself grace along the way," she reminds me.

Our session continues and I feel lighter as she gives me guidance.

"I keep getting reminders of how I look like my mother," I admit, feeling nervous.

"Your resemblance to her must hold significant meaning for you," she suggests. Images of my mother flood my mind and I feel a lump form in my throat.

"It can be a blessing. Other times...It's a painful reminder."

"I can understand that. Your mother lives on through you, Flora," she reassures me.

I hated to ask the question. "Will I ever get over my mother's death?"

She listens and gives an awkward smile, yet her gaze is gentle. "You were sixteen when your mother died of Covid. You were very young. That's a lot for someone that age to take on," she responds empathetically.

"It still feels like yesterday..."

"Grief doesn't have a timeline. It's a journey you take at your own pace. You need to allow yourself to feel and to heal."

My breath becomes shaky. I am grateful for her understanding and the safe space she provides during our sessions, even if I dread them beforehand.

"Thank you," I say, giving her an awkward smile.

"In time, the pain may lessen. The key word is *time.*"

I feel a mixture of hope and sadness as our session draws to a close. I need to take one step at a time in order to heal.

TWO
FLORA

My father throws his backpack on the kitchen table, wearing his hiking gear. The bright colors of his worn cap have faded over the years. He finishes packing, tightens the straps, and ensures everything is in place.

I check to see if I have all my essentials as my father looks up at me.

"Bear spray?" he asks as he zips up his backpack.

"Got it," I reply, patting the side pocket where the canister is tucked away.

I walk to the hallway mirror and apply a layer of cherry lip balm, admiring my outfit for a moment. I have on my black hiking leggings and a black tank top. They both fit snugly and allow easy movement. Over my hiking outfit, I have on my favorite navy blue hoodie. In the reflection, I see my father wearing his dark cream cargo trousers and forest green fleece, looking outdoorsy. He catches me looking at him and gives me a reassuring smile.

"Looks like we have everything. Let's hit the road," he says, giddy. His excitement makes him look cute.

I tie my hair up into a ponytail and grab my own backpack from the table. I look around the kitchen one last time and head towards the door. I chuck my bag in the truck's backseat and jump into the passenger's side. The inside of the truck smells of old leather and musk. My father gets into the driver's seat and rolls down his window. We buckle up our seatbelts and then hit the road.

The sun casts long shadows through the trees onto the road as we drive through the quiet town. My father glances over at me, smiling, and I can't help but smile back. I can tell that he is excited to go on this hike; it brings me joy when I see him happy.

I turn on the radio and find a station that plays cheerful, old music as my father starts bobbing his head to the beat.

"How did your appointment go?" he asks.

"You know, same old, same old..."

I don't like talking about the details of my sessions. I stare out the window, watching the outside pass by. My father can sense my hesitation and doesn't question further.

We pull up to a traffic light and I see two black motorcycles in front of the truck. Two men sit astride on the bikes, both built like gods and covered in dark tattoos. They both wear worn jeans, one in a white T-shirt and another in a black T-shirt.

One of the bikers turns his head back, looking at our truck. He nudges the guy next to him and his gaze follows. Their faces are obscured by their blacked-out helmets and dark visors, giving them a menacing look as their attention lands on us.

"You know them guys?" my father asks, not letting his eyes leave the bikers.

"No?"

Looking at them, I feel uneasy. I don't remember seeing them before. The bikers speed off once the traffic light turns green, their engines roaring as they take a turn further into town. I feel adrenaline as my whole body breaks out into goosebumps.

"Probably just some guys on a morning ride," my father says, driving on.

We enter an area with tall trees on either side of the road. Driving through the forest, the sunlight now only filters through the branches, making the temperature feel cooler.

My father looks up in shock. "Jesus, look at that!"

He grips the steering wheel tightly as he slams on the brakes. I look up and see a massive animal in the middle of the road.

"Is that a moose?" I ask.

My father nods his head with the engine still rumbling. "Yup," he confirms.

The moose is enormous and easily towers over the truck. I can see its coarse, brown fur and its antlers stretched out like branches.

"It's huge," I say, my voice barely above a hush.

My father and I simply sit there silently, watching as the moose makes it to the other side of the road. It looks at us, its breath condensing as it exhales, and vanishes into the depths of the forest.

"They are massive, especially when you're this close," my father says, releasing the breath he's been holding. He presses the gas pedal and continues driving.

"Yeah. There's so much land and wilderness out here. It's crazy. You can go miles without seeing someone," I say, looking out the window and watching the trees go by.

"I can see why your mother always wanted to come back."

My father's eyes remain on the road, but I can tell he is lost in thought. I picture my mother running through these forests as a young girl. I could understand why she wanted to come back, too. We pull into a gravel parking lot and I unbuckle my seatbelt as my father brings the truck to a stop.

We both grab our backpacks from the backseat. I adjust the straps, ensuring it won't slip off while we hike. It feels heavy pressed against my back, but I know it has everything we need.

I look around, taking in everything. The trees tower above us, the air filled with the smell of fresh pine and earth.

My father comes up beside me and we pivot around to face the trail ahead of us. The path leading into the dense forest is narrow, with lined-up ferns and underbrush on either side.

My father takes a deep breath and asks, "Ready?"

"Of course."

Finally, with one last look at each other, we start walking down the path, feeling the gravel crunch under our boots. We slowly hear fewer sounds from the road, more birds chirping, and the occasional twig snapping underfoot.

WE HAVE BEEN HIKING FOR OVER AN HOUR NOW, SO WE TAKE A BREAK as we reach a fallen tree. I feel the rough bark press on my legs as I lean against it, hearing the call of a woodpecker in the distance. The forest around us is peaceful and calm with the trees covered in dark green moss and ivy. My father hands me a bottle of water. I unscrew the cap and take a long sip, feeling the cold water as it flows down my throat.

"So peaceful," I breathe.

My father's eyes scan the forest, his face shining in the sunlight.

"It's beautiful..." he agrees.

The treetops sway in the breeze above us. My father puts his hand on his head, ensuring his cap doesn't fall off as he takes in the sight.

"Have you made any friends? I know you've been going out more."

I feel my chest tighten at my father's question. The truth is, I still had no friends. My father encouraged me to leave the house more and get acclimated. He suggested I visit the local art gallery, the library, maybe even volunteer. Despite visiting these places, I didn't have the courage to speak to anyone. I fear rejection so much that I keep my lips sealed whenever I meet someone new.

I avoid my father's gaze as I shake my head, the weight of disappointment settling down on me.

"Flora..." my father says with a sigh. "Make some friends. Get out there more. Stop locking yourself away watching horrors and painting."

His words sting, but I know he is right. Being at home is a safe haven for me. I could lose myself while painting. I feel my father's eyes soften as he looks at me.

"I don't want you to be lonely," he says gently.

"Well, I have you, so I'm not lonely..."

He takes a deep breath and looks at me. "Flora, I won't be around forever."

It is a truth I can't ignore; he is right.

My thoughts drift back to my sheltered life. I didn't mind being *alone*, losing myself in paintings or books. However, the thought of *loneliness* terrifies me. At home, I always knew my mother and father were present in the background, even if I spent most of my time in my bedroom.

Living with my father at the age of twenty makes me feel like a burden, like an obstacle in his life. Perhaps he wants to pursue his interests and have his own freedom.

"So...Nancy. How do you feel about her?" my father asks, avoiding eye contact and shuffling his feet.

"The woman who works at the local bar?"

"Yeah..."

"Uh, she's nice. Why?"

"Well, I wanted to ask her out for dinner," he says, focusing on a spot on the forest floor.

I never thought this day would come—my father being able to move on from my mother. I can't blame him for wanting companionship; it's been four years since my mother's death. For so long, it has just been me and him.

"She would never replace your mother. Your mother was the love of my life," he says, lifting his head and looking at me.

"Dad, honestly, it's fine. I understand..."

I reach out for his arm and steady my voice. "Mom would want you to be happy," I say.

He takes a deep breath, swallows hard, and nods. "Thank you, Flora."

It took him a lot of courage to ask me that. At that moment, I don't just see my father; I see a man who has endured loss and is now taking his own steps to heal.

"Save me from cooking?" he asks with a faint smile. "I thought we could grab a bite to eat at the bar after the hike."

"Sounds like a good idea."

I pick up my backpack, dusting off a few pine needles that have fallen from the trees above. I sense that my father feels better after getting that off his chest.

"Thank you again, Flora," my father says with gratitude in his eyes.

Before we continue our hike I adjust my straps, making sure the backpack's weight is evenly distributed.

I pass the bottle of water to my father and he tucks it back into his own bag. We set off and resume our hike through the forest.

EVERY STEP BACK TO THE TRUCK FEELS LIKE AN EFFORT. I AM completely shattered by the hike and my legs throb with an ache. My father notices and opens the truck door for me as I throw my bag into the backseat with the last bit of strength I have. I collapse into the passenger seat, letting out a deep sigh.

My father climbs into the driver's seat with a groan. He must feel the same fatigue I do.

We don't speak, a mutual understanding between us as we sit in silence. The cool, fresh air fills the truck. I glance over at my father as he focuses on driving, but I can see a hint of satisfaction in his eyes after completing our hike.

Breaking the silence, I ask, "You mind if we skip the bar?"

"The hike has really taken a toll on you?" I can see the disappointment on his face as he turns around and glances at me.

"My legs are aching..." I admit, giving him a weary smile.

"Well, if you don't mind," he begins, "I want to see Nancy. Is it okay if I drop you home?" he asks, hesitating slightly.

"That's cool. I'll watch a horror movie or something," I reply with a slight nod,

trying to mask my tiredness by smiling. Curling up on the couch with a bowl of popcorn sounds like the perfect way to end this exhausting day.

As we head home, a group of bikers drive next to the truck in the other lane. The two bikers at the front spark a flicker of recognition. One of the riders turns his head sharply to the side for a split second. On another motorcycle, a woman with brown, curly hair clings tightly to another tattooed man, her arms wrapped around his waist.

My father observes them. "There are a lot of bikers in this town," he states.

"Hmm," I reply.

We pull into the driveway and my father parks the truck, remaining in the driver's seat.

I hop out of the truck and feel the evening air hit my face. The bikers come back to mind, with their dark aura and tattoos. I try to ignore my thoughts as I turn to my father. "Want me to cook you anything for dinner?"

"It's okay. I'll grab a bite to eat at the bar," he replies.

Before I can shut the truck door, my father speaks up again, "Are you sure you're gonna be okay, Flora?"

"I'll be fine," I reply, shutting the truck door and offering him a small smile to ease his worry.

He reverses the truck out of the driveaway and shouts out the window, "I'll be back later!"

I turn to face the house, appreciating its imposing size. It is much larger than the house we had back in England. Double the size, in fact. With its pristine, white paneling with matching windows and doors, the house stands proudly on its plot. We left a small brick Victorian townhouse behind in England.

Before, my bedroom was tiny, big enough to fit a single bed and a small dresser. Now, my bedroom is spacious with large, bay windows that let in plenty of light. It's nice having a double bed and a cozy reading nook.

I open the door to the house and step inside. Even though I preferred this house, it still felt unfamiliar with our old furniture mixed with new pieces we've collected since moving.

I feel relief as I sit on the hallway bench. I unlace my hiking boots and tug them off, setting my aching feet free. I wiggle my toes and let out a deep groan.

I push myself up from the bench and walk into the kitchen to grab a glass from the cupboard. I fill it with water, taking a generous sip. I turn to the cupboard and search for a snack. Finding a box of popcorn, I open it and put it in the microwave. I head upstairs to change into something more comfortable, my legs aching with each step. *Ouch. Fuck. Ow.*

I make my way to my bedroom and walk over to the closet, taking out my *Chucky* T-shirt. I take off my hiking clothes and change into my loungewear.

I hear the microwave's faint beeping and go back downstairs. Before I even reach the kitchen, I can smell popcorn. I can't help but feel excited for this chilled evening. Grabbing the popcorn and a glass of water, I head to the living room. I sink into the couch and pull a blanket over my legs. Picking up the remote, I begin to flip through the movie options. I settle on the movie *Misery*, my father and I's favorite. We have always shared a bond over horror movies. There is something about controlled terror. The opening credits roll and I feel a sense of calm wash over me.

My thoughts drift to my father; I hope he is enjoying his evening. As the movie progresses, my phone buzzes. I pick it up and see a text from my father.

DAD

Hi, Flora. Just checking in and making sure you're okay. Nancy says hi.

ME

Hey, Dad. I'm good. Just watching Misery and munching on some popcorn. Tell Nancy I said hello. Enjoy your evening. 🙂

I send the text message and place my phone down, focusing

back on the movie. The minutes tick by and the movie reaches its climax. My phone buzzes once again and I glance at it, expecting another text from my father. Instead, it is a news alert about a local event, something that can wait 'till later. I return to the movie and it quickly comes to an end. I take the empty bowl and glass to the kitchen to clean up. I wander back to the living room and glance out the window, looking out as the moon shines over the backyard. My phone vibrates on the table once more. Picking it up, I see another text message from my father.

DAD

Glad to hear. I love you.

ME

I'm going to bed. I love you, too, Dad.

I decide to turn in for the night. I walk upstairs and crawl into my bed as the day's fatigue finally catches up to me.

I WAKE UP AND REALIZE I MUST HAVE FALLEN ASLEEP STRAIGHT AWAY last night. I glance at my alarm clock: *6:00 a.m.* I push back the covers with a groggy sigh. A pressing need to pee drives me out of bed. I step into the hallway and notice Nancy at the top of the stairs, pausing at the sight of her. She is wearing a loosely buttoned blouse that hangs open just enough for me to notice the lace underneath. Her dark red, wavy hair is a tangled mess, probably from a fun night with my father. Holding her boots in one hand, she glances up at me with an embarrassed look.

"Uhh...Flora," she stammers.

I raise an eyebrow and whisper, "I hope you spent the night with my father and not breaking in..."

"Your dad wanted me to leave before you woke up," she whispers uncomfortably.

I roll my eyes and give her a reassuring smile. "Nancy, it's fine."

She relaxes and gives me an awkward smile before tiptoeing down the stairs.

I shake my head slightly and head into the bathroom, closing the door and letting out a deep breath. I switch the light on and the sudden brightness causes me to squint. Glancing in the mirror it reveals my disheveled state with my hair sticking up in every direction. Turning the faucet on, I splash water onto my face, starting my morning routine. I quickly relieve myself and remain on the toilet for a moment, my mind drifting to my father's new relationship. Nancy is a new source of joy for him that he so dearly needs. She's a lovely woman, the manager at the local bar, and everyone knows her name. I have only met her a few times, but every encounter has been pleasant. Her warm smile and hearty laugh put everyone around her at ease. The most important thing is that she puts a genuine smile on my father's face.

I accept my father's new relationship, but I still wish it was my mother standing at the top of the stairs. I miss her every day. Seeing Nancy take her place stirs a mix of emotions inside me. I know it's unfair to Nancy; she has done nothing wrong. She makes my father happy. I stand up and sigh, flushing my thoughts away with the water in the toilet. I leave the bathroom, still lost in my thoughts, and jump back when I nearly bump into my father, standing topless in the hallway.

He seems flustered and asks, "Flora! How long have you been awake?"

Feeling awkward, I take a deep breath and reply, “Calm down, Dad. I already saw Nancy.”

His face is red from embarrassment. As I walk down the steps, I hear my father mumble something under his breath. He doesn't need to explain himself to me. Reaching the bottom of the stairs, I head towards the kitchen and pour myself a glass of juice. I sigh as I put my glass down and begin to make breakfast.

My father walks down the stairs, pulling a T-shirt over his head. He looks at the floor as he clears his throat. “So...” he utters.

I make it easy for him by suggesting, “You wanna go to the bar for dinner?”

“Yeah? I’d like that very much, Flora,” he replies, visibly relaxing.

It’s a small step in the right direction. It’s an opportunity to support my father and, perhaps, form a connection with Nancy.

THREE

FLORA

We drive down the street and I notice my father is wearing his best T-shirt layered with an open flannel shirt. He's made extra effort—even his beard is neatly trimmed.

My hair flutters as the evening air blows through the window and I try pushing a strand behind my ear. Hopefully, it doesn't go frizzy before we arrive at the bar.

"How was work today?" I ask.

"Didn't run into any burning buildings. However, I did have to help an old lady get her cat down from a tree."

I can't help but laugh. "Okay, that is super cliché."

"It used to be so busy each day in London. Here, it's quiet," my father replies with a shrug.

I could understand and appreciate that he liked the slower pace of life here.

"This might be too soon...but Nancy has offered you a job at the bar, if you want it."

He catches me off guard and I don't know how to reply. I had a job back in England where I worked part-time in a small café and the regulars knew me by name. Working here seems daunting, but maybe this would be a way for me to meet new people.

"I will have to think about it," I finally reply.

My father nods and doesn't press on any further. As we approach the bar, the glow of street lights fills the road. My father parks the truck. "Things will get better, Flora."

"I know..." I say, nodding and giving him a genuine smile.

I hop out of the truck and we head towards the bar. I take in the sight—a brick building with red neon signs and old, rusty green awnings hanging over the windows. This is the only bar in town, making it popular. I'm intrigued by the thought of working here. The gentleman my father is, opens the door for me and I step inside.

It's relatively quiet this evening with only a couple of locals scattered about. One side has all leather booths and wood tables. At the end of the room are two pool tables and an old jukebox, along with a TV mounted on the back wall. "Jerry, Flora!" a voice calls loudly.

Turning my head, I see Nancy behind the bar. She looks different from when I saw her just this morning. Her red hair is now tied back and her makeup is done nicely, giving her a professional look.

My father and I walk over to the bar. He pulls out a stool for me and I hop on it. He then takes the stool next to me and settles in.

"What can I get you both to drink?" Nancy asks with a twinkle in her eye.

"I'll have a beer and Flora will have a white wine," my father replies.

Nancy smirks at my father and states, "I can't serve her wine. You need to be over twenty-one here."

"Oh, yeah, I forgot about that," my father says.

"Just a Cola, please, Nancy," I request.

Nancy nods her head and turns around, grabbing our drinks and placing them in front of us. As the night goes on, more locals enter the bar. The jukebox begins to play a mixture of classic rock and country tunes as my father, Nancy, and I chat and laugh together.

"There's a mini concert here next week and multiple bands are playing," Nancy says, leaning over the bar. My father looks at me, his eyebrows raised. I meet his gaze with a smile.

"Sounds like a plan," he replies.

Nancy's face lights up at his response. "The lineup is going to be good. A few locals will be playing," she says.

She starts cleaning the bar, running a cloth over it as my father and I enjoy some food. He munches on a hotdog while I dig into a bowl of chili. The atmosphere is lively yet relaxed.

Suddenly, the bar door flings open. A group of individuals walk in, immediately catching my attention.

The first two men have tattoos over their bodies; I recognize them as the bikers I keep seeing around town. I catch their attention as they look straight at me with intense gazes. My breath hitches in my throat. The man with light brown hair that swoops over his forehead smirks at me. Feeling nervous, I don't know how to react.

The other man with combed back, darker hair with tattoos climbing up his neck, nudges his friend. They both stride over to the pool tables.

"Crap," Nancy mumbles under her breath.

My father leans over the bar. "Who are they?" he asks curiously.

"The Faulkner brothers," Nancy replies, keeping her voice low. "One of them is on the local motocross team. They aren't good news, nor bad, but they have a reputation. I can't complain, though. They spend a lot of money when they come into town."

Trying to focus on my bowl of chili, I turn around, facing the bar yet feeling flustered.

I feel like someone's eyes are lingering on me, but I don't want to turn around and investigate.

"They usually have a few drinks and shoot a couple of games of pool. They can get rowdy, but they've never caused real trouble," Nancy whispers to my father.

"As long as they don't start trouble here." He glances at the pool table where the Faulkner brothers are.

The smirk from the light-haired brother flashes in my mind, making my heart beat a little faster.

I glance at the pool table as the Faulkner brothers laugh and joke with their friends.

"Jerry!" a voice shouts from behind us.

We look over our shoulders and see Marty walking in.

"Hey! What are you doing here, Marty?"

"Well, I fancied a beer after work," he replies, grabbing a stool beside my father. Nancy gives Marty a friendly nod and passes him a beer. He and my father dive into a conversation about work.

I turn back to my bowl of chili, but feel a presence beside me. Out of the corner of my eye, I see one of the Faulkner brothers. The one with the darker hair and tattoos stands close, towering over me. His scent of smoke mixed with men's cologne wafts over me. I don't know why, but it makes my heart race.

He tosses his credit card onto the bar and says in a deep voice, "Keep the beers coming."

I try to avoid eye contact with him as I feel his intense gaze study me.

Nancy places a few beers on the bar and he picks them up effortlessly between his fingers. His forearms flex, making the veins prominent. Something about his arms makes me feel weak.

"Thanks," he mumbles. As he turns to walk away, his eyes linger on me. He heads back to the pool table where his friends are waiting.

Letting out a breath I didn't realize I was holding, I try to shake off the encounter. My father and Marty carry on talking, not noticing.

I glance back over at the group—the females are all over the Faulkner brothers. One woman with long, brown hair and a tight-fitting dress stands between the legs of the light-haired Faulkner brother as he sits on a stool. She leans in close to him, screaming for his attention, but he doesn't seem interested in her. His eyes glance over her shoulder and lock onto me as he smiles mockingly.

Feeling exposed, I quickly look down at my food. My heart pounds in my chest. I can't help but wonder why he is focusing on me.

"Everything okay?" my father asks. I snap back into reality.

"Yeah, everything's fine."

He reassures me with a pat and returns to his conversation with Marty. I take a deep breath.

Suddenly, the jukebox starts playing *Man! I Feel Like a Woman!* by Shania Twain.

The females in the group jump up and down, clapping their hands. They rush around the bar, grabbing the hands of every lady and pulling them into their dance party. The one who was flirting with the Faulkner brother runs over to me and grabs my hand.

"Come on! Join us!" she excitedly exclaims.

"Oh, no, thank you." A wave of shyness washes over me.

My father turns to me with a grin and says, "Go have fun, Flora."

Reluctantly, I let the woman pull me towards the pool tables where the other women are dancing. They form a circle around me and I join them as embarrassment flushes through my cheeks. As I move to the music, I glance at the Faulkner brothers. They are standing nearby with beers in hand, their eyes fixated on me. The lighter-haired brother smirks at me again—his gaze unwavering and intense. The darker-haired brother watches me with a more neutral expression, but his eyes don't leave me, either.

"Man! I feel like a woman!" the women shout in unison, their voices mingling with the music. They spin around, clapping and cheering.

I glance over at my father to see him sitting at the bar, smiling at me. His conversation with Marty has paused as he watches me. Pure pride and happiness light up his face and it gives me a boost of confidence. I feel like all eyes are on me, but I don't care.

As we continue to dance, more women join in. I feel like a free-spirited woman as we all dance and sing.

Everyone applauds and cheers when the song comes to an end. I find myself feeling breathless as I return to the bar and my father. "That wasn't so bad, was it?" he asks.

I gulp loudly, trying to catch my breath.

"Your daughter can dance, Jerry!" Marty says, patting my father on the back.

Marty looks at me and I blush, looking down and sipping my soda.

"Do you two wanna play some pool?" Marty asks, tilting his head toward the pool tables.

My father jumps down from his stool and says, "Sure."

I follow close behind as they walk over to the pool table, the Faulkner brothers and their friends playing at the next table.

My phone buzzes in my pocket. I pull it out and see that my

Auntie Vicky is calling. "Dad, Auntie Vicky is calling. It's loud in here...I'm gonna take it outside!" I shout over the noise.

I step outside and the cool air hits my cheek. I look down at my phone and see I just missed her call. I try calling her back, holding the phone up to my ear. Looking around the parking lot, I see a group of men on motorcycles pull up. They jump off their bikes, remove their helmets, and start walking over to the bar. They stop outside the door, leaning against the walls. I try calling my auntie back, but it goes straight to voicemail.

I put my phone in my back pocket and walk over to the bar door.

One of the men with dark blond hair steps in front of me, blocking me from entering the bar. "Well, well, well. Hello," he says with a smirk.

"Excuse me..." I say.

"Oh, she's British," he remarks. He looks at his friends with approval as they all surround me and chuckle lowly.

"Let me pass," I demand, looking up at him. They all tower over me, trying to intimidate me. He studies me briefly and then steps aside with a mocking bow. "After you," he says.

I walk past them, ignoring his sarcasm, and re-enter the bar. I quickly rush over to my father and Marty who are still setting up the pool game.

"Everything okay?" my father asks, looking up from the table.

"Yeah. Auntie Vicky didn't answer," I say, trying to sound nonchalant as I brush off the encounter outside.

Marty hands me a pool cue and asks, "You ready to show us your skills?"

Taking the cue, I force a smile. "Absolutely," I reply.

After we begin the game, I can't help but often glance at the Faulkner brothers and their group.

I line up my shot and catch my father's reassuring smile.

The song *Black Velvet* by Alannah Myles plays in the background, adding a sultry atmosphere to the dimly lit bar.

As I take my first shot, the three ball echoes and drops into the corner pocket. I can't help but smirk as pride fills me.

With a smug face, I look up at my father and Marty. "Well done," my father says, smiling.

Nancy walks over and starts collecting empty bottles. She nods towards a booth where a group of rough-looking men sit. "See that group in the booth?" she whispers to my father. I perk my ears, eavesdropping while pretending to line up my next shot. My father nods.

"Well, they're from another motocross team."

Nancy gathers the last of the bottles. "The teams never see eye to eye." Her brows furrow with concern as she glances warily at the men. My father's eyes look over at the men sitting in the booth; a younger, cockier bunch. Then, his eyes shift to the Faulkner brothers.

We continue our game, ignoring the tension between the motocross teams filling the bar.

"Wanna join me outside, Jerry?" Marty asks. "I'm going to smoke."

My father shakes his head lightly and smirks. "Are you going to be okay, Flora?" he asks, hesitating to leave me inside the bar alone.

"I'll be fine. Besides, I can work out how I'm going to win." I giggle.

As my father and Marty make their way to the door, the warm light from the bar spills out into the night, illuminating their figures.

I lean over the pool table and focus on my next shot when I feel a sudden, sharp poke in my side.

Startled, I see the light-haired Faulkner brother leaning over the adjoining pool table, lining up his shot. His pool cue must have jabbed me by accident.

"Shit! Sorry. Did I poke you?" he asks with a smirk. His friend passes by and he hands off the cue.

"It's okay..." I say, my voice coming out softer than intended. I feel the heat rushing up to my cheeks as they blush.

"Are you Australian?" he asks with a raised eyebrow, clearly intrigued.

"Uhh, British," I reply. I look up at him, realizing how tall he is. He towers over me, his height imposing as he looks at me with a mixture of curiosity and amusement.

"Nice. I'm Dax Faulkner...by the way," he replies confidently, extending his hand towards me.

I shake his hand firmly. "Flora Lockley," I respond. His grip is strong and wielding. I feel a strange flutter in my stomach.

The other, taller Faulkner brother strides over, standing beside Dax. He looks me up and down, evaluating me. My heart races at his presence; his eyes have a certain intensity.

"This is my brother, Lyka. Well, I say brother, but I'm adopted."

Lyka rolls his eyes and crosses his arms over his chest, maintaining his stern, distant demeanor.

I feel overwhelmed standing between these two handsome brothers. Dax's light hair and easy charm contrast sharply with Lyka's darker, brooding presence. I don't know where to look for a moment, my eyes darting between them.

As I focus, I notice Dax's eyes are a light brown, almost golden. His gaze is steady; it feels like he's looking straight into my soul.

"I guess you're new around here?" Dax asks. Lyka remains beside him, silently observing.

"Yup. I moved here four months ago."

"Nice...How do you find living here?"

"It's nice, I guess...You're the guys I keep seeing on the motorcycles, right?" I ask, curiosity getting the better of me.

The brothers look at each other, exchanging a knowing glance as their smirks deepen.

"That's us—"

"LYKA FAULKNER!"

Dax grabs my wrist and quickly pulls me behind him, not giving me time to react.

"*Shit!* Get behind me," he urges, his face now serious as his protective instincts kick in. I stumble backward slightly as Dax presses me against him and the edge of the pool table, his body shielding me from whatever is about to unfold. I manage to peer through the gaps of Dax's massive arms and see the dark-haired blond guy from the parking lot walking over with aggressive energy. I hold onto Dax's forearm as he comes closer.

Lyka remains standing beside us, his demeanor calm and unbothered.

"What do you want, Jonny?" Dax asks with restrained anger.

Jonny is followed by several of his friends. They fan out and surround the pool table on either side, trapping us. I let out a loud gulp, feeling scared.

"Did you fuck my girlfriend?" Jonny snarls as he moves closer to Lyka, sizing him up.

Lyka lets out a deep chuckle that echoes through the now silent bar.

"This has nothing to do with me..." I mumble.

I try to move away, but Jonny's friend steps closer to me. His gaze turns predatory as he reaches out and touches my hair. I flinch back, letting out a little noise. Dax moves swiftly, his arm snapping back to shield me. "Touch her again and I'll break every bone in your hand," he hisses through gritted teeth.

"NOT IN MY BAR! Take it outside or I'll call the cops!" Nancy screams from behind the bar.

Jonny and Lyka remain locked in a tense standoff. Their faces are inches apart, their breathing heavy.

Lyka chuckles. "She loved every minute of it," he taunts, his words dripping with provocation.

In an instant, Jonny snaps. He swings at Lyka, but Lyka is quicker and deflects Jonny's fist. Violence erupts into chaos as punches are thrown, shouts echo through the bar, and glass shatters everywhere.

My hands grip the edge of the pool table as Dax fiercely struggles with one of Jonny's friends. My heart pounds in my chest as I glance over and see Lyka and Jonny locked in a brawl.

The female patrons scream in fear as the fight spills over into every corner of the bar. Nancy rushes forward and attempts to intervene. Suddenly, I feel a hand grip the top of my arm. I look up and stare into a stranger's eyes. I don't know this person and I don't know what to do. I feel panic as I struggle against his hold. Dax turns around, his fist connecting with the stranger's face with a powerful punch. The man staggers backward and releases me.

Blue and red flashing lights cast a glow inside the bar.

"THE COPS!" a female voice shouts out.

Everyone involved in the fight scatters and runs towards the door. Dax looks back at me with a smirk, his white T-shirt now covered in blood.

My father pushes through the crowd and bumps shoulders with Dax, rushing over to me. Nancy appears beside me, reaching out. "Are you okay, Flora?" she asks, out of breath.

I stand there, stunned and speechless, trying to process everything.

"She's bleeding!" my father exclaims, looking down at my T-shirt with wide eyes.

I look down at the blood on my T-shirt, searching for an injury.

Am I hurt? I don't feel any pain.

"Wa...Wait, it's not my blood," I manage to stutter, my voice trembling.

Was it Dax's blood?

My father pulls me close and embraces me. I turn my head and look at the bar door. Red and blue flashes illuminate Nancy's figure as she approaches the officers.

Marty pulls up a chair and gestures for me to sit down. "If I were in here...I would've handled those troublemakers," Marty says with confidence.

The image of Dax's smirk and the blood staining his T-shirt flash in my mind.

Are Dax and Lyka okay? Did they get hurt?

Nancy speaks to the cops as my father watches over me, his hand resting on my shoulder. He then heads to the bar to get me a glass of water while Marty cleans up the shattered glass from the floor. A female officer with a notepad strides over to me.

"I need a statement from you. I've been told you saw the whole thing," she says, her tone firm.

I look up at her, suddenly reluctant to share what I witnessed.

"I didn't see anything. My eyes were closed."

The officer clicks her tongue, her eyes scanning me from head to toe as if trying to read my thoughts. "You have blood on your T-shirt and you didn't see anything..."

I shake my head, not saying a word. My father returns and hands me a glass of water.

"You know I can arrest you for obstruction of justice," the officer warns, her eyes narrowing as she looks down at me.

Something snaps inside me. I stand up from the chair and

place the glass of water on the pool table. “I didn't see anything!” I exclaim, brushing past the officer and jogging towards the door.

“Flora? Flora!” my father calls after me as he follows.

I push open the door and step outside to the gathered crowd, my eyes drawn to Jonny who’s pressed against a patrol car in handcuffs. I anxiously scan the crowd, but can't see Dax or Lyka anywhere.

“Come on, let's get you home,” my father says gently, pushing me toward the truck.

We walk towards the truck and I climb into the passenger seat, my mind racing with all kinds of thoughts. The flashing lights fade into the background as we drive away.

“Are you sure you're okay?” my father asks as he looks at me worriedly.

I nod, staring out the window at the streets passing by.

“Yeah, I'm okay. Just wanna go home.”

My thoughts keep returning to Dax and Lyka, their smirks, and the chaos that follows them.

I LIE IN BED, CHECKING THE LOCAL NEWS ON MY PHONE. EVERY FEW minutes, I refresh the page. I keep looking for any mention or updates about the bar brawl.

Dax and Lyka Faulkner.

Why can't I get them out of my mind? Why didn’t I just tell the officer what happened? I couldn’t...Dax protected me. I wasn’t about to rat them out.

So far, there's nothing new. Just a brief mention of a disturbance at the bar and the involvement of local motocross teams.

I can't help but feel flustered thinking about Dax and Lyka. Dax's smirk, the way he protected me during the fight. Lyka's brooding personality, the way he taunts others. The night's events play over and over in my mind.

What kind of world have I stumbled into?

I close my eyes, still gripping my phone.

FOUR

FLORA

The week passes by quickly. Nothing ever comes from the bar fight and I am able to put Dax and Lyka out of my mind. I can hear my father and Nancy laughing in the kitchen downstairs. I look in the mirror, trying to figure out what I should wear for tonight's mini-concert. Two outfits dangle from my door, representing two different aspects of me.

One option is an oversized T-shirt with the logo of an old band, cut-off denim shorts, and my black, worn Doc Martens. It looks effortlessly cool, a little dangerous, and is comfortable—ideal for the night.

The second option is a delicate, floral dress. It will pair nicely with a light blue jean jacket and ankle boots. Am I going grunge or do I prefer a softer look?

I chose to wear the huge T-shirt and shorts. I tie my hair in a disheveled ponytail and pull two long strands out, framing both sides of my face. I look in the mirror one last time, feeling confident.

I go downstairs and step into the kitchen where Nancy and my father continue to talk. She turns in her chair and looks at me.

"Very rock 'n' roll. I like it," she says, smiling.

"You look great, Flora," my father says, looking up briefly.

"Ready to rock?" Nancy asks, straightening herself. She's dressed in a trendy outfit, ready for the evening.

I feel my nerves kick in as I reply, "Yeah, let's do this."

As we head out the door, my father winks at me and I feel anticipation building up for tonight. I am ready to let loose and have fun tonight, rock 'n' roll style.

WE WALK UP TO THE BAR'S PARKING LOT WHERE IT'S ALREADY crowded with people chatting away. Through the crowd, I see Marty standing and waiting for us. He is wearing a whiskey sign T-shirt and jeans, looking cool and casual.

He greets me tenderly by leaning in and kissing me on the cheek, taking me by surprise. "You're looking good, Flora, " he whispers. I blush at him, feeling a flutter of excitement.

Marty turns to my father and pats him on the back. "Good to see you, man," he says.

Nancy takes my father's hand as he asks, "We all ready to have a good time?" We all nod in agreement. My father leads Nancy inside the bar with Marty and I following closely behind. The atmosphere immediately transforms. The air is thick with mist from the fog machines. The music is loud and energetic, making me feel the beat thumping in my chest. Bright lights flash with the beat of the music, casting patterns across the crowd. I follow my father as he heads towards the bar, pushing through the crowds of people. He orders four beers, the bartender moving quickly to fill the order.

"If anyone asks, you're twenty-one," he says, winking at me with a wicked grin.

Nancy shakes her head with easy resignation. "You're such a bad influence!" Nancy shouts in his ear as she nudges him jokingly.

We make our way through the busy crowd, holding our drinks, getting closer to the stage where everyone moves to the music.

The stage looms above us as we find a spot at the front. I take a sip of my beer while Marty stands beside me. A few feet away, my father and Nancy begin dancing. Watching them enjoy themselves is a nice sight to see.

The singer announces his next song, *All These Lies*. The crowd goes wild and starts jumping up and down.

I realize people are quickly coming between me and my father. I scan the area to spot him amidst the crowd. Marty can see I am worrying and places his hands on my waist. "We've lost my father and Nancy," I shout over the music into his ear.

Marty looks over the crowd. "They'll reappear," he reassures me. I nod, trying to relax.

He starts dancing and I feel his body move closer to mine. We dance up against each other, lost in the moment. The lights flash in time to the music, lighting up our faces.

My bottle feels light as I take the last sip from it. Marty's hand remains on my waist and I lean into him, letting myself be carried away by the moment.

Marty leans down, his lips close to my ear. "Having fun?"

"Yeah! I've nearly finished my beer, though."

Marty grabs my hand as we make our way through the crowd, heading back towards the bar. Seeing the long line, I let out a sigh. "Do you mind if I go to the bathroom while you grab more beers?" I ask.

Marty gives me a thumbs-up and joins the line.

I head to the bathroom to see a long line forming against the wall. I put one foot up against the wall, resting my weight on the other leg. I spot a gap in the crowd and see Lyka leaning against the wall opposite me. He looks at me and grins, his eyes locking onto mine. My heart feels like it just skipped a beat. I never noticed before, but his eyes are a light, almost icy, blue. He holds my gaze, unwavering. I'm frozen, unsure whether to go over there or not. I notice he has a healing cut on his eyebrow, I'm guessing from the bar brawl. *I wonder if Dax is here, too?*

A woman with jet-black hair and tattoos appears out of nowhere, wrapping her arms around Lyka's neck. He doesn't respond to her touch; his arms remaining at his sides. His eyes remain locked on me as they kiss and I'm unable to look away. He smirks while continuing to kiss her and stare at me, the woman remaining oblivious.

His eyes never leave mine, even when they break the kiss for a moment. I can tell he is getting some twisted pleasure from this.

Why is he staring at me? What is he trying to prove?

Marty appears in front of me holding two beers. Before I can think it through, I put my arms around his neck and pull him into a kiss. His tongue meets mine as he wraps his arms around my waist, the cold glass of the beer bottles pressing against my back.

I lean my head to the side, standing on my tiptoes. I look over at Lyka who is still watching with a dangerous glint in his eye.

Two can play that game, fucker.

He looks pissed off as he stops kissing the woman. A surge of people moves in front of him, obscuring my view. I push Marty away when reality hits me. He looks down at me, flustered and confused.

Oh my god! What the fuck did I do?! He's my father's friend!

"Flora..." he begins.

"Marty, that shouldn't have happened. I'm sorry."

"I think it's best if we keep this between ourselves," he suggests.

"Yes. I totally agree," I say, nodding.

He smiles and bobs his head to the music, trying to lighten the mood.

"Why don't you go find my father while I wait in line? I still need to use the bathroom."

"Sure. If I find him, I'll wait for you at the bar," he replies.

Marty disappears into the crowd and I stand on my tiptoes, looking for Lyka. He's gone.

The line moves and it's almost my turn. I can feel the music pounding through the walls, but it doesn't compare to the beating in my heart. My mind goes crazy with thoughts of what just happened. The kiss with Marty was impulsive; we shouldn't have done that. But the way Lyka looked at me while kissing another woman was intense.

Was he trying to provoke a reaction from me? I realize I played right into his twisted game.

It's finally my turn. I close the door behind me and take a deep breath. I speedily use the bathroom and wash my hands, not lingering around as it's dirty. I hope Marty won't say anything to my father; that will make things awkward.

Navigating through the crowd, I head towards the bar and accidentally bump into someone.

"Oh, shoot. Sorry," I say.

I look up and see Jonny with a bruised eye, his friends standing ominously behind him.

"Hello, Miss British," Jonny sneers with sarcasm.

I try to walk past him, but one of his friends steps in front of me, trapping me as he blocks my path.

"The Faulkner brothers not with you?" Jonny asks, tracing his finger under my chin. I jerk my face away, glaring at him. He makes my skin crawl.

"I don't even know them," I hiss back with defiance.

"Oh, so you're up for grabs then?" he asks, something flashing in his eyes.

"Fuck you!" I yell.

He grabs the top of my arm tightly, his grip strong as his expression darkens.

Without thinking, I spit in his face, my saliva landing below his eye. He freezes, not knowing how to react. His grip on my arm loosens and his eyes burn with fury as he wipes his face with the back of his hand.

"*Trust me*, you're gonna pay for that," he declares.

I push him with all my strength and dart past him, the crowd closing in around me as I run.

I rush past people and look over my shoulder, making sure that Jonny isn't following me.

Catching my breath, I stop at the bar area, scanning the crowd. I spot Marty, Nancy, and my father standing at the other end of the bar as I make a beeline towards them.

"Why are you out of breath? You okay?" Nancy asks.

"Yeah, it's just very hot in here," I say quickly.

I couldn't tell them about Jonny. My father would only make a scene and I don't want the drama.

"Well, why don't you step outside for some fresh air with Marty while Nancy and I get more beers?" my father suggests.

Relief washes over me when I realize Marty hasn't said anything to my father.

"Sounds like a good idea," Marty says, almost too eagerly.

Marty puts a hand on my lower back, weaving us through the crowd towards the exit. We step outside and the cool, refreshing air hits my face. I can't help but cough as it's quickly interrupted by the cigarette smokers outside.

"Come here," Marty says, guiding me away from the crowd.

The noise from the bar is muddled as we turn around a corner. I lean against the brick wall as Marty stands in front of me.

"Everything okay?" he asks.

"Marty...About earlier..." I start to say. He moves closer before I finish my sentence, placing one hand against the brick near my head.

He gently guides my chin with his other hand, forcing me to look into his eyes. Somehow, our lips meet and his hand moves to my cheek.

What am I doing? Stop! Flora, stop! He is twice your age!

I don't even like him like that, but his tongue meets mine and I lose myself for a moment.

My back presses against the brick wall and Marty suddenly stops kissing me.

"Fuck...I want you, Flora," he says, kissing me again before continuing. "However, you're twenty *and* my friend's daughter. We shouldn't be doing this."

We both study each other for a moment. He's right; we shouldn't be doing this.

I haven't kissed a guy since I was seventeen at Holland's house party.

Grabbing my hand, Marty leads me further around the corner out of sight from everyone now. He places one of his hands under my thigh, lifting my leg up against his hip as he starts kissing my neck.

I can feel his other hand inching over the waistband of my shorts to my panties.

"Marty..."

"Flora," he murmurs against my neck.

I feel his finger start to move under my panties and I gasp. "I...I...I can't. I've never done this before," I stutter.

"What, outside?"

"Uhh, no. I'm a virgin..." I whisper, gulping loudly.

He stops kissing me and removes his hand from my shorts, taking a step back as he thinks.

"I'm sorry," he finally says as I look down. He steps forward and cups my cheek. "No, Flora. I'm sorry. I shouldn't have let it get this far."

I place my hand on top of his, looking at him with innocent eyes.

"Don't look at me with those eyes. Knowing you're a virgin...fuck. I want you more," he whispers.

I don't know what I'm thinking. Was I about to lose my virginity to Marty? No. Not outside in the dark.

I feel nervous and let out a giggle. "I think it's best we go back inside."

"You're right. Your father is probably wondering where we are," he says, his voice tinged with reluctance.

We head back to the bar with Marty entering first. I hang back, wanting to catch my breath before I head back inside.

I sense someone is watching me. I turn my head to the side and see Lyka sitting on his motorcycle. He smirks as he takes a long drag from his cigarette, his eyes locking onto mine.

Did he see me and Marty? Does he get pleasure from taunting me?

I want to know what he finds so amusing. I want to go over there and confront him. As I take the first step toward him, Marty steps outside, calling my name.

I give Lyka one last glance and then turn back to Marty. "Sorry, I'm coming."

I brush past Marty and step inside as the music pounds

through the speakers. From a distance, I can see my father and Nancy near the bar, enjoying themselves.

"Sure you're okay?" Marty asks, leaning down and whispering in my ear.

"Yeah," I reply, forcing a smile.

Lyka comes back into my mind and I can't shake the image of him.

His smirk. His fucking smirk.

What is it about him that gets to me?

My father hands me a beer as we walk over to him. "Flora! There you are," he says with a grin.

"Just needed a breather, Dad," I reply, taking a sip of the beer.

Marty glances at me and gives me a reassuring nod. Nancy looks between us and catches on, giving me a knowing look. I look down, not knowing how to react.

I just glance around the room again, searching for Lyka, but he's gone.

THE REST OF THE EVENING IS DRAMA-FREE. THE CONCERT ENDS AND MY father offers Marty a ride home.

Nancy and I make our way to the truck and settle into the back seat.

My father and Marty smoke a cigarette about ten feet from the truck. I bite my cheek and anxiety gnaws at me, thinking Marty could be telling my father about earlier.

"I wonder what they are talking about..." I mutter.

"Did something happen with you and Marty?" Nancy asks.

"N—No..." I say. My cheeks flush as I struggle to keep my cool.

Nancy's eyebrows raise. "Flora. You came back with smudged lipstick." I look up at her, panicked. "Don't worry, your father didn't catch on. Also, I won't say anything."

"It was just a kiss," I reply, hoping to downplay the incident.

Nancy reaches over and puts her hand on top of mine. "You're a big girl, my lips are sealed. Just be careful."

"Thanks, Nancy."

I am grateful for her understanding. I realize I can trust her as we form a little bond at this moment. My secret is safe with her.

I take a deep breath and clear my throat. My heart races as my father and Marty head back to the truck.

"Ready to head home?" my father asks, climbing into the driver's seat. Nancy and I nod, looking at each other with a smile.

I lean back into my seat and let out a sigh of relief as we drive to drop off Marty first. All I can say is that tonight has been a rollercoaster.

FIVE
FLORA

Moonlight shines through the window and fills the living room. I am slouched on the couch with a blank over me, my attention elsewhere while my father watches a show.

"You've really come out of your shell since we moved here. It was nice seeing you have fun," my father says, still watching TV.

"Well, you'd be pleased to know I might take Nancy's offer... You know, working at the bar."

It's a small step, but it's a step forward.

My father's face lights up and I can't help but smile. Before he can say anything, his phone buzzes loudly. He jumps up from the couch and heads to the kitchen.

"Hello, you..." I hear my father say from the other room. I'm guessing he is talking to Nancy on the phone.

I'm craving something sweet, but we have no candy in the house. I walk to the kitchen and see my father leaning against the counter, his phone pressed to his ear.

"I'm gonna walk to the store to get some chocolate," I mouth quietly.

I grab my hoodie from the closet and slip on my trainers. Before I leave the house, my father gives me a thumbs-up.

I leave the house feeling the cool air on my face. The moon casts long shadows across the sidewalk with the crickets chirping as I walk.

My hair tangles with a rush of wind hitting me as a sleek, black motorcycle speeds past.

Was that Dax or Lyka? Damn! Why are they occupying my mind?

Bright, fluorescent lights make me squint as I enter the store. Walking down the aisle, I spot chocolate and pick up two bars. I pay and leave the store.

Outside, I see Dax leaning casually against his bike. His golden eyes meet mine and a cigarette dangles from his lips. He winks at me and I can't help but blush. He flicks his cigarette to the ground and gestures with his head, inviting me over.

I stash the chocolate bars in my hoodie's pocket and walk over to him, feeling nervous.

He studies me as we stand there in silence. We both look at each other, exchanging smirks. Dax retrieves his helmet and extends his arm, holding it in front of me.

"I...I...Uh. I've never been on a bike," I stutter.

Dax places the helmet on my head without hesitation and adjusts the straps under my chin.

Effortlessly, he lifts me onto the back seat of the motorcycle. I feel a rush of adrenaline as he swings his leg over the motorcycle and settles into the driver's seat.

I cling to Dax's waist without hesitation. The motorcycle engines come to life and we drive off.

The world around us dissolves into a blur of houses and streetlights. As we soar down the streets, I feel like a bird set free.

I grip Dax tighter, my fingers digging into him. Surprisingly, he doesn't seem bothered by my hold. My heart pounds in my chest as he leans into the road's curves.

I am amazed at his skills as he maneuvers the motorcycle. We leave town and head through the forest, the trees a blur of green as we speed past. I let out a little, excited giggle. Dax hears and lets out a deep chuckle.

Effortlessly, Dax pulls off a quick maneuver and turns the bike around, the tire kicking up smoke as we speed back into town. I am pure adrenaline and my heart is going crazy.

Dax slowly drives down my street and pulls up outside my house.

How does he know where I live?

He helps me off the bike and removes the helmet from my head. I quickly pat down my hair, hoping it doesn't look a mess. That was truly an experience, the rush. It felt like being on an intense roller coaster. The streetlight shines down on us as Dax leans up against his bike.

"Fun?" he asks, his voice laced with amusement.

"Uh, yes!" I bite the inside of my cheek. "How did you know where I lived?"

Dax crosses his arms and replies, "It's a small town..."

I fidget nervously. He moves closer, towering over me, and I instinctively look up.

"Whoa, you have different colored eyes...cool," he remarks.

Dax reaches out and brushes a stray strand of my hair away from my face. I feel a spark between us for a moment. His light brown hair falls soft on his forehead, framing his strong jawline. His golden brown eyes seem to glow. His features are sharp. He is more than just handsome—he is a force of nature; drawing me in with an irresistible pull that leaves me breathless.

Is it bad that I want him to kiss me? No, Flora. What am I thinking? First Marty, now him?

Dax withdraws and his gaze shifts to my house. "You better go in," he whispers.

I don't want to look away from Dax's eyes, but I turn around and glance up at the window. My father stands at the window looking down, his expression unreadable.

I pivot back around to say goodbye to Dax. However, he is already straddling his bike. He starts the engine and speeds off down the road.

"Bye, then," I murmur, confused, raising my hand in the air.

I sigh as I walk up to the front door. I really don't want to face my father—I know I am going to be met with questions.

His face darkens as he holds the door open for me. I take a deep breath and walk into the kitchen.

"So. That was the guy from the bar brawl. Right?" he accuses sharply, following me.

I don't know what to say. I freeze.

"You said you were going to the store. Why were you on his bike?"

I cross my arms and feel defiance rise within me. "You said I needed to make friends, right?" I retort.

"Yes. But not with people who get into bar brawls. Not people like him!" he replies, slamming his hand down on the kitchen table.

"It's not a big deal. He got into one fight!"

"People like him are a big deal. They're bad news, Flora!" My father raises the volume of his voice.

"You fucking wanted me to make friends. I start to and you fucking hate it!" I shout back.

I can feel frustration welling up inside me.

"Don't you dare swear at me! You are not to see him again, Flora!" His voice is firm.

I clench my fist and turn away, not wanting to look at him. "I fucking hate you right now! I'm twenty. You can't tell me what to do!"

I storm up the stairs and slam my bedroom door shut with a loud thud. I collapse onto my bed and cry. I've never spoken to my father like that before. I want to say sorry, but I am too angry right now.

The house is eerily quiet. Suddenly, I hear the front door slam shut. The truck's engine starts outside and I realize that my father has left.

I lie on my bed as tears stream down my face. My phone buzzes in my pocket. I get it out and I see I have a text message from my father.

DAD

Gone for a drive.

ME

Okay.

I feel remorseful, yet angry at my father. I cry into my pillow as I lie there, curled up on my bed and wishing my mother was here. I surrender to the emotions and let it all out. My eyes feel heavy as I sob.

I DON'T KNOW HOW I FELL ASLEEP. HEARING MY FATHER DOWNSTAIRS getting ready for work puts my mind at ease, despite our unresolved tension.

How would my mother have handled this situation? I wish

she were still alive; she would have been calmer and more understanding than my father.

I'm ready to face my father and the day. I get out of bed and head to the bathroom.

Walking down the hallway, I hear my father shout, "Flora... I'm going to work, okay?"

I pause at the bottom of the staircase and look down at him. "Okay," I reply with a blunt tone.

"We can talk when I get home..." his words trail off.

I silently acknowledge his words. I turn around and continue towards the bathroom.

"Flora, I love you," he shouts up.

I hesitate for a moment, my hand on the bathroom door. I want to respond, but for some reason, I don't. I shut the door behind me, biting the inside of my cheek.

The sound of the front door closing cuts through the house. A sudden surge of regret washes over me and I bolt out of the bathroom. I rush to my bedroom window, pulling it open. I lean out, hoping to catch my father before he leaves, but it's too late. I watch as the truck drives down the street.

I linger at the window and I whisper into the wind, "I love you, too, Dad."

I SIT IN THE BATH, LEANING MY HEAD AGAINST THE EDGE, CLOSING MY eyes, and letting my thoughts drift. Dax appears in my head, riding on his bike. I felt a rush of intoxicating freedom. He is undeniably hot. I wanted to kiss him, or maybe it was just the adrenaline from the ride playing tricks on my mind.

Then there was Lyka. His presence lingers in my thoughts.

Taunting me with that smirk, like he knows something I don't. The Faulkner brothers were constantly on my mind. Dax with his golden eyes and Lyka with his icy blue stare. They had a way of getting under my skin.

I open my eyes to the sound of the occasional faucet drip. Reaching for the plug in the bathtub, I pull it. I stand up, step out of the tub, and feel a chill. I grab a black towel from the rack and wrap it around my body.

All of a sudden, I hear a knock at the front door. Wrapped only in a towel, I decide to investigate. Tiptoeing down the stairs, I open the door just a crack and peek around the door. Marty stands there, glancing around the yard.

"Marty..." I say, my voice filled with surprise.

"Can I come in?" he asks.

I nod and open the door fully, my naked body still hidden behind the towel. As he enters, I take a step back and tighten the towel around me.

"Aren't you supposed to be at work?" I ask.

"I'm working the night shift this week," he replies, his eyes never leaving mine.

I feel uncomfortable as we stand there in silence.

"I can't stop thinking about you," he continues, stepping closer.

I look down and reply, "Marty, we can't."

"I know. The fact we shouldn't makes me want you more," he confesses.

My eyes well up with tears and I feel confused. "Look at me," he whispers.

Grabbing my waist and pulling me close, our bodies press together, the towel the only barrier between us.

I breathe deeply and can smell him, manly and musky. His lips touch mine.

He takes my hand and whispers in my ear, “I’m here. It’s okay.” He leads me upstairs.

Holding the towel tightly with my other hand, my mind is going crazy with thoughts. We reach the top of the stairs and I feel the moment's weight settling over us. Marty pushes my bedroom door open and leads me over to my bed.

“Marty...”

He doesn't say anything, he just cups my face and kisses me gently. “Flora, I want you,” he breathes.

Grabbing both my hands, my towel loosens and falls to the floor in a heap. My naked body is exposed and my breath catches in my throat. No man has ever seen me naked before.

Marty steps back, his eyes taking in every inch of me.

Am I about to lose my virginity?

His hand caresses my neck and I lean into his touch. His thumb brushes past my lip and I open my mouth, sucking it.

“Have you ever had an orgasm before?” he whispers.

I swallow hard. I have, but alone. Never involving anyone else. I would always focus on my clit, but I’d never insert my fingers inside.

My cheeks feel hot as I blush and nod. Marty’s eyebrows lift in surprise.

“Yourself, or?” he probes.

“Uh...myself.”

He breathes in deep and lets out a groan, his lips finding my neck.

“What's the most you’ve done with someone?”

“Only kissed,” I admit.

His lips trail along my neck, causing my skin to tingle. His other hand slides up my back, pulling me closer until our bodies touch.

“I can make you feel good,” he offers.

My body arches towards him, seeking more of his touch. Marty's mouth moves lower, planting kisses along my collarbone and down to my chest.

He takes a step back and pulls off his T-shirt in one motion, tossing it on the bed. His hands move to his belt as he unfastens it and drops it to the floor. He unzips his pants and pushes them down, revealing the outline of his erection through his underwear. I've never seen anything like it. I can't help but examine his body. He steps closer to me. His hand moves to my neck, pulling me into an urgent, demanding kiss.

He breaks the kiss as his hands move lower to my waist, pulling me against him.

"Flora, I need you," he breathes.

Marty's hands slide down my sides, resting on my hips. He pulls back as his eyes lock onto mine. I take a deep breath and nod, giving him the consent he wants.

He grips my thighs and lifts me. He lays me down and his body hovers over mine. *This moment will change everything.* Marty stands up and slides his underwear down, kicking them away. As he straightens up, my eyes are drawn to his erection.

"Are you on anything?" he asks.

I shake my head no. I feel anxiety fill my body.

"It's unlikely you will get pregnant the first time."

"Uh, please wear a condom," I say.

He lets out a sigh, bending down and retrieving his wallet from his pants. He takes out a condom, tears the packet open with his teeth, and quickly rolls the condom onto his cock.

I open my legs for him and he positions himself between them. I feel his body press down on me as he lowers himself.

"I'll go easy on you," he whispers.

I feel a knot form in my stomach from his words. I'm scared and nervous.

I don't think I'm ready.

The tip of his erection nudges against my entrance. I tense up.

I'm not ready! Say something, Flora! SAY SOMETHING!

Marty lifts his head and I look into his eyes. "You look just like your mother. So goddamn beautiful," he murmurs.

My heart sinks. I feel like I have just been punched in the gut. He wants my mother, not me.

"I can't. Stop," I say, pushing against his shoulders. But he only presses harder against me, trapping me underneath him.

"It's okay," he coos.

"No! I'm not ready!" I cry out.

"Shh..."

I tense up and my entire body becomes rigid.

"STOP, MARTY!" I shout, my voice echoing around the room.

I can tell he is frustrated as he lets out a grunt, finally releasing me and rolling off to the side. I sit up, grab a large pillow, and hug it like a shield.

Marty's face is cold and detached as he stares at me. Tears spill down my cheeks as I cry. "I'm not my mother!"

Without a word, he picks up his clothes and gets dressed. Once fully clothed, he looks at me and mutters, "Sorry."

He leaves my bedroom, closing the door behind him. I hear him make his way downstairs and leave.

I grab a pillow, hug it tightly, and begin to cry. My mind races and I feel the sting of his words. *You look just like your mother.*

Tears well up in my eyes again. I feel so foolish, so naïve. I am so glad I didn't have sex with Marty. It makes me feel sick knowing I nearly let him take my virginity. He didn't want me, he wanted my mother.

I feel shaky as I stand up, grabbing the towel from the floor and wrapping it around myself. I head to the bathroom, locking the door behind me. I look at myself in the mirror and my eyes are puffy.

"You're not her. You're not your mother. You are you, Flora," I whisper to myself.

I head back to my bedroom and close the curtains. I sit on the edge of my bed and pick up my phone. I start texting Nancy. I know I can never tell my father, but Nancy is the only person I can trust with this. I wish my mother were still alive.

ME

Can we talk later? Please don't tell my father.

NANCY

Of course. Pop by the bar tonight. I won't say a thing.

I PUSH THE WHOLE MARTY SITUATION TO THE BACK OF MY MIND. Wanting to make amends with my father, I prepare his favorite meal, sausage and mashed potatoes.

I stand at the kitchen counter, peeling and chopping potatoes with a dishcloth draping over my shoulder.

I look up at the clock and see my father is due home at any moment. I can't wait to see his face when he sees the effort I've put into making dinner.

Suddenly, I hear a knock at the front door and pause. I turn down the heat on the stovetop.

I bet he forgot his keys.

I wipe my hands on the dishcloth and throw it on the counter. I walk towards the door and open it.

Nancy stands there with her back turned. I can tell her shoulders are shaking as they move up and down.

"Nancy, I was going to drop by the bar later..."

My heart drops when she turns around, her eyes red and tears streaming down her face. Two officers walk up the path and stand behind her, their expressions serious.

"Flora. I am so sorry," she cries out, her voice breaking.

I look past her and at the police officers, feeling confused. I try to make sense of the situation.

A male officer steps forward. "Can we come in, please?" he asks calmly.

Nancy rushes toward me, wrapping her arms around me as the officers follow her in.

"Your father was in an accident, Miss Lockley," one of the officers says quietly. Nancy pulls away, still crying.

"Ok...what, like he got burnt in a fire?"

"No. He was in a car accident."

"Well, is he at the hospital?"

Nancy lets out a whimper and sobs. The officer's face drops and I let out a gulp, trying to calm my nerves.

"Miss Lockley, your father passed away at the scene. I'm sorry," the officer says.

The room spins around me as my heart sinks. I place my hand on the wall, propping myself up. My knees buckle and I drop to the floor. It feels like the whole world is collapsing around me.

No. This can't be true.

Nancy kneels beside me. She holds me tightly as I scream in her chest. "NO! NO!" I scream, my voice raw and filled with agony.

The officers stand silently, giving me space to process the news. My father's death crashes down on me. Nancy presses me into her chest, her blouse soaking up my tears.

I push away from her and look up at the officers. “What happened? How?” I wail.

“We think he swerved into a tree to avoid hitting an animal.”

The horrific image of my father in the car burns in my mind. “Was his death quick?” I ask. I cling to hope that he didn't suffer.

Nancy grabs me and pulls me in tight as she sobs. “DID HE FEEL PAIN?” I scream out.

“We...we can’t say for certain,” the officer stutters as he looks down at me with pity.

I grab onto Nancy as I shake, tears bursting out of my eyes and mixing with hers. The room falls to complete silence. My stomach somersaults and I gag. The need to throw up hits me like a tidal wave as the realization sets in.

I spring up and dash across the room to the sink, gripping at the edge as I vomit. Nancy follows and holds my hair, rubbing my back. My sobs grow less loud and develop into whimpers. Nancy says nothing, remaining with me.

As the nausea starts to subside, I twist on the faucet and splash the cool water onto my face. Nancy passes me a towel and I pat my face dry.

“I’m here,” Nancy says softly, pulling me in for a hug.

The officers approach us. “If you need anything, please do not hesitate to reach out,” the other officer says.

I find it impossible to speak so Nancy steps in. “Thank you, officers,” she says in a strong voice.

As they leave, I cling to Nancy. *He didn’t hear me say I loved him this morning.*

“He went to work thinking I hated him,” I say in a croaky voice.

Nancy places her chin on my head as she tightens her embrace. “No, no. Don’t say that. He loved you so much, Flora.”

"But our last words were so angry...I told him I hated him."

"He knew you didn't mean it. Parents understand that sometimes we say things in the heat of the moment. He knew you loved him and he loved you with all his heart."

"I should have said I loved him when he left. I should have..." My voice trails off.

Suddenly, the door flings open and Marty rushes through.

"I heard...I heard," he says quietly, his voice thick with emotion.

Unaware of the complicated events between Marty and me, Nancy gently pushes me towards him. Stumbling towards him, my legs feel like lead. Marty catches me in his arms and he holds me. Despite earlier events, I find myself leaning into him.

"Flora, I am so sorry," Marty says as Nancy steps back, giving us some space.

Marty strokes my back in a soothing motion. "I'm here for you, Flora. Whatever you need, I'm here," he states in a reassuring tone.

I nod against his chest and a numb feeling washes over me.

Nancy leans against the kitchen table and says, "I will help with the funeral and anything else you need."

Still holding me in his embrace, Marty says, "If you want, I can stay here and look after you."

No. Hell no. What, so he can try and take my virginity when I am most vulnerable?

Nancy nods in agreement. "That's a good idea. You shouldn't be alone right now, Flora," she says in a gentle voice.

"No...No...I'll be okay."

"Are you sure?" Marty asks in a concerned whisper.

I pull back from Marty's embrace. "Yes...I just need some alone time."

Nancy steps forward, her voice filled with empathy. "We just want to ensure you're not going through this alone."

"I know," I utter.

Marty and Nancy share worried glances, but choose to respect my decision.

"Alright, but remember, if you need anything, Flora, anything at all..." Marty says sincerely.

I nod and feel a wave of gratitude for their support.

Marty gives me one last squeeze and I nod to Nancy. They leave me in the quiet of my home. As the door closes, I feel empty. Taking a deep breath, I steady myself. I sit at the kitchen table in the silence of the house. I snatch a glass and throw it at the cupboard. The glass shatters into pieces, my heart pounding as the shards scatter across the floor.

I bow my head and put my hands together as if I'm praying. "Why...Why me, God? First, my mother and now my father. What have I done to deserve this?"

I stay hunched over the table, feeling the cold reality of my loss.

I am all alone and dead inside.

THE FUNERAL SONG *THE LIVING YEARS* BY MIKE + THE MECHANICS keeps repeating in my head. I sit on the couch in my black dress, drenched from the rain during the service. The fabric of the dress clings to my skin. Marty stands by the window, looking out at the rain as he loosens his tie. He hasn't said much since we got back. He glances back at me occasionally, as if trying to find the right words to say. Nancy sorts through paperwork in the kitchen for me.

I stare at nothing as I sit there. My father's voice is now

silent forever. The image of his coffin being lowered into the ground refuses to leave me.

Feeling numb and lonely as the rain continues to beat against the window, I close my eyes, wanting everything to go away. However, the song, coffin, and rain remain in my head.

Nancy enters the room and she sits next to me, placing her hands on mine.

"You're cold and wet. Let's get you out of these clothes," she says softly.

She leads me upstairs, taking my hand. We enter my bedroom and I sit on the edge of my bed.

Walking to my closet, she picks out some loungewear and places it next to me.

"I just need to use the bathroom. I'll give you a moment." She exits the room and shuts the door behind her.

I take off the wet dress, my body feeling weak and drained as I pull on the T-shirt and leggings.

Suddenly, I hear the rumble of motorcycles outside as I peer out the window. Outside, I see Dax and Lyka. They are both dressed in black with Dax holding a card in his hand.

Marty rushes out of the house towards them, angrily. He and Dax are face to face, his hands moving in a heated manner. I want to go out there and intervene, but I feel too weak and drained to do anything.

I can see Dax clench his fist, but Lyka steps in and places a hand on his shoulder. Marty grabs the card from Dax's hand and throws it into the mud. Lyka pulls back Dax and they get on their motorcycles, speeding off.

I walk over to my bed and sink into it. Nancy returns and sits beside me, her hand resting on my back. "Your aunt texted, she sends her love. It's a shame she couldn't fly over."

"Hmm," I respond.

"Are you going to take her offer and move back to London?"

"I don't know..."

The thought of moving to London felt overwhelming. I own this house now, my father had a life insurance policy that pays me a substantial amount. I would rather be poor and have my mother and father here than rich and lonely.

"I don't know what to do," I admit.

"It's a big decision. You don't have to make it right now. No one expects you to have all the answers today. Let yourself grieve." Nancy pats my back one last time and then stands up. "I'm going to leave you in peace. If you need me, call me. Day or night," she says softly. She walks over to the door and pauses to look back at me.

"Thank you, Nancy." I give her a small smile of gratitude.

I hear her footsteps descending the stairs and then the sound of the front door closing. I scream out and cry, my sobs echoing in the empty room. The pain is unbearable. I feel completely alone.

I hear my door creak open and I jolt up, feeling startled. I see Marty standing at my bedroom door.

"I forgot you were here," I mumble, wiping away my tears. I feel embarrassed and vulnerable.

"Come here," he says, walking over to my bed.

I don't know why, but I shift toward him and reach out. He pulls me close into his chest and I bury my head in his shirt.

"It's okay, I'm here. Let it out." His fingers brush away my tears as I sob. He lowers his head and somehow, his lips meet mine.

No! What is he doing?! I can't!

I pull back, shove him away, and break the kiss. I look up at him, angry.

"No, Marty!" I cry out.

"I promised your father I would take care of you if anything happened to him."

His words fill me with rage and I abruptly stand up from the bed. I glare at him as I clench my fists. "Take care of me? Take care of me?!" I repeat. "What, by wanting to fuck me because I look like my mother?"

Marty gets up from the bed and places his hands on my shoulder. My body jerks at his touch.

"Flora, you are vulnerable at the moment."

"Exactly! My father just died and you're trying to fuck me!" I hiss.

"Just let me take care of you," he pleads, his hand tightening on my shoulders.

He just wants to fuck me.

I shove his hands off me, taking him by surprise. "Fuck off! Just leave!" I say through gritted teeth.

Marty's jaw clenches. I am scared, but I refuse to show him. "Go!" I say in a firm voice, pointing toward the door.

His eyes darken and he walks away as I follow closely behind. I watch him descend the stairs and hear him grunting with each step. He walks outside into the rain and I follow him outside.

I am soaked as I watch him enter his car. He punches his passenger seat hard and drives off.

My legs tremble as I stand there, the rain mingling with my tears. I just want to collapse, but a white card catches my eye, lying half-buried in the mud. I walk over and pick it up. The card is soaked, the paper fragile and starting to disintegrate. I carry it carefully as I hurry back inside.

I close the door and stand in the hallway, dripping water onto the floor. I look down at the card as my hands shake. Slowly, I peel it open, the wet paper tearing slightly at the edges. The ink has bled, but I can still make out the words:

SORRY TO HEAR ABOUT YOUR FATHER. DON'T HESITATE
TO REACH OUT. WE LIVE AT CEDARWOOD CABIN.
DAX + LYKA

The two brothers who I couldn't stop thinking about at one point. Now, it feels like a distant memory. I can't summon any emotion to connect with the card. The house's silence presses in around me. The only sound I can hear is the rain.

SIX
FLORA

Two months have gone by since my father's funeral and I've hardly left the house.

Nancy has been a saint and has been checking on me regularly. My aunt finally stopped begging me to move back to London.

Could I start fresh in London or should I stay here? I don't even know anymore.

I stare at the plate of toast in front of me that's gone cold. I've hardly eaten anything since my father's passing. I look at the sleeping pills on the table. The doctor prescribed them to me, but I haven't touched them. The house smells of stale coffee and untouched meals.

A darkness has taken over me. I feel so empty, like I'm being sucked into a black hole.

I wrap my arms around myself and cry, closing my eyes and taking a deep breath.

Why me? Why? Both my parents were taken from me...

I open my eyes and look at the sleeping pills again.

"I could escape all this," I mumble to myself. I can't bring myself to take them. Not yet.

But I am so lost in grief, I just want this black hole to release me.

I SET MY BACKPACK ON THE KITCHEN TABLE—EVERYTHING IS PACKED. I pace to the mirror, inhaling deeply before I look at myself. I decided to wear my father's flannel, his scent still clinging to the fabric.

I move closer to the mirror and take a long look at my eyes. One of them belonged to Dad, another to Mom. My dark blond hair doesn't look half bad, considering I haven't taken much care of it lately.

I pace over to the table, sling on my backpack, collect the keys from the holder, and open the door. Turning one last time to glance around the room, I want to cry, but I swallow it down.

I place my backpack in the passenger seat and get into my father's truck. Since moving here, I have rarely driven because I dread driving on the other side of the road.

I turn the radio on and *Stop and Stare* by OneRepublic fills the truck. I find myself relating to the lyrics as I pull out of the drive and roll down the window.

I start my drive into the forest and barely notice the town as I pass through it. The drive doesn't feel that long and I arrive quickly. I pull up to the graveled parking lot, looking around to see that no one's here. I jump out of the truck, grabbing my backpack.

Ahead of me is the forest. The trees are bending to the wind and the air is fresh. I take a deep breath and fill my lungs. Under my boots, I feel the gravel and stones crunch with each step. After walking for a bit, I stop and feel the heavy weight of my backpack. I swing it off and let it drop to the ground. I open the main compartment and reach inside, grabbing a bottle of vodka.

I take it out, unscrew the cap, and take a full swig. The vodka burns as it goes down my throat.

Carrying the bottle of vodka, I continue walking as the path in the forest takes me deeper.

I feel my head starting to lighten up and my steps become unstable. I stop to stretch out my hand and feel the bark of a nearby tree. I look at the fallen tree log, the same log my father and I shared during our last hike. I start crying.

I stumble towards the fallen tree and fumble in my pockets for my phone. I finally pull out the phone as my hands tremble. I just want to see my parents' faces one more time.

It slips out of my hand and the phone falls. Bouncing off a rock, I watch as the screen shatters. I bend down and pick it up, letting out a frustrated groan as I stare at my smashed phone. The world around me seems to blur. My head feels light and detached. Leaning against the fallen tree, I lower my body to the ground. I lift the vodka bottle to my lips and take another deep gulp. I close my eyes for a moment as my head pounds. I fight to stay conscious.

I unzip the pocket of my backpack and reach inside for the small bottle of untouched sleeping pills. Bringing the bottle closer to my face, I squint at the label, but I understand exactly what I am doing. This moment has been meticulously planned for the past three days. I lied to Nancy, telling her I was off to London and that I couldn't say goodbye as it would only hurt more. I've thought through every detail and weighed up my options. And now, at the brink of it all, I feel a sense of peace.

I want to be with my parents.

I place the bottle of sleeping pills beside me. Reaching for the vodka bottle again, I take another sip. My hands tremble as I pick up the bottle of pills. I fumble with the childproof lid, finding myself unable to open it. This fucking lid is the barrier between me and my final act.

Frustration wells up in me and my eyes become heavy. I close them, seeking a brief respite.

My heart aches as my parents come to my mind. The vodka bottle and pills slip from my hands, rolling into the underbrush. I lean against the fallen tree and close my eyes, my head falling back with a soft thud. As consciousness slips away, a sense of peace washes over me.

I surrender to the darkness.

MY BODY BOUNCES UP AND DOWN, ROLLING SIDE FROM SIDE-TO-SIDE. My head feels dizzy, like it's spinning. I struggle to open my eyes, and when I do, my vision is blurry. Shapes and colors blend together, but I slowly realize I'm inside a vehicle being transported somewhere.

"Count again and make sure!" a deep male voice says, his tone edged with concern.

"Twenty-eight pills. All accounted for. I've counted twice now," another male voice responds, sounding serious.

The realization hits me. I hadn't managed to take any of the sleeping pills. I try to focus on the voices.

Am I dead? Am I in heaven? Am I dreaming? Who are they?

My throat burns and I can still taste the vodka. Swallowing is painful, as if I'm forcing down shards of glass. My body feels numb, my limbs heavy and unresponsive.

My mouth feels dry as I let out a groan. The sound catches one of the men's attention.

"We'll take her back to the cabin," one male voice says.

"I better not regret this," the other male responds bluntly.

My eyes flutter closed, the motion of the vehicle makes me feel nauseous.

The first voice says, calmer now, almost as if trying to reassure himself, "We're doing the right thing." The other male grunts in response.

I want to speak, but I feel too sick and dizzy.

The vehicle swerves slightly, making my dizziness more intense. I swallow hard. I clench my fists, nails digging into my palms, desperately trying not to throw up.

SEVEN
FLORA

I open my eyes and notice the flow of a warm, crackling fire. My head feels dizzy as I manage to sit up, look around, and take in my surroundings. I am in a huge, cozy cabin.

"Whoa! Steady," a calm voice says. I look to the left and see Dax walking over. My head starts throbbing as I reach to touch it.

"Some water..." Dax offers, holding out a glass.

I can feel my hands tremble as I reach out for the glass. I bring it to my lips and take a sip. Straight away, the water soothes my sore throat.

"Thanks," I say, my voice weak.

"How are you feeling?" Dax asks, his voice gentle as he sits next to me.

"Dizzy, and my throat hurts."

"I'm glad we found you in time. You gave us quite a scare."

I don't know what to say, so I look around the cabin. "Where are we?"

"Cedarwood Cabin. We thought it was a good idea to bring you here. Somewhere safe."

I nod, keeping quiet. I'm guessing this is where they live. The card they left me said something about Cedarwood Cabin.

"Thank you," I say with gratitude.

Dax gets up from the couch and walks into another room as I settle back against the cushions.

I take in my surroundings as I look around. The massive cabin has two stories and a balcony overlooking the living room area with a stone fireplace in the center. A deer antler chandelier hangs from the ceiling. Every soft furnishing is light cream with either bear, deer, or moose woven into the fabric. This cabin looks like something out of a film.

How can they afford this?

They must live here with their parents; it's going to be awkward meeting them. I take another sip of water as I hear footsteps from above me. I look up to the balcony and see Lyka walking across. My eyes follow him as he makes his way to the wooden stairs. I nod my head as he descends down the stairs.

"Hi," I say quietly.

Lyka looks at me and rolls his eyes, his expression hard and unwelcoming. I watch him walk away, feeling confused.

Left alone again, I take another sip of water. The cabin, with its rustic charm and luxurious touches, feels almost surreal. Despite the beauty around me, the interaction with Lyka leaves me feeling more isolated than ever.

All of a sudden, I feel nauseous, like I'm going to throw up. The intense feeling makes me stand up in a panic.

"I'm going to be sick!" I exclaim. I frantically look around for the bathroom. Everything blurs around me as my stomach makes noises and churns. Dax bursts back into the living room and, without hesitation, grabs my arm as he leads me to a door on the far side of the room.

I run, stumbling to keep up with him. Dax pushes the door open, revealing a small bathroom. I feel relief once I see the toilet. I rush forward, fumbling with the lid and barely managing to lift it. I collapse and throw up. Vomit fills my mouth, mingling with the taste of vodka. My throat burns. I grip the sides tightly, my knuckles white as I try to steady myself. The sound of my retching echoes in the small bathroom.

Dax rubs my back with one hand, his other holding back my hair as he remains quiet. I start to tremble and feel weak as the sickness subsides. I stay there for a moment with my head in the toilet. Dax moves and hands me a damp washcloth. I take it, feeling grateful yet embarrassed.

"Just take your time. You're safe," Dax says with a calm tone.

I push myself back from the toilet and nod weakly. I feel grateful for his support.

"This is so embarrassing. I'm so sorry."

"Don't be sorry. Let's get you back to the couch. You need rest," Dax replies. He helps me to my feet, his arm steady around my limp body.

We make our way back to the living room where Lyka stands leaning against a door frame, arms crossed over his chest, staring at me with disapproval.

Why the fuck is he judging me? I feel embarrassed already.

Dax lowers me on the couch and I sink down, feeling exhausted yet relieved. Lyka pushes off the door frame and walks away with a huff.

"I know what you tried to do in the forest," Dax begins as he sits in the armchair across from me. His face glows from the fire and his eyes are filled with compassion. "Lyka and I won't mention it to anyone. But I think staying here for a few days is best until you recover."

My breath catches in my throat as my defenses crumble. I look away from him, not wanting to make eye contact. "I'm ashamed," I mumble as my eyes fill with tears.

"Don't be. I know how you feel. When my mother...well, my adoptive mother, died from sepsis, my whole world came crashing down. I didn't want to be here."

My tears spill over and I wipe them away. "I know that feeling too well. My mother died from Covid."

Dax leans forward in the armchair and looks at the fire. "So, you don't have any other family in America?" he asks.

"No. I have an auntie in London. However, it's an estranged relationship," I explain. "She used to contact me regularly once we moved here. She wanted me to move back to London after my father died, but I haven't contacted her back...even though that's where people think I am right now."

Dax gives me an awkward smile and I can tell he doesn't know how to respond. The silence between us grows. The only sound you can hear is the fire crackling and the occasional creak of the wooden cabin settling.

I shift the conversation. "So, do you live here with your father, then?" I ask.

"No. Our father died of liver disease five years ago. The alcohol killed him after he turned to the bottle. He wasn't much of a father after my mother died. Lyka stepped up, looking after me."

Guilt hits me and I feel terrible after my recent actions with the vodka. "Oh. I'm so sorry. I'll stop asking questions."

Dax lets out a dry chuckle. "It's fine. Lyka and I have moved on. That's life."

I wish I could move on like they had.

He stands up from the armchair, walks over to a wooden box in the corner of the room, opens it, and retrieves a blanket. He places it beside me. "Get some rest. I'll cook you up something." "Thank you," I murmur, placing it over my legs.

Dax heads towards the kitchen and I settle back into the couch. I glance toward the staircase, half-expecting to see

Lyka's disapproving figure. Instead, the space is empty. For the first time in two months, I allow myself to relax.

I BLINK HARD A COUPLE OF TIMES AND FINALLY MANAGE TO OPEN MY eyes. Lyka leans over me, his cold stare greeting me. I quickly raise my torso from the couch and the blanket slips down my shoulders.

"Fuck! Jesus, Lyka! You scared me," I gasp.

"Dax made you some food," he mumbles, walking away.

Do I have to follow you then? Yes? No? Asshole.

I push the blanket to the side and stand up slowly, still feeling rough. With each step, dizziness hits me harder.

I enter the kitchen which has the same rich wood that defines the rest of the cabin. Deer heads adorn the walls. In the center stands a stone island with smooth, light wooden stools surrounding it.

Dax is already at the island and pulls out a stool for me. "I made you some chicken noodle soup. Hopefully, it will make you feel better."

I take a seat, my eyes falling on the bowl in front of me. The soup smells delicious. The golden liquid has tender chicken, noodles, and vegetables with steam rising off it.

"Don't worry if you can't finish it. The main thing is you need to drink plenty of water," Dax explains, his voice soft but firm.

I lift the spoon and take a sip, the warm broth soothing my sore throat. Dax sits next to me with his own bowl. Across the island, Lyka sits there with a grumpy, intense, rugged allure. His tattoos snake up his massive arms. His light blue eyes, piercing and cold, sharply contrast his black hair, which is stylishly pushed back. Despite his grumpy demeanor, his edge makes it hard to look away.

Dax, on the other hand, presents a more approachable figure. His light brown hair falls casually on his forehead and his golden eyes hold an inviting warmth. Even though he was adopted, there was a surprising resemblance between him and Lyka. I observe them, feeling an unexpected flutter in my stomach. It is strange and unsettling. There's something about them. My eyes flutter back to Lyka. He sits there, still glaring at me.

Stop staring at me, Lyka. Fine, I'll make small talk. Asshole.

"So, Lyka, who was that girl with the black hair and tattoos at the concert?" I ask.

"Why, jealous?" he retorts. His eyes flash with amusement as he smirks arrogantly.

"No." I scoff and roll my eyes.

Dax interjects. "Sounds like Jenna. That's Jonny's old lady." He seems unaffected by the tension between me and Lyka as he continues to eat his soup.

Lyka finally stops staring at me, picks up his spoon, and starts eating.

"Ahh. So...are you seeing her?"

"No, I just fuck her," Lyka replies bluntly, a smile spreading across his lips.

"Wait. So, is she with Jonny or not?" I ask, turning to Dax for clarity.

Dax sighs. Lyka jumps in, his tone dripping with smugness. "She always wanted to be with me. I just fuck her to wind Jonny up. All I have to do is snap my fingers and she comes running."

I roll my eyes, feeling a mix of disgust and pity for Jenna.

"Well, aren't you just classy, Lyka," I mutter.

My comment must have struck a nerve because Lyka suddenly leans forward on his stool, his eyes narrowing with malice. "Foolish little girl," he says, his tone dripping with cruelty.

"Lyka!" Dax shouts.

"Do you have a problem with me, Lyka?" I counter.

Lyka rolls his eyes, dismissing me without another word. He returns to his soup and looks disinterested.

"Just ignore him. I do," Dax says, trying to lighten the mood with a joking tone. I manage to finish my soup, though my stomach feels uneasy. I take a sip of water, hoping to settle it. "Thank you, that was nice," I say, offering Dax a grateful smile.

Dax takes my bowl, stacking it on top of his own. He walks over to the sink and places them down. "So, I'm gonna sleep on the couch tonight. You can take my bed."

"Oh no, I couldn't do that. I'll sleep on the couch–"

"No, you're a guest," he insists, cutting me off.

"The couch isn't comfortable. What about if you share a bed with your brother?" I suggest, glancing at Lyka.

Lyka looks up from his bowl, his expression hardening. "I don't share."

"Of course you don't," I say sarcastically, unable to hide my irritation.

"Didn't your parents have a bedroom?" I ask, hoping to find a solution. Dax hesitates, an awkward smile playing on his lips. "Uhh, yeah. Lyka and I have left it untouched since Dad died..."

The room falls into an uncomfortable silence.

DAX TURNS ON THE FAUCET, THE WATER BEGINNING TO FLOW AS I LEAN against the cool bathroom wall. A warm bath is a good idea after my rough day.

“About Lyka...don’t worry about him. He’s like that with everyone,” Dax reassures me.

I give an awkward smile, unsure of how to respond. I walk to the window and I glimpse outside. The view takes my breath away—nothing but an expanse of lush green trees stretching as far as the eye can see.

“Oh, wow. It’s beautiful,” I gasp.

“Yeah. We’re lucky.” Dax walks up beside me. His tall frame casts a shadow on the window. “The nearest neighbor is miles away. It’s a fifteen minute drive to town.”

“Very deep in the forest, then...”

“Oh yeah. Just the way we like it.” Dax chuckles.

He walks back to the bathtub and turns off the faucet. I watch him for a moment, struck by the veins running down his arms. Before leaving, he stands near the door, his hand resting on the frame as he speaks. “I’ll leave you to it. Fresh towels are over there,” he explains, nodding toward a rail.

Before he turns around to leave, he adds, “Oh. I also laid out one of my T-shirts and some shorts for you on my bed.”

“Thank you, Dax. Again, I’m so ashamed of what I tried doing in the forest–”

“Listen. Let's not talk about it anymore. However, don’t feel ashamed. Okay?”

I watch as he quietly shuts the door behind him, leaving me alone. I walk over to the door and lock it. I take a deep breath and peel off the layers of clothes. Eventually, I stand naked and exposed in front of the mirror, looking at my skinny body from the weight loss of not eating for the last two months. I feel mixed emotions as I look at myself. There is a part of me that feels relieved that my plan didn't go through. However, at the same time, I feel uneasy knowing the Faulkner brothers are seeing me in such a vulnerable state.

I turn away from the mirror and step into the bathtub, the

warm water enveloping me. I sink down until the water reaches my breasts, closing my eyes to shut out the world outside.

The sound of water trickling from the faucet fills the room. I lean my head against the tub, drifting into the tranquil waters.

I wash my body quickly with the soap, hoping it has not been used on the brothers' ball sacks. I decide not to wash my hair, anticipating they'll drive me home tomorrow. I finish rinsing off and step out of the tub. I pull out the plug, wrap a towel around my body, and pick up my clothes from the floor.

I open the bathroom door and peer down the hallway, but see or hear no one. I walk down to the first door, which is slightly open, revealing a cozy bedroom. A fireplace casts a warm glow as I enter, turning my head to the right. There, sitting by the window and smoking, is Lyka. He stands up abruptly, eyes scanning me up and down, causing my heart to race. Memories of uncomfortable encounters with Marty flood my mind and I grip the towel tighter.

"Shit, sorry. I thought this was Dax's room," I mumble, feeling nervous.

I exit the room and hurry to the next door down the hallway. This time, the bedroom door is closed. I knock, open the door, and look around, taking a moment and looking around the room. I see the T-shirt and shorts that Dax has put out for me on the bed.

Like the rest of the cabin, the bedroom has a rustic charm. A stone fireplace stands against one wall. The wooden double bed is adorned with dark green bedding. A standing bookshelf in the corner catches my eye with books adorned with small figurines and trinkets.

The room feels peaceful, a sanctuary amidst the wild beauty of the forest outside.

I set my clothes on the bed and glance around. A framed

photograph on the bedside table catches my eye—a snapshot of Dax and Lyka together, their smiles carefree.

I change into the T-shirt and shorts quickly.

I hear a knock on the bedroom door as I'm in mid-thought. "Come in," I say loudly.

Dax pokes his head around the door. "Everything okay?"

"Yeah, thanks. The T-shirt is a little big...but it will do." I giggle as the garment hangs loosely on my body.

"You look good..." Dax says in a flirty tone, then quickly shaking his head as if catching himself. I look away as I blush.

"Are you sure you don't mind me staying in your room?"

"Honestly, it's fine."

"Okay. Are you going to be dropping me back tomorrow?"

He slips his hands into his jeans pockets. "Not sure yet. I want to make sure you're fine first," he replies, his eyes meeting mine with a hint of concern.

I nod, unsure of how to respond to his kindness.

"Well, I'll let you get some sleep. If you need me, you know where to find me."

"Thanks, Dax," I say softly, appreciating his effort to make me feel at ease.

He gives a final nod before walking out. The room falls into silence, the only sound the soft crackle of the fire.

I turn around, look at the inviting bed, and crawl onto it. The bedding is thick and cozy. I take a deep breath, inhaling the faint scent of pine and wood smoke. My thoughts begin to settle as I lie there. My eyelids grow heavy. Despite the unfamiliar surroundings, I feel a sense of calm.

EIGHT
FLORA

I WAKE UP FEELING MUCH BETTER THIS MORNING, THE DIZZINESS HAS completely disappeared.

The cabin is silent and I can only hear the birds outside chirping. Quietly, I get out of bed, needing to use the bathroom.

I walk down the hallway as the wooden floorboards creak under my feet. Just as I reach the bathroom, the door swings open and out walks a woman. I recognize her. It's Jonny's girlfriend, Jenna. She stands there in only a red, lacy bra and underwear, exuding confidence. I can understand why Lyka is attracted to her. Jenna smirks at me, looking me up and down with an evil glare. I feel awkward, not knowing what to say or do. It's clear she spent the night here. Before I can say anything, I hear the door behind me creak. I turn around and see Lyka standing in his doorway, topless. He has perfect six-pack abs and a V-line leading down to his lower body. His eyes meet mine, but he doesn't say a word.

Jenna nudges my shoulder deliberately as she walks past me. She walks to Lyka, who steps aside to let her pass as she disappears into the room.

Lyka lingers for a moment, his eyes still locked on me. He

smirks like he is taunting me. I roll my eyes at him, feeling frustration welling inside me. He slams the door behind him, echoing through the silent cabin.

I take a deep breath and steady myself before entering the bathroom. I try and push Jenna and Lyka out of my mind.

I finish on the toilet, I wash my hands, and splash some cold water on my face. I then step back into the hallway, ready to face whatever the day might bring.

I walk into the living room and see Dax fast asleep on the couch. He looks peaceful, his messy hair sticking out in all directions. I tiptoe past him to the kitchen, but a floorboard creaks loudly.

"Morning," Dax says, his morning voice deep. He rubs his eyes and squints.

"I didn't mean to wake you," I say, apologetically.

The blanket falls from his chest as he sits up, revealing his toned, tattooed torso.

What is it with the men in this cabin and their amazing bodies?

Dax swings his legs over the side of the couch. He pats the cushion next to him and I take a seat beside him. Just then, we hear shouting from Lyka's room.

"Lyka! Lyka!"

"Ahh, that sounds like Jenna," Dax says, shaking his head.

"It is. I bumped into her while going to the bathroom." I give him an awkward smile. Dax looks around the room, clearly unsure of what to say next. He seems expectant to change the subject. "Breakfast?" he offers, tossing the blanket aside. I nod in agreement.

Dax jumps up from the couch and I can't help but notice he's wearing just his underwear. I look down and see his morning wood pressing up against the fabric.

"Oh, uh..." I stutter, looking down and quickly averting my eyes.

Dax looks down at himself and chuckles. “Just gonna go to the bathroom,” he says with a grin.

I give him a closed-lip smile. I don’t know where to look, I feel so awkward.

Wow...*Fuck. He looked big! I have only seen Marty’s, but Dax is bigger.*

I hear more shouting and banging from Lyka's room. I try to block it out, instead focusing on the fire that is just dying embers. A few minutes later, Dax returns, dressed in gray sweatpants and a T-shirt. “Alright, let's get some breakfast going,” he says with a smile, heading towards the kitchen. I follow him as Dax opens the fridge, pulling out the ingredients. “How do you feel about pancakes?”

“Pancakes sound amazing.”

As Dax stands at the stovetop cooking the pancakes, I realize I haven't seen my phone since being here.

“Do you happen to know what happened to my phone?”

“We found it smashed near a rock, it doesn't even turn on. I asked Lyka to see if he can fix it. He's good with technology stuff,” he replies, flipping a pancake. “Make yourself at home, by the way.”

“Oh, okay...” I mutter, feeling a mixture of relief and frustration. At least they found it, but now I'm even more cut off from the outside world.

Why am I even worried? It’s not like anyone is going to contact me. They think I’m in London.

I walk over to the cupboard, grab a glass, and then head to the fridge to pour some orange juice. I stand next to Dax and lean my back against the countertop.

“How old are you and Lyka?”

“I'm twenty-nine and Lyka is thirty-three. You?” he asks, glancing at me briefly before turning back to the pancakes.

“Twenty.”

“Wow, you're young. Can't even legally drink yet,” Dax teases with a smile.

“Uhh...I guess. It's weird here. In England, we can drink at eighteen,” I say, shrugging.

“Lucky Brits,” he says sarcastically, raising an eyebrow.

He flips the pancakes again, the golden brown surfaces sizzling slightly as they land back in the pan.

“You wanna eat these outside on the balcony?” he asks, plating the pancakes. “Sure,” I respond, feeling a little thrill at eating outside with the forest view.

Dax takes two plates and walks over to the back door. I hold it open for him as he steps out, following closely behind. I am taken back by the view as we step onto a dark, wooden balcony. The sight is breathtaking—nothing but endless trees. The sun shines through the tops of the trees, creating beautiful shadows. Dax places the plates onto a wooden table with benches.

I take a seat on one of the benches and feel the roughness of the wood on the back of my legs. The air is fresh as I take a deep breath. Dax sits across from me and we both dig into our pancakes.

“If you don't mind me asking. What do you and Lyka do for work?” I ask, taking a bite of a pancake.

Dax pauses for a moment. “I compete in a lot of motocross games, Lyka does a lot of woodwork making furniture, and we both hunt,” he explains, his tone casual but filled with pride.

“Men with many talents?” I ask in a joking tone.

“You could say that,” he replies, a small smile playing on his lips.

“So, I'm guessing Jonny is on another motocross team?”

“Yeah. He's hated me for a long time; he just can't beat me. And he hates my brother for obvious reasons.”

“Is Lyka adopted, too?” I venture, hoping I’m not overstepping.

"No. His mother and father wanted another child, but couldn't. In the end, they adopted me when Lyka was four and I was a newborn baby," Dax explains.

"Oh! I'm sorry to hear that, Dax," I say awkwardly, not sure how to respond.

"It's cool. Before you ask, I know your next question...My mother dropped me off at a fire station when I was just two weeks old," he continues, his eyes fixed on his pancakes.

He looks up, his golden eyes meeting mine. "I'm over it. Lyka's mother and father gave me a life. They were my real parents."

I feel a lump in my throat. I look out at the forest, trying to process everything he shared. "That's really amazing, Dax. To have had that kind of family, I mean," I say, turning back to him.

"Yeah, it is. They gave me everything I needed. Lyka and I... We've had our ups and downs, but we're brothers."

"Having each other's back and being close is nice to see."

Dax chuckles, shaking his head. "Yeah, *close* is one way to put it. We're both stubborn as fuck, but we'd do anything for each other."

"I wish I had brothers or sisters."

Dax looks over at me, his expression thoughtful. "So, you said your mother died of Covid? You mentioned your auntie, but do you not have anyone else? No grandparents?" he asks.

I take a deep breath and the loneliness overwhelms me. "Nope. No one else. I am all alone in America."

Dax's face softens. I can tell by his facial expression that he feels empathy. "I'm really sorry to hear that. I can't imagine how hard that must be."

I can feel tears form in my eyes, but I don't want them to spill over. "It's been rough. After my mom passed, it felt like my whole world fell apart. She was my rock. And now, with my father gone, too, I just feel like there is a huge void inside me."

Dax reaches out and places a comforting hand on my hand. "I get it. Losing family is never easy. But you're not alone. You've got us, at least for a little while."

As we finish our breakfast, the conversation shifts to lighter topics. Dax tells me about some of the motocross races he's won, his face lighting up as he recounts his favorite moments. Lyka suddenly walks out onto the balcony in his underwear, the sun highlighting his tattoos. He lights a cigarette, takes a deep drag, and leans over the railing, exhaling a cloud of smoke into the air.

"Sounds like someone had a good night," Dax states.

Lyka takes another drag and nods. His eyes seem so distant. Jenna walks out fully dressed in a black leather jacket and black ripped jeans. Her heavy boots thud against the deck as she walks up to Lyka. She turns, her eyes narrowing as they land on me and Dax.

"Anyway..." I begin, trying to break the awkwardness.

"Wait, aren't you the British girl who crossed my boyfriend Jonny at the concert?" Jenna accuses in a sharp tone. She attempts to wrap her arm around Lyka's waist, but he shifts away, avoiding her touch.

"I think you heard wrong. He made a comment and grabbed me, so I spat in his face," I reply bluntly.

Dax raises both his eyebrows, a chuckle escaping his lips. He seems impressed by my retort.

"And your *boyfriend*?" I continue, not missing a beat. "Yet you're here, fucking Lyka." The words come out sharper than I intended, but I don't regret them. Lyka smirks, his eyes gleaming with a mix of amusement and approval.

Jenna glares at me, her lips curling into a sneer. "Dax, keep your bitch on a leash."

I scoff, unable to believe her audacity.

"Watch your mouth, Jenna," Dax warns.

She ignores him and moves in to kiss Lyka, but he turns his head away, her lips landing awkwardly on his cheek. She storms back into the kitchen.

Lyka takes one last drag of his cigarette, flicks the butt over the railing, and follows her inside. The balcony door slams shut behind him, leaving Dax and me again alone.

“Well...that was something,” Dax says.

I shrug. “She had it coming.”

Dax chuckles and shakes his head.

“Let’s hope that will be the last we see of her for a while,” Dax says. I nod, sharing the mutual feeling.

Lyka walks back onto the balcony, sitting beside me on the wooden bench. His demeanor is guarded.

I guess Jenna has gone, then...Thank god.

“I've invited some people around tonight,” Lyka announces.

“Alright, cool,” Dax responds.

“Will you be dropping me back soon?” I ask, my gaze shifting between Lyka and Dax, searching for their response.

Dax and Lyka look at each other, communicating silently. Lyka doesn't say a word. He just turns away, looking into the forest.

“We’ll give it a few more days. We wanna make sure you’re fine first,” Dax replies.

“I know what I did in the forest was stupid. I can’t thank you two enough for helping me. However, I don’t want to be a burden,” I explain, my voice filled with gratitude and shame.

“It’s just a few days. It’s not like you have anyone to go home to, Flora.”

I flinch at his words, but I can tell he meant no harm in what he said. He was right, and deep down, I knew it, too. I had no family waiting for me. The thought of going back to an empty house filled me with dread.

Reluctantly, staying here might be the lifeline I need, even for a few more days.

"Well, what about food? I can pay toward the costs."

"Flora...Me and Lyka have enough food for some time. We don't need your money. We've got a freezer full of animals we've hunted," Dax reassures me.

I feel guilty; these two brothers have already done so much for me. The least I can do is offer to contribute.

Lyka reaches into his pocket and pulls out a pack of cigarettes, pushing it toward Dax. Without a word, Dax places one between his lips, lighting it.

"Just enjoy your time here. Take a break," Dax says after exhaling a stream of smoke.

Taking a break in this beautiful cabin, deep in the forest seems nice and ideal. Hopefully, it will be enough to restore my mind from the dark thoughts that linger.

I REALIZE I HAVE TO GO COMMANDO, NOT WANTING TO WEAR MY WORN panties again as I get dressed. I step into the hallway and hear quiet voices coming from the living room.

"It's all working, yeah?" I hear Dax ask.

I peek around the corner and see Lyka and Dax standing in front of the TV. Lyka looks up and notices me. He quickly switches it off and crosses his arms.

"Everything okay?" I ask.

Dax turns around and gives me a closed-lipped smile. "Yeah..."

Lyka only grunts in response. He sits on the couch and immediately goes on his phone. I glance around the room and notice their massive collection of movies. Rows upon rows of DVDs and Blu-rays line the shelves. Intrigued, I walk over to the shelves, running my fingers along the various movie cases.

"You have so many horrors..."

"Ahh, you like horrors, then?" Dax asks, moving closer and standing behind me.

"My favorite is *Misery*."

Dax looks over at Lyka and raises his eyebrows. "Lyka loves that film, too..."

Lyka glances up from his phone, giving a small grin with a flicker of approval in his eyes before returning his attention to his screen. Seeing another expression other than grumpiness from him feels odd, but I'm not complaining.

"You're welcome to watch anything you want," Dax says.

"Thanks, Dax."

I look back at the movies, seeing what other titles they have.

"I was thinking we could ride around the forest to the lake," Dax says, breaking the silence.

"Wait. You have a lake?"

"We don't *own* the lake. It's just off our land, a short ride from here. We sometimes go fishing there."

I shrug my shoulders and reply, "Sure."

Dax nudges Lyka with his foot and he looks up from his phone. "You coming?"

Lyka stands up and huffs. "Yeah," he replies bluntly.

Dax grabs a set of keys from the side table. We exit the cabin onto the porch that wraps around the building and the fresh, forest air hits me. At the front of the cabin, five Adirondack chairs are arranged around a stone fire pit, strings of lights hanging from the surrounding trees. It's a beautiful scene, so tranquil. We descend the wooden steps and I follow Dax and Lyka towards a stone garage. Lyka steps forward and lifts the garage door, revealing an array of vehicles inside.

There's a dark, emerald green Land Rover, two motocross bikes, two sleek, black motorcycles, and four ATV quads.

How do they afford all of this?

"We do well enough with our jobs and hobbies," Dax says, as if he can read my thoughts.

"We'll take these," Lyka says, walking over to the ATVs as he inspects them.

Dax grabs a helmet and a pair of gloves, handing them to me. "Safety first," he says with a wink.

I put on the gear and walk over to the ATV as my nerves start setting in. Dax gives me a quick rundown of how to operate it. The engines roar to life and we drive out of the garage onto a dirt path leading into the forest. My heart races; I've never been on an ATV before.

The ride is intoxicating. The ATV easily handles the rough ground and I feel a sense of freedom as we speed through the forest.

After a short ride, we arrive at the lake. It's a tranquil spot with clear, blue water reflecting the sky and the surrounding trees. It almost takes your breath away.

Dax and Lyka park their ATVs and take off their helmets. Dax walks over to the water's edge and skips a stone across the surface. "Beautiful, isn't it?"

"Yeah," I reply, my voice filled with awe. "It's incredible."

Lyka leans against his ATV, lighting a cigarette. He takes a deep drag and exhales, his eyes fixed on the lake. There's an intensity about him that I can't quite figure out.

We stand there for a while, just taking in the beauty of the lake and the forest around us. For the first time in a long while, I feel a sense of calm wash over me.

Dax breaks the silence. "We come here often to fish and relax. It's a good place to clear your head."

My eyes don't leave the lake, I'm still in awe at the view. "I can see why."

I gaze into the distance and my eyes widen in dismay and fear. Across the lake, I spot a bear and her two cubs leisurely going through the underbrush. It's the first time I've ever seen a bear in person, and even from this far away, the sight is both majestic and terrifying. My mouth opens in silent awe.

Noticing my reaction, Lyka follows my gaze and quickly understands.

"Hey! Mama bear!" Dax shouts. I'm guessing he shouted to let the bear know we were close.

The bear hears Dax's call, lifts her head, and looks in our direction. Without hesitation, she ushers her cubs back into the safety of the forest.

"Whoa...That's the first time I've seen a bear. Scary," I say, my voice breaking, betrayed by my fear.

Lyka shakes his head and scoffs, clearly unimpressed.

"Well, you better get used to seeing animals like that," Dax says. "We're deep in the forest. There are bears, wolves, coyotes, snakes, deer, elk, moose—"

"I've seen a moose, they're massive!" I interrupt.

"Yeah...You don't fuck with moose. More dangerous than bears, if you ask me."

"I always find it crazy how many animals you have around here that could easily kill you. We only have sheep and cows in England," I muse, shaking my head.

"Well, every place has its dangers. Here, you just have to learn to live with it."

We stand there as the lake reflects the clear sky. I can't help but feel respect for this place's untamed beauty. I glance to my right and notice a small, rustic, brown cabin nestled among the trees. Its presence seems almost hidden, blending seamlessly with the forest.

"Ooo, what's that?" I ask, looking at them both with curiosity.

"That's a fishing cabin. If you ever get stuck out here, you can stay in there. It's pretty basic, just a bed and fire." Dax explains.

I take a few steps closer to get a better look. It's old and weathered.

"We use it mostly during the fishing season or when we want to escape. It's warm and dry," Dax says.

Lyka, leaning against his ATV, takes a drag of his cigarette and adds, "It's a good spot if you need some alone time...No one bothers you out here."

I start walking towards it, and as we reach the cabin, I peek through the window. Inside, I can see a simple interior. A single bed is positioned against one wall, covered with a blanket. A small wood-burning stove sits in the corner, its chimney extending through the roof. There's an old wooden table with two chairs and a few shelves holding fishing gear and basic supplies.

Dust covers everything, making any object or piece of furniture have a slight gray hue.

"It's a good place to fuck someone," Lyka says, stubbing out his cigarette.

I roll my eyes and cross my arms. "Lyka...You're either grumpy or fucking someone."

Dax chuckles, raising his eyebrows and glancing at Lyka for his response.

"Just because you ain't getting any..." Lyka says in his deep, gravelly voice, a hint of a smirk playing at the corners of his lips.

Glaring at him, I feel a spark of defiance flare up. "Or maybe I don't want to."

"Calm down," Dax interjects, still smirking but clearly trying to diffuse the situation.

The atmosphere changes when Jonny suddenly appears behind the small cabin, his friends following close behind.

"Look...it's the Faulkner brothers," Jonny taunts. An evil grin spreads across his face and I want to slap him. He irritates me.

Lyka's smirk is wiped off his face as he quickly moves to stand protectively next to me, his arm pushing me slightly behind him. I've never seen this side of him before, but it's clear he's ready to defend me.

"What do you want?" Lyka asks in a threatening tone.

"Nothing, just out on a walk," Jonny hisses back.

"What, deep in the forest?" Dax retorts, stepping forward. His eyes narrow, his body tense and ready for whatever might happen.

Jonny's friend steps to the side, his eyes locking onto mine. He gives me an evil smirk. "Hey Jonny, isn't that—" he starts to say, but Jonny cuts him off, his gaze never leaving Dax.

"Yup. The British doll. You know she has a wicked tongue, spitting at me like that. Maybe I should teach her some manners and rip it out," Jonny sneers, his eyes filled with a twisted amusement. His words make my skin crawl and I feel scared. I can feel Lyka's arm pressing me more firmly behind him.

Lyka's protective stance becomes even more pronounced, his arm acting as a barrier between me and Jonny. His muscles are tense; I can sense his readiness to act if things escalate.

Dax steps up to Jonny, their faces inches apart. "Get the fuck out of here," Dax growls through gritted teeth.

I hear a sharp click and my eyes dart to see Jonny flip a switchblade open. The blade glints in the light and my heart skips a beat. Lyka notices it, too. I grab onto him, gripping his arm tightly.

"What are you gonna do, Jonny?" Lyka asks, his voice steady.

Dax's eyes follow Jonny's hand and he steps even closer, his face inches from Jonny's. "Cut me, I fucking dare you," he challenges.

"You better back off, Jonny," Lyka warns.

Jonny's friend looks uneasy, glancing between Jonny and Dax. "Jonny, come on, man. Let's just go," he mutters, trying to pull Jonny away. But Jonny seems locked on Dax, the knife still out and threatening.

"You think a knife scares me? Go on, try it. See what happens," Dax hisses.

The standoff feels like it stretches forever, every second ticking by. My heart is pounding in my chest. Finally, Jonny seems to waver. With a snarl, he retracts the blade and steps back, shoving the switchblade into his pocket. "You're not worth it, Faulkner."

Dax doesn't move, his eyes still locked on Jonny, watching his every move. "Get the fuck out of here," Dax repeats.

Jonny and his friend finally turn and walk away. I release the breath I didn't realize I was holding, my grip on Lyka's arm loosening.

Dax stands there for a moment longer, making sure they're really gone, before he turns back to us. His face is a mixture of anger and concern, the adrenaline still evident in his eyes. "Are you okay?" he asks, his voice softer as he puts a reassuring arm around me. "We need to be more careful. They might come back."

"Agreed." Lyka nods.

But amidst the fear, there's the realization that Dax and Lyka would do anything to protect me.

I jump onto the ATV, gripping the handles as we return to

the cabin. We pull up and park in the stone garage. I dismount and a wave of sleepiness washes over me.

"Hey, you don't mind if I go take a nap, do you?" I ask, handing the helmet back to Dax.

"You don't have to ask. Use my bed."

Feeling grateful, I nod and head into the cabin. As I walk down the hallway, my eyelids grow heavier with each step. Suddenly, I hear footsteps behind me. I turn around and see Lyka trailing a few paces behind.

"What?" he grumbles, catching my eye.

"Nothing," I mutter.

Lyka's eyes darken, and without a word, he storms past me, his shoulder bumping into mine.

What the fuck is his problem with me?

He slams his bedroom door with a loud bang that vibrates through the cabin.

I sigh as I shake my head and continue to Dax's room. I kick off my shoes and fall onto the bed, sinking into the mattress. Pulling the covers over myself, I let out a long sigh. The bed smells faintly of Dax's cologne. My eyes flutter closed and I drift off almost instantly.

NINE

FLORA

I AM STARTLED AWAKE. I RUB MY EYES AND I FEEL GROGGY. THE SONG *Regulate* by Warren G and Nate Dogg plays loudly. As I get out of bed, I can smell the strong scent of cannabis. It's an odd feeling that cannabis is legal in this state. I hear people chatting outside, so I follow the noise and exit the cabin.

Stepping onto the porch, I take in the scene. Around the fire pit sits a group of people. Lyka is in his element; a girl with long, brown hair perches on his lap, laughing at something he's said. Dax, sitting down with legs spread comfortably, takes a deep drag from a joint. The rest of the group, three other guys and two girls, are scattered around in some chairs with others on the ground.

I walk over slowly and awkwardly. Lyka spots me and nudges the blond guy next to him. "Move," he commands bluntly.

"No, no, it's fine. I'll sit on the ground," I protest while smiling. I don't want to cause any trouble.

Lyka turns his head to the blond guy, his eyes narrowing. "I said fucking move."

The guy sighs and rolls his eyes, but obeys, moving to the ground. I feel uncomfortable, but take the now-empty seat.

The blond guy hands me a beer. I accept, but I am feeling a little hesitant as I look down at the alcohol.

"Think that's a good idea?" Dax voices.

"It's only beer. I'll be okay," I reassure him.

"What are you, her babysitter?" the girl on Lyka's lap taunts, her tone dripping with sarcasm.

Lyka chuckles to himself, clearly amused.

"I'm Tammy, and that's Lina and Sav." The girl on Lyka's lap introduces herself and then points to the other girls. I look over at them and give a polite smile.

God, this is so fucking awkward.

Dax takes a drag from the joint and passes to the blond guy who moved for me. "You forgot about the guys," he says, exhaling.

"I'm Jack," the blond guy says, taking a drag on the joint and passing it back to Dax.

"I'm Robin," a voice calls from across the fire. I glance up to see a very tanned, good-looking man with a confident smirk on his lips.

Another guy chimes in, "You can call me Dickie."

I feel awkward with these strangers around me as they look and study me, making me feel on edge.

"The guys are on my motocross team," Dax explains.

Tammy whispers something into Lyka's ear and he grins, his hand resting possessively on her thigh.

I sip my beer, trying to relax my awkwardness and nerves.

"So, Flora, how are you finding our little corner of the world?" Robin asks. The fire lights up his face and makes his eyes twinkle.

"It's...different," I reply honestly.

“I hear you are staying at the cabin for a bit?” Sav asks, looking up from the fire, her eyes curious.

“Uhh, yeah,” I reply, feeling the whole group's attention shift towards me.

“Have Dax or Lyka tried it with you?” Tammy asks, her tone teasing but pointed. I notice Lyka's grip on her thigh tightening, a silent warning.

“What? Oh, come on!” Tammy exclaims. “It's only a matter of time before you do,” she adds, smirking as her eyes shift to Dax and Lyka.

“The Faulkner brothers have slept with every girl here,” Lina chimes in, laughing as if it's the most natural thing in the world.

Dax shifts uncomfortably in his chair, the comment making him uneasy.

So it’s not just Lyka who gets around.

“Flora doesn't have to know that,” Robin interjects, shaking his head. He looks over at me, an apologetic smile tugging at his lips.

“Doesn't Flora mean *flower* in Latin?” Jack asks, smoothly changing the subject. His eyes meet mine, giving me a friendly smile.

I nod my head and smile, grateful for the distraction. “Yes, it does,” I confirm, sipping my beer.

“That's a beautiful name,” Robin compliments. “Very fitting.”

Lyka and Dax look at each other quickly.

“Thanks,” I say, feeling a bit more relaxed. The fire crackles and the smells of burning wood mingle with beer and cannabis.

“How did you end up here with these two then?” Sav asks.

“It's a long story,” I start, glancing at Dax. “Let's just say I needed a change of scenery and Dax and Lyka offered to help.”

"Hmm. Sounds like there's more to it." Tammy raises an eyebrow.

Lyka speaks up, sensing my discomfort. "It's none of your business, Tammy."

Tammy's face shows she is slightly annoyed, but doesn't push further. She turns her attention back to Lyka before looking at me and holding the joint out in front of me. "Pass that to Sav," she orders.

I take the joint from her awkwardly, not knowing where to hold it. Sav reaches over, takes it from me, and giggles.

Tammy starts kissing Lyka's neck as Lina moves herself between Dickie's legs, sitting together in an intimate pose. The atmosphere is charged with casual intimacy.

I catch Tammy's eye as she looks at me, sensing my discomfort. I give her a polite and awkward smile.

"I bet you find this awkward, don't you, Flora..." she says with a hint of mischief.

I don't know how to respond. "Umm," I say, hesitantly.

"It's how we live out here. It's a small town. We all kinda please each other, if that makes sense," she continues as she nuzzles closer to Lyka.

Dickie kisses Lina's cheek and states, "You only live once, right?"

I can't stop myself from asking, but the question slips out. "Do you all fuck each other then?"

Everyone bursts out laughing, making me feel embarrassed and stupid. Dax face palms, chuckling. "It's just a bit of fun..." Lina states.

"What happens in Cedarwood cabin stays in Cedarwood cabin," Lyka confesses with a smirk.

Robin shakes his head at them all. "Just ignore them, Flora," he says, his tone reassuring.

"What? It's not like she's a virgin!" Tammy states.

I can feel my cheeks turning red. The laughter dies down and everyone looks at me, expecting me to answer, but I don't.

"Oh my. You're a virgin?" Sav asks. I can't help but feel like she's mocking me.

I wanna just curl up and die of embarrassment.

Lyka and Dax exchange a quick glance before returning their attention to me, their expressions unreadable.

Robin suddenly gets up from his chair and asks, "You wanna come grab some more beers with me?"

"Yes, please."

I feel grateful he is trying to take me out of the spotlight. I follow Robin toward the cabin, leaving everyone else behind talking quietly as I walk away.

As we enter the cabin, the music becomes muffled. Robin leads me into the kitchen where a cooler is filled with beer and ice.

Robin grabs a couple of beers and hands me one. "You okay?" he asks.

"Oh, yeah. I'm just not used to this kind of...openness, I guess."

"Yeah. It's a lot to take in. Everyone is pretty chill, especially when you get to know them." He chuckles.

I take the cap off the beer and take a swig. "It's just different, that's all. By the way, thank you for getting me out of there. It was so awkward."

"It's cool. I could tell you needed a breather."

I can hear the sounds of music and laughter outside, probably mocking that I'm a virgin. However, I feel at ease with Robin as we stand in the kitchen.

Breaking the silence, Robin asks, "What do you do for fun? Got any hobbies?"

"I used to paint a lot. I love hiking and being out in nature."

"Hiking, huh? There are some great trails around here. I could take you some time."

"Yeah, that sounds nice. I'd like that," I reply, feeling more relaxed.

"I'm sorry if my earlier comment made you uncomfortable," Robin says. "You are very pretty—just like your name," he adds.

I look at his tanned arms and my eyes meet his as he moves his thick, black hair out of his face.

"Thanks." I giggle, feeling myself blush.

Robin places his hand on my waist and moves closer. I freeze, unsure how to react, but I feel my stomach flutter. *Is he going to kiss me?*

I suddenly hear a creak from behind me. Robin quickly removes his hands from my waist and steps back as we turn around to see Dax standing in the kitchen doorway. He crosses his arms and his expression is unimpressed.

"Everything okay?" Dax asks.

Robin backs away from me, cracking his neck. "Yeah, dude." Their eyes lock.

"Sav wants you," Dax says.

Robin lets out a huff and leaves the kitchen frustrated, brushing past Dax without another word. I follow him, but Dax grabs my arm, stopping me.

"Flora. He only wants one thing."

I look up at him, seeing genuine concern in his eyes. "Thanks for looking out for me." I try to brush him off, but I feel a mixture of gratitude and confusion. *Why did Dax care so much?*

Dax loosens the grip on my arm and looks down at me. "Just...be careful," he says.

"I will."

He steps back slightly and moves a strand of my hair behind my ear. "Let's head back outside. The others will wonder where we are."

We walk back out to the porch where the laughter and conversation still continue. As I sit by the fire, I notice Robin and Sav talking quietly on the other side of the circle. Robin glances my way briefly, but his attention quickly returns to Sav.

Tammy is still on Lyka's lap, whispering in his ear. Lyka's eyes meet mine for a moment, something unreadable passing through them before he looks away.

Dax sits down next to me, offering me a reassuring smile. I take a deep breath, feeling more at ease. Suddenly, raindrops begin to fall, pattering against the leaves.

"Shit. Let's get inside," Dax calls out.

We all rush towards the cabin. Once inside, you can hear the intensity of the downpour. We gather around the living room, everyone feeling the effects of the beer and cannabis.

Dax puts some music on and the beat of *Gimmie More* by Britney Spears starts playing. Tammy and Sav dance on the rug in the center of the room. Their movements are sensual, drawing the attention of everyone around. They move closer together, their arms draping over each other's shoulders as they sway.

I glance over at Lyka who is watching them dance. Lina pulls me up, her grip firm yet playful. "Come on, Flora. Dance," she whispers. I feel the effects of the beer and feel giddy. I let my body move to the music.

I notice Dax watching me dance and his eyes flicker with enjoyment. I feel more confident as he watches me. On the other hand, Lyka shifts in his seat, his expression hard to read. Tammy catches on and grabs my hand, pulling me towards her. She moves her hands up and down the sides of my body.

Lina and Sav continue their dance, their movements synchronized.

Tammy's face is suddenly close to mine. She leans in and kisses me, her tongue exploring my mouth. I've never kissed a girl before and the experience is surprising. When she finally pulls away, she looks at me with a smirk and a glint of mischief. I can feel all eyes on us.

"That's fucking hot," Jack says, sitting on the floor.

Lyka's expression shifts and he abruptly stands up. His movements are swift as he crosses the room, his gaze locked on Tammy. Without a word, he grabs her arm with a firm grip. Tammy looks surprised as Lyka pulls her down the hallway toward his room. Lina and Sav stop dancing, their playful smiles fading as they watch Lyka and Tammy disappear.

The music still plays, but it feels distant now. Breaking the stillness, Lina moves over to Dickie and casually sits on his lap as he wraps an arm around her waist.

"Let's put on a movie," Dax suggests. The idea is agreed upon and we gather around the couch. Dax picks a light and funny movie, and as the opening credits roll, we settle into the cushions. The sound of the rain outside is a comforting backdrop. As we lose ourselves in the movie, we all hear muffled sex moans from Lyka's room.

DAX

I sit at the kitchen island, drinking a beer. The cabin is quieter now, but I can hear faint sounds of laughter and chatter outside where Sav, Jack, and Robin are smoking.

Lyka walks in nonchalantly, only wearing his boxers, and heads straight for the fridge. "Where is everyone?" he asks.

"Flora, Dickie, and Lina have gone to sleep. The others are outside smoking."

Lyka nods, taking a huge sip from his glass. He places the empty glass back on the counter with a satisfied sigh. He turns around, biting his bottom lip. "You got any condoms? I've run out and I'm not going in Tammy bareback."

His question catches me off guard, but I quickly stand up from the stool, reach into my pocket, and pull out a condom. I toss it over the counter. “There you go.”

“Thanks, man,” Lyka says, grabbing the condom with a hint of relief. He then tucks it into the waistband of his boxers. He turns to leave, then hesitates, looking back at me with a curious expression. “You good?”

“I caught Robin getting close to Flora,” I tell him.

Lyka's expression turns from casual to serious. He walks over and sits on a stool.

“What do you mean...*close*?”

“He was touching her waist,” I reply, waiting for his reaction.

His jaw tightens and his fist clenches. I can see the anger building up inside of him.

Robin suddenly appears at the kitchen doorway, his eyes darting between Lyka and me. “Everything alright?” he asks.

Lyka stands up from the stool, his eyes locked onto Robin. “*What the fuck* were you doing with Flora?” His voice is cold.

“What's wrong? Jealous? The little virgin might not want the Faulkner brothers?” Robin taunts.

“Shut the fuck up!” Lyka growls, his eyes narrowing.

Robin smirks. “For once, someone in this town doesn't want you two. You fucking hate it!” he replies.

I stand up from the stool and it falls behind me. I feel the adrenaline kick in. “I know your plan...Take her virginity just so you can boast about it,” I say with fury.

Robin lets out a sinister chuckle, his eyes gleaming. “I promise to be gentle with her...Maybe.”

His words provoke me and I see red. Every ounce of anger and protectiveness surges through my body to my fists. I rush toward him, tighten my fist, and punch him straight in the face. The force of the blow sends him stumbling backward.

"You ain't going near her again. Got it?" I shout through gritted teeth. I look at my knuckles and they are covered in blood. Lyka throws a cloth at me and I wrap it around my hand.

Robin recovers and he glares at me. Lyka stands beside me, ready to back me up.

"I'll be gone first thing in the morning when I'm sober and can drive," Robin mumbles, his voice barely audible. He looks defeated as he turns and leaves the kitchen.

I feel Lyka place a hand on my shoulder to calm me down. However, I am too wound up and shove him off. I take a deep breath and sit back on the stool, trying to calm myself.

"I just want to protect her...for her to be safe with us. I don't know why," I confess.

I turn my head to Lyka and his expression is unreadable, as always.

"She's in a dark place. We've both been there. We know what it's like to feel helpless, Lyka."

Lyka's eyes meet mine, and for a moment, the room is filled with an unspoken understanding. The darkness we've both faced forged a bond you can't put into words.

Tammy walks into the kitchen wearing one of Lyka's T-shirts. She moves with confidence, completely oblivious to what just happened. She walks up to Lyka, wrapping her fingers around his hand. She tugs on Lyka's hand and pulls him towards the hallway. "Come on, Lyka."

Lyka hesitates for a moment and he looks back at me. There's a brief flash of something in his eyes—apology, perhaps, or regret. But then he allows himself to be led away, following Tammy back to the bedroom.

I take another sip of my beer and Sav slowly walks in. She takes the beer bottle from my hand, lifts it to her lips, and takes a sip. "Everyone has passed out." She giggles, her eyes sparkling with amusement.

I manage an awkward smile, unsure of how to respond. Robin and his words still linger in my mind.

Sav moves closer to me, placing the beer bottle on the counter as she stands between my legs. Her hands rest on my shoulders and she leans in, her lips brushing against my neck.

"Sav..." I say. I push her gently, giving her a warning.

"Dax...It's been so long since we've fucked," she murmurs against my skin.

My mind drifts to Flora, her image flashing in my mind. I shouldn't be doing this. Guilt gnaws at me. *Why am I thinking of Flora?*

Sav's hand trails down my chest, moving to my jeans. She feels for my cock and starts rubbing.

"I can't..." I whisper.

Sav stops, her eyes locking onto mine with desire. She takes a step back, her hand still grasping mine. She pulls, her eyes pleading. "Come on, Dax," she whispers. I can tell she's putting on a seductive voice. I feel a mixture of emotions inside me—guilt, desire, confusion. I take a deep breath and follow her.

FLORA

I wake up in Dax's bed and my head feels dull from last night's beer. I glance down at the floor and see Lina and Dickie laying near the foot of the bed, cradling each other while they sleep.

The room's quietness is shattered when I hear chanting from Lyka's room.

"Yes, yes, yes!"

The unmistakable sounds of Tammy and Lyka fucking echoes through the cabin. I roll my eyes, feeling irritated.

I look over at the nightstand alarm clock which reads six in the morning. My throat suddenly tightens up and I feel thirsty. Carefully, I step over Lina and Dickie, hoping not to wake them. I quietly make my way out into the hallway. I look to my right and see Robin sprawled on the floor with a rug covering him. Jack is slumped against a door with a couch cushion under his head. I can't help but let out a little chuckle at the sight.

I head towards the living room and kitchen. As I approach, the faint sound of moaning can be heard. I turn my head and see Sav and Dax on the couch. As I get closer, the sounds become unmistakably clear.

Sav is straddling Dax, her movements slow as she grinds against him with her head thrown back. "Dax...yes," she murmurs, lost in the moment.

I am caught off guard and don't know where to look. My eyes look around, trying to focus on anything. Dax opens his eyes and notices me, quickly pushing Sav off him. He looks surprised and embarrassed, and I feel the same way. "Shit. Shit. Shit," he mutters.

Sav looks at me with annoyance as she stands, raising her hands in the air. "Sorry," I mumble as I walk backward toward the hallway.

I make my way back to Dax's room, stepping over Lina and Dickie once again. Crawling back into the bed, I pull the covers over my head, wishing I could erase the last few minutes from my memory. One single tear falls onto the pillow. The muffled sounds of Lyka and Tammy's fucking still reach my ears, blending with my thoughts of Dax and Sav.

EVERYONE HAS LEFT THE CABIN AND IT'S NOW EERILY QUIET. I STAND IN the bathroom, brushing my teeth. I look up at my reflection, trying to collect my thoughts and shake off the awkwardness of the morning.

As I'm lost in thought, I catch a glimpse of movement behind me. Robin is standing in the doorway with a noticeable black eye. My brow furrows in confusion.

“What happened to you?” I ask.

Robin shifts uncomfortably, his eyes darting to the side. Dax appears out of nowhere, his face stern. I can't shake the feeling that something happened between them.

“Ahh, I fell after you went to bed,” Robin mumbles, avoiding my gaze. The explanation feels fake and how he glances at Dax makes me suspicious. I feel a pang of unease.

Robin breaks the silence and says, “Anyway, Flora, I’m going. It was lovely meeting you.”

I watch him leave and I have so many questions. Dax stands there, his expression softening slightly as he looks at me.

“Are you okay?” I ask him.

“Yeah, I'm fine. Robin just had a bit too much to drink last night. We had a...disagreement. It's nothing for you to worry about.”

I want to press further, but Dax’s demeanor suggests he’s not in the mood. “Okay, if you say so...”

“By the way, I’m sorry you saw that earlier with Sav,” he mumbles.

“Why are you sorry? I don’t care,” I reply, trying to sound normal, but a slight edge to my voice betrays my true feelings.

Dax's eyes search mine as if hoping for a different answer. “Sure you don't care?”

“No? It’s like you want me to care...”

The truth is I did care a little, but I don’t know why. I didn’t expect him to behave like that. Even after learning that he and Lyka have slept with all of their friends.

Dax steps closer, trying to look into my eyes, but I walk past him, eager to escape the atmosphere. He stops me, his hand gentle yet firm on my arm. He looks down at me and his eyes are intense. He brushes his finger against my chin, making my heart skip a beat. I instinctively move my face away, the confusion of my emotions too much to handle.

"Could you please drop me home today? I've decided I'm going to return home to London," I whisper as I look away from him.

Dax bites his lips and nods. I can see the sadness in his eyes...and something else. He lets me walk past him. I head back to the bedroom to gather my things, my mind going crazy with thoughts and emotions I can't quite figure out.

TEN
FLORA

I glance around the bathroom, making sure I have everything. I decided this morning to move back to London to live with my aunt. I put my backpack on and head to the living room.

Dax and Lyka are standing in front of the TV with expressions of shock and disbelief across their faces.

They don't register my presence as I walk in. "What?" I ask, curiously. Turning to the TV, I instantly understand their shock.

A news channel is broadcasting a breaking story:

"A new strain of the Coronavirus has been discovered with a much higher fatality rate. The President has put America on lockdown for three weeks. You must only leave for essentials."

My backpack slides off my shoulder. "Oh my God," I whisper to myself as I allow the information to sink in. Lyka and Dax turn to me.

"I thought the world was going to live with Covid now," I

utter, my voice tinged with disbelief. Just when it seemed like everything was going back to normal, this happens.

"What do you want to do, go home or stay here?" Dax asks in a supportive tone. It's clear he wants me to be comfortable with whatever decision I make.

"For three weeks? Just the three of us?" I ask. But the idea of being alone with my dark thoughts for that long feels unsettling. I've been fighting hard to keep them at bay. The thought of returning home without my father being there and three weeks of being alone...

"We have everything we need. We don't need to leave the cabin," Dax reassures me.

I feel uneasy and take a deep breath. The idea of traveling now seems risky. "Covid killed my mother. I know what it can do to people. I guess I have to stay here," I say, shrugging.

They both exchange glances. "We'll make it work. Don't worry," Dax says.

"Yeah..." Lyka adds.

"One problem. I don't have any spare clothes or underwear." Being stuck here for three weeks without any clean clothes feels daunting.

"It's fine. My mother had a whole wardrobe of clothes she didn't wear. I think they will fit you."

"Oh, Dax. I couldn't." The idea of wearing someone else's clothes feels intrusive, especially considering she is dead.

"It's fine. Some of it is brand new and still has the tags on."

"Okay...well, what about underwear?" I ask, feeling uncomfortable.

Dax pauses. "I guess you could wash your bra often and wash your panties daily. Or...wear some of my underwear?" He looks up and gives me a smirk. Lyka chuckles under his breath and shuffles his feet.

Dax tries lighting the mood and raises both of his hands. "Hey, it's not a bad idea...Better than going commando, right?"

I can't help but laugh. "I guess you're right. Thanks, Dax. I'll take a look at the clothes and figure something out."

Lyka suddenly speaks up, "Don't think you are getting an easy ride staying here for three weeks. It's not a vacation. You can help around the cabin."

"I'll help out wherever I can," I agree immediately.

Lyka nods before turning and heading to a door near the stairs. It's a heavy wooden door with a sturdy lock. He pulls a key from his pocket, unlocks it, and steps inside, closing it behind him. The lock clicking back into place echoes slightly in the living room.

"Where does that door go?" I ask Dax, curiosity getting the better of me.

"Oh, just to the basement. We grow cannabis down there. It's best you don't go down there...it's not safe," Dax explains.

I nod, acknowledging what he just said. I reach the couch and sink into the cushions.

"Dax, wait...You can't sleep on the couch for three weeks..."

"I mean...if you're offering, I'll happily stay in bed with you," he says, winking and raising his eyebrow with a playful glint in his eyes.

"Nice try. Seriously, I'll take the couch," I insist.

"Honestly, it's chill."

Dax walks over to the couch and extends his hand. I grab it and he helps me up with ease. "Let me show you where we keep our stock."

"Stock?" I echo.

I feel his palm against mine as he leads me through the kitchen toward a door I've never noticed before. We step through the door and I'm greeted by a room with shelves packed with canned goods, snacks, and household items. It's like a mini store, with so many supplies that it would put most convenience stores to shame. At the far end of the room, there are three large chest freezers.

"All our frozen meat is in there," Dax explains, pointing to the freezers.

The shelves hold multiples of every item. "Why do you have this stockpile? It's like a store..."

"Well, after the previous lockdown, we like to be prepared. We also get harsh winters out here. Plus, Lyka and I hate going into town."

I walk over to a section of the shelves stocked with condoms and period products. I glance back at Dax, raising my eyebrows.

"What? You always gotta be prepared. We have a lot of female guests," he says, shrugging it off.

"Of course," I mutter, amused but not entirely surprised.

"Hey! Better to have it and not need it, than to need it and not have it. Right?"

"I guess you're right..." I shake my head.

Dax shows me where everything is kept. Shelves are dedicated to different types of foods, baking supplies, bottled water, and a section for cleaning supplies. I am surprised at the level of organization.

"You could survive out here for months without ever needing to go into town," I say, running my fingers along the canned goods.

"That's the idea. We like our privacy, and this way, we can stay self-sufficient. Plus, you never know when you might need to hunker down for a while," Dax says, leaning against a shelf and crossing his arms.

"That makes total sense. Especially with everything going on now."

"Exactly. With the new lockdown, we don't have to worry about running out of essentials."

We exit the stockroom, stepping back into the main cabin. “You got any more things to show me that I don't know about?” I ask. Dax turns around, a mischievous glint in his eye. “Well...we have the barn where Lyka does his woodwork, there's also a mini gym, and, behind the barn, we have a hot tub.”

“Okay...This place just keeps getting better.”

Dax grins and opens the back door as I follow him. We descend the balcony steps and I glance around, taking in the forest. Ahead of us, I see a large, wooden barn, its structure sturdy. As we approach the barn, I notice its double doors are slightly ajar. Dax pushes the doors open and I step inside, the smell of fresh-cut wood and sawdust greeting me. The interior is spacious, with various woodworking tools neatly arranged on one side. A large workbench dominates the left side of the room, covered in half-finished projects and pieces of wood.

“Lyka spends most of his time in here, that is, when he is not fucking some random girl. He’s pretty talented with woodworking. He made most of the furniture in the cabin,” Dax explains.

I run my fingers over a beautifully carved, wooden chair, admiring the intricate details. “This is amazing,” I say, genuinely impressed.

Dax leads me further into the barn and we reach an area with gym equipment, including a treadmill, a set of free weights, and a bench press. On the other side, there's a ping-pong and pool table. “We try to stay active, especially during the winter when we're cooped up inside,” Dax notes.

“I bet you guys have some intense matches.”

“Haha, you have no idea. Lyka’s got a mean backhand in ping-pong, and you already know we are pool sharks.”

We exit the barn and Dax leads me to a small clearing behind it. Nestled under trees is a hot tub surrounded by a wooden deck with several lounge chairs and a small table. It looks so inviting and relaxing.

"This is our little oasis. It's great after a long day, especially when it's freezing in the winter."

I look around, taking in the peaceful setting.

"You guys have everything you need out here. This place is incredible."

"It's our haven away from the world," Dax says with a satisfied smile on his face.

"You know, Dax...While we're in lockdown, you and Lyka can't bring any girls here to, you know, fool around with."

Dax grins and shakes his head. "I have my right hand."

The mood feels lighter and we both laugh at the banter. I walk up to the hot tub and run my hand along it. "Can I try it out tonight?"

"My right hand or the hot tub?" Dax asks with a playful tone, smirking.

"The hot tub!"

"Haha. I'm just joking, sure."

"Oh, shit! I don't have any swimwear," I say, rolling my eyes.

"You can go in naked...Perhaps just wear your bra and panties?" Dax suggests.

"Maybe..."

Dax and I start walking toward the cabin when the door opens. Lyka steps out, heading toward the barn. He acknowledges us with a nod as he passes by.

"Lyka!" Dax calls out. "Flora's thinking about trying out the hot tub tonight."

Lyka stops walking as he turns around and looks at me. A small smile tugs at his lips before he continues walking to the barn. Dax and I head inside, the scent of burning logs greeting us as we step into the living room.

I STAND IN THE BATHROOM WEARING A ROBE, PREPARING FOR AN evening in the hot tub. Suddenly, dark thoughts flood my mind with memories of my mother, father, and past. The darkness overwhelms me and I feel like I'm being sucked into a black hole. My chest tightens and I find it hard to breathe.

I sit on the edge of the tub, trying to steady myself. Tears fill my eyes and I'm unable to hold back my sobs. My crying echoes around the bathroom loudly. I bite my hand, trying to hold in the noise.

The door suddenly opens and Dax rushes in. "Hey, hey," he says calmly while kneeling beside me.

"I'm...I'm...sorry," I say, my voice trembling. Feeling embarrassed and vulnerable, I wipe away my tears.

"It's okay," Dax replies, placing his arm around my shoulder. He is full of concern as he cups my face. His finger caresses my cheek and wipes away my tears. I glance up and see Lyka standing in the doorway, his arms crossed and his expression unreadable like always. Dax nods at him and a silent communication passes between them. Lyka lingers for a moment longer before turning and walking away, giving us privacy.

"If you want to talk, I'm here," Dax offers softly.

I try to push the darkness away and take a deep breath. "I'll be fine. Let's go outside to the hot tub. Shall we?" I say, trying to ease my thoughts.

Dax hesitates, his eyes searching mine for any sign that I'm not okay. But I maintain the smile on my face, trying to convince him. Eventually, he nods, standing up and offering me his hand. "Okay," he agrees, though his concern doesn't fade.

He helps me get up to my feet and I take his hand as we walk through the cabin. As we step outside, the cool air hits my skin and I wrap my robe around me tighter.

The string lights illuminate the pathway to the hot tub, casting a soft, magical glow over the surroundings.

Dax lifts the cover, revealing the steaming water. "Here you go."

I hesitate. I can feel Dax's eyes on me. With a deep breath, I untie the robe, let it open, and it falls to the ground revealing my black bra and panties. I catch a flicker of something in Dax's eyes. I quickly slip into the hot tub, the warm water instantly wrapping around my body.

Dax drops his robe, revealing his navy swim shorts. His fit, toned body covered in tattoos takes my breath away. I quickly look away as I don't want him to see my reaction. The water ripples around him as he lowers himself into the hot tub.

He settles into the opposite corner. The night air feels pleasantly cool on our exposed skin. I lean my head back on the side of the tub and close my eyes for a moment, trying to let the stress and the dark thoughts of earlier melt away.

Neither speaks for a while, simply soaking in the night and the water's warmth.

"How are you feeling?" Dax asks, breaking the silence.

I open my eyes and glance at him. He looks calm, yet his eyes are full of empathy.

"A little better. I'm sorry...Sometimes, it just hits me out of nowhere."

"You don't have to apologize."

I find myself relaxing more and my shoulders start to ease. "Thanks, Dax. I mean it."

Dax leans over and places his phone on the side. "I'm gonna play some music, let me put it on shuffle." The song *I Feel Like I'm Drowning* by Two Feet starts playing through the speakers.

I close my eyes again, leaning my head back and letting the tranquility of the night wash over me. Suddenly, I feel a splash of water hit my face, startling me. I open my eyes and squint at Dax.

"Did you just splash me?"

"No?" he replies with an innocent look before winking at me.

"Oh, it's on!" I narrow my eyes and start splashing him.

"Hey!" he exclaims, moving closer to the middle of the hot tub and splashing me back. Our laughter echoes around the trees.

I meet him in the middle, trying to outdo his splashes, both caught up in the moment. I lose my footing on the slippery surface and stumble. With a surprised scream, I fall onto Dax, causing him to lose his balance. We both slip, the water splashing around us. I land on his lap and place my palms against his chest to steady myself.

We are face to face and everything is still. I feel his breath on my face and my heart races. One of his hands rests on my waist, holding me steady, while the other caresses my thigh. His golden eyes lock onto mine and neither of us moves. I swallow hard as my body reacts to his touch.

His thumb moves up and down on my thigh, sending shivers up my body. I feel goosebumps form on my skin.

"Are you okay?" he whispers softly.

I bite my bottom lip. "Yeah, I'm fine."

His hand tightens around my waist and I can't help but lean in as our foreheads touch. Neither of us makes a move to pull away.

"Dax..." I start to say seductively.

He removes his hand from my thigh and traces his finger over my lips. His eyes search mine as if he's trying to read my thoughts. The moment stretches on and I want to kiss him. I wrap my arms around his neck, preparing myself.

The sound of a twig snapping jolts us out of our moment and we both turn our heads toward the forest as a fox emerges from the trees. For a brief second, it feels like the fox is a silent witness to our almost-kiss, but then it darts away, disappearing into the night. I gulp and quickly move off Dax's lap. My heart is still racing.

"Um...I'm gonna head inside. I'm feeling sleepy," I stutter, my voice sounding shaky. I try to avoid eye contact with him.

"I just need to put the cover over the tub and lock up. I'll be in soon..."

We both pretend that we didn't just have a moment together. I climb out of the hot tub and grab my robe, wrapping it tightly around myself.

I hear the forest sounds as I walk back to the cabin. The moonlight casts a soft glow over everything.

I reach the cabin and my mind goes crazy, repeatedly replaying the moment in the hot tub.

His lips, eyes, and touch. Oh, fuck! Get out of my head.

I rush towards the bedroom. As I walk down the hallway, I hear a faint moaning. The sounds become clear as I get closer and I realize they're coming from Lyka's room.

I bet he has a fucking woman in there!

The door is slightly open and I glance inside. The lamp casts a dim light over the room. Lyka is fully naked, lying back on his bed with his feet on the ground. His tattooed body looks amazing; his head is tilted back into his pillow and his eyes are closed. He is completely lost in the moment as he moves his hand up and down his cock.

I feel breathless. I want to step back, but I can't tear my eyes away. The way his body clenches with each stroke, the quiet moans that escape his lips. His cock is big, the tip glistening with pre-cum.

His hand movements get faster and his breathing becomes ragged as his other hand clenches the sheet. His moans grow louder and I almost want him to say my name. I can't help but feel aroused watching him.

Lyka's strokes become more frantic as he works his cock. I watch as he grabs a tissue from the bedside table, placing it on the tip of his rosy, swollen cock. With a final, loud groan, he releases, his body shuddering as he comes. I feel a strange mix of emotions swirling inside me—arousal, guilt, and a hint of envy.

I hear the sound of the back door shutting. I panic and quickly back away from Lyka's door.

I move down the hallway as silently as possible. I glance back over my shoulder, expecting Lyka to appear in the doorway, but the hallway remains empty.

Thank God!

As I reach my bedroom, I carefully close the door behind me, leaning against it to catch my breath.

I try to shake off my arousal and guilt. The sound of his moans, the way his body moved. The room feels like it's going to swallow me whole and I find myself pacing, unable to settle. Eventually, I force myself to sit on the bed, my thoughts still whirling around.

ELEVEN

FLORA

I sit at the end of the bed, my mind drifting back to the events of last night: Dax and I in the hot tub and Lyka lying on his bed, lost in his own pleasure. The intense thoughts linger in my mind.

How do I feel about Dax? I know I wanted to kiss him.

"Damn aerial!" Dax shouts with frustration, pulling me back to the present.

I walk into the living room where I find him hunched over the TV, fiddling with its controls. The screen projects an unyielding blue.

"What's up?" I ask.

He looks up with an irritated face. "A damn mouse has chewed through the aerial cable again. We won't be able to get live TV until it's fixed." He sighs as he brushes his hair out of his face. "I'll have to go up on the roof later and have a look."

"Good thing you've got loads of movies," I offer.

Dax's face lights up slightly. "Yeah, we do. At least we won't get bored."

Lyka suddenly appears from the hallway and immediately

reminds me of last night's events. I feel a flush of embarrassment at the memory of watching him.

“Gonna be a storm later. Just got the notification on my phone,” Lyka announces in his deep voice.

“Will it be bad?” I ask, trying to avoid making eye contact with him.

“Maybe a few fallen trees,” he replies as he stares at me, confused, trying to understand why I won’t look at him.

“We’ve got everything we need. It’s cool,” Dax responds.

He walks towards the kitchen, leaving me alone in Lyka’s presence.

Lyka moves towards the front door. Calling out to him, I ask, “Hey, Lyka.” My voice is much louder than anticipated.

He pauses and turns to me with the door held open.

“Did you manage to fix my phone?” I inquire, continuing to direct my eyes away from his.

Lyka shakes his head and exits the cabin.

I walk into the kitchen and notice my bra and panties hanging out to dry, but they’re still damp. A spike of embarrassment hits me as I realize I have to go commando today.

“I thought you could see me in action today?” Dax asks with a hint of excitement.

My mind races. *Action? What does he mean?* I furrow my brows in confusion.

“There’s a miniature motocross track behind the house in the forest,” Dax explains, noticing my confusion.

“Yeah, that would be cool.”

Dax takes out his phone and states, “The storm isn’t due till tonight, so we’re all good. I'll make some sandwiches before we head out.” Dax grabs a loaf of bread and prepares lunch. I watch him work as he prepares some sandwiches.

“What fillings do you like?” he asks as he glances up at me with a smile.

"Surprise me."

Dax nods and adds layers of ham, cheese, lettuce, and a smear of mustard to the bread. He then wraps the sandwiches in wax paper and places them in a small cooler with water bottles.

I CARRY THE COOLER AND A PICNIC BLANKET WHILE DAX STANDS IN HIS motocross gear, carrying his helmet. He looks undeniably hot in his gear.

He walks over to the garage and grabs his motocross bike as I walk alongside him. I glance over at Lyka, who is topless and chopping wood. I can't help but bite my bottom lip, blushing at the sight of him. I quickly look away, hoping Dax doesn't notice.

"Yo! I'm gonna show Flora the track," Dax shouts.

Lyka wipes the sweat from his forehead with the back of his hand and nods. There is something about his topless body and manliness that makes my stomach flutter.

How the fuck am I going to cope with living with these two for three weeks?

It's been less than twenty-four hours since lockdown started and I already have had too many thoughts about them.

Holding the handlebars to his bike, Dax and I walk deeper into the forest. We come to a hill and I look down to see the track with dips and jumps.

"You can see the whole track from here. Make yourself comfortable," Dax says.

I flick out the blanket, spread it on the ground, and place the cooler on top. I lower myself and stretch out my legs, watching as Dax puts his helmet on.

Fuck! Fuck! Fuck!

Seeing him in the whole outfit with his helmet, not being able to see his face, turns me on.

He mounts his bike, kick-starts it, and rides onto the dirt track. He controls the bike well and confidently, making the first jump as if he has done it countless times before. I feel breathless as I watch him. He navigates the track's twists and turns with ease, his engine echoing around the forest.

As Dax circles back around, I take in the scenery, looking up at the tall trees above. My heart skips a beat as I watch his bike fly through the air and land smoothly. I am so impressed by his talent.

Dax pulls up beside me, removing his helmet. His face is flushed and he looks impressed with himself.

"Whoa, that rush! What do you think?" he asks, out of breath.

"Okay...that was incredible. I can see why you win a lot. You're really good."

Dax can't help but grin with pride. "Thanks. It's a lot of fun. You should try it sometime."

"Uh, I'll stick to watching for now."

Dax dismounts his bike and sits beside me. He reaches into the cooler and pulls out a couple of sandwiches, handing one to me. We eat in comfortable silence.

You can hear the forest around as the breeze hits the trees and birds sing. As we finish lunch, I look back toward the cabin and thoughts of Lyka come to mind—the sight of him working and his muscles flexing. I feel a mixture of emotions and don't even know what to think. Dax lays back on the blanket, looking up at the sky.

"Just saying...this isn't such a bad way to spend lockdown," he says, breaking the silence.

I join him, lowering my torso and lying on the blanket next

to him. I look up, taking in the blue sky that peaks through the trees above.

I know they say the calm is before the storm, but today is so beautiful!

"Well, in the previous lockdown, all I did was eat and paint."

"You paint?" Dax asks, turning his head to look at me.

"Yeah, watercolors. I haven't painted for a while, though."

"My mother used to paint, too. We have some watercolor paints in the barn. Maybe you could get back into it."

"Maybe..."

I love his encouragement despite my hesitancy. It's been a long time since I felt the urge to create. We lie there in silence, taking in the forest views.

Dax breaks the silence. "Tell me about your paintings, Flora."

"I..." I hesitate for a moment. "I used to paint landscapes mostly. Places I visited, places I imagined. I guess it's my way to escape. Creating a world that feels safe and beautiful."

"I'd love to see your paintings sometime."

His interest makes me smile. "Maybe I'll show you some. That's if I find the courage to dig them out."

A fly buzzes near my face and I flick my hand. "Truth be told...when my mother died, I just painted with the color black. I haven't painted at all since my father's death."

Dax sits up and places a hand on my knee, his eyes filled with genuine concern and empathy. Talking about my parents hurts and I feel a hard lump form in my throat.

"After my father died, I just couldn't bring myself to do it anymore. It just felt pointless, you know?"

"Maybe being here will help you paint again, hopefully in color."

I look into Dax's eyes, wanting to wrap my arms around and

hug him. He smiles and his playful demeanor returns. "Plus, we've got a pretty awesome hot tub here. That's gotta count for something, right?" he asks, trying to cheer me up and change the subject.

I laugh. "You're right. It does."

Dax stands up, extends his hand out, and I grab it. "Come on. Let's head back."

When Dax and I returned to the cabin, we settled in to watch *House of Wax*. Halfway through, Lyka joined us, his hair slightly messy and sawdust sprinkled on his flannel from working on his wood projects all day.

By now, the storm has arrived and is in full swing. I stand in the stockroom, scanning the shelves for some snacks. My stomach rumbles, craving something sweet. My eyes land on a packet of candy just as Lyka enters the room. He reaches above me to grab a packet of mixed nuts.

"Enjoy watching?" he asks quietly.

I feel a rush of panic and my heart skips a beat.

Fuck! Oh my god! He knew I watched him please himself. Oh, fuck!

I try to think of an excuse. "Uh..." I stutter.

Lyka looks at me with a confused expression. "*Misery* is my favorite. However, I do like *House of Wax*, too."

"Oh, yeah! The movie..." I reply, trying to sound nonchalant.

Lyka gives me a strange look, but says nothing more. He exits the stockroom, leaving me alone with my mind going crazy. I'm surprised he even spoke to me. He is normally so blunt and stern. I take a moment to catch my breath, steady myself, and then head into the kitchen. The wind outside is howling and rain violently lashes against the windows.

I lean against the counter, unwrap the candy, and take a bite. Dax walks into the kitchen. “Find something good?”

“Just some candy,” I reply.

He grabs a couple of beers from the fridge and hands one to me. “Damn, it's stormy outside,” he says, clinking his bottle against mine. “Cheers to surviving the first day of lockdown.”

“Cheers,” I echo, feeling more at ease. We both take a sip.

Dax and I walk into the living room. Lyka is already settled on the couch, munching on his packet of mixed nuts and scrolling through his phone. I take a seat beside him, sinking into the cushions as Dax rummages through the stack of DVDs, looking for our next movie.

I turn to Lyka and ask, “Any news on the lockdown situation?”

He glances up from his phone and simply shakes his head. Dax finally finds a DVD and pops it into the player. He then sits on the couch next to me as the movie begins.

“Don’t you guys have a computer or internet here?” I ask.

Dax chuckles, glancing at Lyka before answering. “Our parents were old school. They hated technology. But, we had phones as we got older, so it wasn't a big deal.”

I nod, understanding the sentiment behind it. The movie plays on, filling the room with laughter and lighthearted banter.

TWELVE

FLORA

The storm is raging outside as I lay in bed. Each thunderclap is loud, the rumbles shaking the cabin. Flashes of lightning illuminate the room, casting shadows across the walls.

A loud bang outside the window startles me and my heart races. Jumping out of bed, I run to the living room. Dax is fast asleep on the couch, the chaos outside having no effect on him. I nudge his arm, trying to wake him up. His eyes flutter open, squinting as he tries to make sense of the situation.

"Flora..." Dax mumbles, half asleep.

"Dax, I'm scared," I whisper.

Suddenly, a thunderclap echoes through the cabin and the walls vibrate. Scared and without thinking, I climb onto the couch and sit beside Dax.

He blinks a few times and sits up. "Hey, it's okay," Dax whispers while shifting to make room for me. He can sense I'm scared and wraps an arm around me, pulling me closer. "It's outside. We're safe in here. The storm can't hurt us," he reassures me.

I feel safe with Dax beside me. I focus on my breathing, trying to calm myself down.

"Sorry. It's just that the storms in England are nothing like this..."

I feel myself getting tired in the safety of Dax's arms, making my eyes start to close.

"Let's get you back to bed. You can't sleep sitting up," he says quietly, nudging me.

We both get up from the couch and he leads me into the bedroom. Another thunderclap crashes, louder and closer than before. Instinctively, I grab his hand.

"Dax...can you stay in here with me tonight?" I can feel the fear and vulnerability sneak up on me.

Dax pauses and bites his cheek as he studies my face. "Of course, I'll stay."

He lifts up the blanket and helps me back into bed as I crawl under the covers. Dax walks to the other side of the bed and looks at me for approval. I nod and he climbs into the bed.

The mattress dips under his weight and I turn to face him. Our bodies are close, but not touching.

"Thanks," I whisper.

The wind and rain are the only sounds you can hear. We look at each other for a moment, only inches apart.

A rumble of thunder scares me and I can't help but flinch. I move closer to Dax, pressing my body against his. I rest my head on his chest, feeling his heartbeat beneath my ear. He wraps his arms around me, holding me close as he rests his chin on top of my head.

"I'm here," he whispers.

His arms encircling me makes me feel safe. Dax pulls back slightly and looks down at me. I tilt my head up, meeting his gaze.

We're face to face, lips centimeters apart as our breaths mingle. I don't know how it happens, but our lips meet. The kiss is soft at first, his lips inviting.

Dax's arms tighten around me, pulling me closer as our kiss deepens. His hand moves up my back, his finger tangling in my hair. I feel a rush of emotions spread through me.

We are both breathless as we break away from the kiss. Dax rests his forehead against mine and I feel his warm breath on my lips.

We hold each other for a moment and our connection grows. Our lips meet again, this time more intensely, as our tongues explore each other. I feel the heat radiate from Dax's body as he grips me tightly. I can't help but let out a quiet moan, which seems to spur him on.

My hands wander under his T-shirt and my fingers move up his abs. He feels incredible, his body is so defined.

He responds by grabbing the back of my neck. Just when I thought our kiss couldn't get more intense, it does. His free hand moves to my waist and slides under my top. I arch into his touch, craving more.

Dax pulls back for a moment, his breathing heavy and his eyes full of desire. We hold our gaze, both knowing this is something we want. He sits up, pulling his T-shirt over his head and tossing it across the room. A shaft of lightning casts a shadow across his chiseled body. I sit up, feeling breathless. He touches my chin, guiding my lips to his for another passionate kiss.

His hands move to the hem of my top and he pauses, looking at me for approval. I smirk and raise my arms, allowing him to lift it over my head. My top is pulled away, revealing my bare breasts. He breathes deeply, taking in the sight of me. I wrap my arms around his neck and straddle his lap. I feel the hardness of his cock pressing up against his underwear. I can't help but let out a moan as we kiss again. His hands roam up and down my back until they move to my hips, gripping them firmly. I grind against him, feeling my shorts rub against his hard cock. My body reacts on cue and I feel myself getting wet, my nipples puckering.

"Fuck. Stop," he mumbles. I can hear the hesitation in his voice.

I look at him, confused and out of breath.

"Flora, are you sure you want this...with me?" he asks, swallowing hard. His eyes search mine.

My heart pounds in my chest as I nod. "I'm sure."

His thumb brushes over my skin as he cups my cheek. "Oh, Flora. I'm not worthy of you."

I can see the self-doubt on his face. I lean in closer, my lips brushing against his ear. "Dax. I want this..."

His eyes search mine and he pulls me closer. "Are you sure?" he asks again.

"Yes. I want you, Dax."

He kisses my neck and I lean my head back, letting out a deep moan.

"Flora, I'm going to be so gentle," he murmurs between kisses.

I grind against him, feeling his cock strain through his underwear. Our hands lock together, our fingers entwining. My movements pick up speed and I can hear his breathing get heavy.

Suddenly, with a swift motion, Dax flips me over. His hand caresses my thigh and he slowly pulls down my shorts. The air hits my exposed skin, making me quiver. I feel vulnerable yet excited. I spread my legs for him, my wet pussy on full display. I watch his eyes as he takes in the sight.

He brushes his hand past my stomach and then caresses my pussy, his touch making me gasp.

"I don't want to hurt you," Dax says, biting his bottom lip.

"It's going to hurt at first. I know," I reply, propping myself on my elbows. "But I trust you."

We move together, rising onto our knees. I reach and tug his underwear down as his erection stands tall and hard. We both look at each other before I reach out, wrapping my hand around his cock. His eyes never leave mine as he inhales sharply.

"Flora..."

I release my grip on his cock. His fingers move to my pussy and he spreads my lips open. I let out a soft moan as he touches my clit.

With his other hand, he gently pushes on my torso. I relax, lie down, and open my legs for him again.

"Wow. You have such a beautiful pussy," he whispers.

I offer myself to him completely and he holds my legs open, his hand gripping my thighs. He moves between my legs, his tattooed body towering over me. His fingers rub my clit, and pleasure consumes me. My mouth is wide open, but no noise comes out.

Fuck, I want to orgasm. I've only ever made myself orgasm before.

I arch my back as his fingers continue to move on my clit. Pushing my hips towards him, I feel my orgasm building up. I close my eyes, lost in the sensation, as my breathing becomes heavy. His fingers pick up speed, moving from side to side.

Finally, my whole body trembles as I have the most intense orgasm of my life. I let out a cry and my legs quiver. Dax holds me close and wraps his arms around me.

I lie there and look up, seeing he's impressed with himself. A smile spreads across his face as he reaches into the bedside table drawer and retrieves a condom. He kneels in front of me, holding out the condom. "Wanna put it on?" he asks.

"I've never..." I start to stutter.

"It's okay, I'll do it."

He tears open the condom packet, pulling it out and slowly

rolling it down his cock. The band grips tightly around his erection. His eyes meet mine, seeking confirmation.

"Flora. Are you sure you want to do this?"

"Dax. I'm sure," I reply. I feel butterflies form in my stomach.

Dax lowers his body on top of mine, positioning himself carefully. One hand supports my head, while his fingers caress my cheek. "If you want me to stop, you just say so."

My heart races and I nod, biting my bottom lip and feeling scared. I feel the tip of his cock at my entrance. He moves his hand from my face as he guides himself.

I begin to shake as my nerves get the better of me. "Relax, Flora," Dax whispers. Slowly, he begins to thrust his hips forward, his cock inching into my pussy. I feel a mixture of pain and pleasure as he enters me.

A loud gasp escapes my lips as my pussy adjusts to his size.

"Are you okay?" he asks, his eyes searching mine for any signs of discomfort.

"Mhmm."

Fuck. His cock is big!

I feel deep pressure and my pussy stretches as he penetrates me. Dax's hips move slowly with each thrust. I feel myself relaxing more, the pain gradually giving way to pleasure.

"Ok. I'm gonna move a little faster now," Dax whispers.

I wrap my legs around his hips, drawing him closer and inviting him deeper. His pace quickens.

Moaning loudly, I'm unable to hold back. "Dax. Dax."

"You're so tight. You're making me want to come," he groans in my neck.

I arch my back, meeting his thrusts. My hands grip the sheets beneath me as I lose myself. The room fills with the sounds of my wet pussy and moans. I let go of the sheets and cling to him.

I feel Dax's hands under my back as he flips me over, positioning me on top of him. Straddling him now, I look down and notice a bit of blood on the base of his cock. My heart skips a beat and I let out a huge gulping sound.

“Oh–” I start to say, my voice sounding scared.

“It’s okay,” he reassures me.

Before I can process his words, he thrusts his hips up, catching me off guard. I throw my head back, my eyes rolling back in pleasure as a cry escapes my lips. “Dax!”

His hips thrust hard, his stiff cock sliding in and out of my pussy. I wrap my arms around his shoulders and our bodies move closer.

Dax catches his breath and flips me over again. I lie on my back with my head pressed into the pillow.

I can feel my pussy tightening around his cock, each thrust making me quiver.

“I’m going to come, Flora,” he grunts.

His hips pound into me over and over. I can feel his balls hit against my skin.

“Dax!” I cry out in pleasure.

His body collapses onto mine as he comes, our bodies sticking together with sweat. He lifts his head, eyes locking onto mine as he strokes my face.

He leans in and kisses me tenderly, his lips meeting mine. “I want this every night, Dax,” I confess, my voice shaking.

“That good?” he teases, chuckling with a smirk on his face.

“Yes,” I breathe out.

“Only if you want to, Flora.”

Yes, it hurt. But fuck, it felt incredible. Dax is amazing.

“Okay, I’m going to pull out. It might hurt,” he warns, his eyes filling with concern.

He eases himself out of me and I feel a slight pressure and discomfort. I look down and see a trace of blood on the sheets beneath me and on the condom. A mix of emotions floods me—satisfaction, vulnerability, and a lingering ache.

Dax reaches over me and grabs a tissue, wiping away the blood from my pussy. His touch is so caring. He takes the condom off, ties it off, and throws it away.

He leans down and kisses my sore pussy and I freeze, not knowing how to react.

He raises back up and settles beside me, pulling me close into his arms. We lie there in the aftermath, our breathing heavy and our hearts still racing. I feel exhaustion settling over me and my body feels tender.

"Are you sore?"

"A little, I'll be okay. I'm just so exhausted and sleepy."

He kisses the top of my head and strokes my hair while holding me tight in his arms. "Get some rest now," he murmurs.

I close my eyes, feeling content. As I drift off, I listen to the beat of his heart.

DAX

Flora is sound asleep and she looks so peaceful. I carefully slide my arm from under her body, making sure I don't wake her. I get out of bed and my cock still throbs. Damn, her pussy was so tight. The way it gripped around my cock...everything about her is perfect.

The thought of being her first fills me with pride and guilt. I've never taken someone's virginity before, but I made sure to be as gentle as I could.

I pull on my underwear and walk to the kitchen. The smell of cannabis hits me as I enter. Lyka is at the back door, smoking a joint and taking a deep drag. I walk over and give him an awkward smile as he hands me the joint. I take a drag, feeling the smoke fill my lungs.

"I heard," he says bluntly.

I don't know what to say. I hand him back the joint and look out to the forest.

"Was she tight?" he asks, his tone almost taunting.

I nod my head and avoid looking at his eyes. He shakes his head and grunts, clearly unimpressed.

"What, Lyka?"

"Nothing."

Lyka finishes the joint, flicks it outside, and walks away. I can feel the tension between us. He stops and turns around, his eyes showing frustration.

Say something, Lyka. What are you thinking? I know you want her.

Lyka shakes his head and walks away without saying a word. I watch him pace down the hallway, feeling his disapproval.

I walk over to the fridge and pull out a bottle of water. Flora comes to mind. My cock still throbs. The way her body felt beneath mine, the sounds she made. The look in her eyes was full of trust. The images replay in my mind and I can't help but feel aroused.

I lean against the kitchen counter, trying to clear my head of its thoughts. I finish the bottle of water and throw it in the trash. With a deep breath, I leave the kitchen and return to the bedroom. The hallway is dark and quiet. I pause when I reach the door, gathering my thoughts before pushing it open.

Flora is still fast asleep, her body curled up. I feel guilt creep up on me as I watch her. I walk over to the bed and quietly slip back in, trying not to wake her. I lie there and pull her close. I want to keep her here, forever. She stirs slightly, but doesn't wake. I kiss her forehead and whisper, "Good night, flower."

THIRTEEN

FLORA

I walk over to the garage to find Dax bent over his bike, tinkering with it. He looks up and sees me, a massive grin spreading across his face. He wipes his hand with a cloth, steps forward, grabs my waist, and pulls me in for a kiss.

"How are you feeling?" he asks.

"Honestly, I'm fine. You don't have to ask me every hour, Dax."

"I bet you won't wanna go back to London after lockdown is over..."

"What happens in Cedarwood cabin stays in Cedarwood cabin, right?" I respond sarcastically. Dax shakes his head, rolls his eyes, and scoffs. I hear heavy footsteps and Dax notices, too. We both turn around and see Lyka walking past. He looks more distant than normal as his eyes briefly meet mine. He scans me up and down before he continues to the barn without saying a word.

"Did you tell him?" I ask sheepishly.

"Flora, you were screaming my name last night. Even with the storm, we all could hear it."

I grab the cloth from his hands and throw it at him, giggling. “Oh, shut it,” I say playfully.

Dax laughs and goes back to tinkering with his bike. Despite the playful banter, guilt settles in my stomach as I glance in Lyka’s direction. *Did he feel betrayed? Or was it something more? Surely not...He is always grumpy with me.*

I find myself wondering if either of us feels something. I turn my attention back to Dax. “So, what are you working on?”

“Ah, just tweaking the suspension. Making sure everything’s perfect for the next ride.”

Dax focuses back on the bike. As he works, my mind keeps drifting back to Lyka's expression.

“I’m gonna take a shower,” I tell him.

Dax looks up from his bike. “Want me to join?” he asks, his eyes locking onto mine with a playful glint.

Biting my bottom lip, I look him up and down. Without a word, I take his hand. He tosses his tool into the metal box and we head back to the cabin together.

THE WATER CASCADES OVER US, BOTH FULLY NAKED. DAX’S COCK IS hard, the condom already in place. He pushes me up against the cold tiles and the sensation sends a shiver through my body. His lips meet mine and our tongues touch. I push him back and whisper, “Now I want to try out your right hand.”

Dax lifts one of my thighs, holding it securely. His lips advance down to my neck while his other hand moves slowly to my pussy, parting my folds open. One finger slips inside and I let out a whine.

"You're still so tight." He starts pulsating his finger, feeling my pussy walls.

"Dax..." I moan, digging my fingers into his shoulders for support.

He withdraws his finger from my pussy and brings it to my lips, prying them open. Without hesitation, I suck on his finger, tasting myself. "*Fuck*, Flora," he growls.

I roll my tongue around his finger and he removes it from my mouth.

"I want you to fuck me, Dax."

The tip of his cock lines up to my entrance and he thrusts forward, entering me with a single, swift motion. My body arches against the cold tiles and I cling to his shoulders, biting my bottom lip.

Dax powerfully thrusts into me over and over. I can't help but let out repeated moans that echo off the tiles.

My leg wraps around his waist and I pull him deeper inside me. The friction of his cock sliding in and out of me makes my eyes roll back in pure bliss.

"Dax! Fuck! Fuck! Fuck!" I cry out.

He groans against my neck. "You're so fucking perfect, Flora."

As he continues to fuck me, he buries his head between my neck and shoulder. Our loud moans blend with the sound of the water.

Suddenly, I notice something dark out of the corner of my eye through the wet, glass panel. I wipe the condensation with my hand to see Lyka standing at the door, watching us.

I don't know why, but I get a thrill from being watched. I don't say anything to Dax; I'm too lost in the sensations.

As my body moves up and down, I lock eyes with Lyka. His expression is unreadable through the droplets of water. His stare is burning. Knowing he's watching us turns me on even more.

Dax's pace quickens, thrust after thrust as he nears his climax.

"I'm coming! I'm coming!" he exclaims.

With a harsh groan, he comes and I feel his cock pulsating inside me. He rests his head on my shoulder and breathes deeply. I hold the back of his head and kiss his shoulder. The water continues to cascade over us.

I look at the door, expecting Lyka to still be there, but the space where he stood is now empty.

Did I imagine Lyka watching us? Surely not. He was there, right?

Dax lifts his head and his eyes meet mine.

"Are you okay?" he asks, out of breath.

"I'm fine...I'm not a porcelain doll. You're not gonna break me."

Dax pulls his cock out gradually and whispers in my ear, "Don't tempt me, flower."

"Flower?" I raise both my eyebrows, confused.

"Well, that's what you are, my flower," he says as he presses his finger under my chin, tilting my face toward his. I can't help but chuckle at my new nickname.

"Let's get you cleaned up. Shall we?" he says, bending down, picking up a shower puff and a bottle of body wash.

He squirts a large amount of the body wash onto the puff, working it into a lather. The scent of coconut fills the air. Dax stands up and starts gently scrubbing my arms.

"Turn around," he commands.

I comply, turning my back to him. He works the puff over my shoulders and down my back. His touch is intimate, yet tender.

He reaches around me, his chest pressing against my back as he lathers my front as I lean back into him. He takes his time, making sure every part of me is clean. After washing me, he guides me under the showerhead, rinsing off the soap.

He spins me around, his mouth meeting my breasts as he kisses them, making my nipples pucker up straight away. He slowly traces his lips over my whole body, worshiping it.

FOURTEEN

FLORA

A WEEK HAS FLOWN BY. ONLY TWO MORE WEEKS LEFT AND BACK TO THE real world. Me and Dax have been fucking nonstop. We've fucked in almost every room except Lyka's. The tension between us and Lyka has been unstable. He has been in his own world, spending long hours in the barn and avoiding us as much as possible. He keeps slamming doors and skipping meals, acting like a teenager who has been told off.

This morning, we all stand in the kitchen, the silence thick and uncomfortable. Lyka heads for the back door, his body language radiating frustration.

"Lyka..." Dax calls out, breaking the silence.

Lyka turns around. He doesn't say a word, just stares at us, his glare unyielding.

"I'm going on a hunt today. Can Flora help you in the barn?" Dax asks.

Lyka's eyes scan me up and down. He nods, exits through the back door, and slams it shut behind him. The sound vibrates through the cabin, causing me to flinch.

"You can help him sand down some furniture," Dax says, trying to lighten the mood.

I smile at him, even though it feels forced. I am hesitant about spending the day alone with Lyka, but I know dark thoughts will return if I'm not in someone's company.

"I better go get ready," he says.

Dax jumps off the kitchen stool and walks over to the firearms cabinet. His hands move confidently as I watch him easily handle the weapons with me standing a few paces back.

"There's something scary about being in the presence of guns," I mutter.

He glances back at me with a slight smile, his eyes flickering with understanding. "You've never shot one before?" he asks, turning his attention back to the cabinet to retrieve a box of ammunition.

I shake my head. "I wouldn't want to," I reply honestly, folding my arms and leaning against the back of the couch.

"Do you have to go out and hunt?" I ask. "I thought we had everything we needed."

Dax finishes loading the bullets into a pouch. "I always like to stay on top of our supply. You'll be fine," he says, pausing to kiss my forehead.

He moves into the kitchen to prepare for his hunt and I watch silently as he gathers his gear.

AFTER DAX LEAVES, I GATHER MY COURAGE AND HEAD TO THE BARN. I'm hoping Lyka is out of his mood by now. I can see the barn doors slightly ajar. I take a deep breath and step inside. *Lord Give Me a Sign* by DMX plays on a speaker.

The pungent smell of sawdust and wood polish hits me. I glance to the side and see tools arranged on a workbench nearby. Several pieces of furniture around the barn are unfinished.

Lyka is at the far end, working on a chair. His muscles flex, making his veins pop out of his arm. The sight takes my breath away, yet it is intimidating.

I approach him and fiddle with my fingers. "Hey."

He doesn't look up, continuing his work with focus. "Grab some sandpaper and start standing down that table to the left of me."

I find a piece of sandpaper and start working on a nearby table. The silence between us is heavy, punctuated only by the sound of sandpaper against wood.

Looking up at him, I muster the courage to speak. "Lyka... I'm sorry if—"

"Don't," he interrupts me. "Just work."

I bite the inside of my cheek and feel a mixture of guilt and frustration. I keep silent as we continue to work. It feels like the minutes are stretching into hours.

A long metal rod with the letter *F* catches my eye. Curious, I walk over and pick it up.

"What's this?"

Lyka looks up and rolls his eyes. "It's a branding iron. Once I've finished a piece of furniture, I brand it with that...*F* for Faulkner," he explains and returns to his work.

I place the branding iron on the table and pick up the sandpaper. I start humming to the music, which apparently makes Lyka annoyed as he starts clenching his jaw. Anger and annoyance wash over me, making me huff in frustration. The tension between us has been building for days and I can't take it anymore.

"What's your problem with me, Lyka?" I demand, gripping the sandpaper tightly in my hand. Lyka stops working and looks me up and down, clenching his jaw.

"I mean, you hardly talk to me. If you do, you're blunt. Yet when you kiss someone, you look me dead in the eyes. What is that about? What do you get out of it?" I ask, my voice rising.

Lyka stands there in silence, his lack of response only fuels my anger. I walk up to him, closing the distance between us until we are face to face.

"Tell me, Lyka. What have I done to you? You're acting like a fucking teenager..."

"Shut the fuck up, Flora. I'm warning you," he says through gritted teeth.

"No, I won't! Tell me. Why are you such an asshole to me?!"

Our faces are inches apart as his eyes bore into mine. It feels like the entire world has shrunk to just the two of us.

"I saw you watching me and Dax fuck in the shower. What is it...jealousy? Angry I didn't pick you?" I hiss.

Lyka's face hardens, his chest heaving as he breathes. The air is almost suffocating me, and I turn to leave.

"Asshole," I mumble under my breath as I walk toward the door. I feel so frustrated I don't even want to look at him.

Suddenly, I hear a whooshing sound. A small ax flies past my head, missing me by centimeters and embedding itself into the wall with a loud thud. I freeze, my mouth wide open in shock. I turn back, eyes wide with a mix of fear and anger.

"YOU COULD HAVE FUCKING KILLED ME!" I scream with rage.

"If I wanted to kill you, I wouldn't have missed," he says through gritted teeth. His eyes are dark and his face is full of fury.

My heart pounds in my chest and I breathe in and out, trying to calm myself down. "You're insane!"

Lyka rushes towards me. I stumble backward, my back pressing up against the wall. The barn now feels small, as if it's closing on me.

"You walk in here, say what you want, and push my buttons. What did you expect to happen?" Lyka says, his eyes never leaving mine. He places his hand above my head, pushing himself up from the wall as he towers over me, trying to intimidate me.

"If you're trying to scare me, Lyka, it's not working."

A sinister laugh escapes his lips. "You have no idea who you're dealing with, Flora."

Lyka pulls the ax from the wall with ease. Without a word, he storms out of the barn. I follow him, anger boiling inside me.

"You don't scare me!" I exclaim.

"Fuck off!" he snaps as he heads towards the trees.

Determined not to let him walk away from this, I catch up to him. I reach out and shove his shoulder, making him stop. He grunts and turns slowly, his eyes empty. I push his chest, feeling his fury.

"You...won't...do...shit," I taunt.

He clenches his jaw and his face fills with rage. Dropping the ax, his hand shoots out and grabs my throat. With force, he slams me against a tree, my head and back colliding against the rough bark.

My eyes fill with tears and I gasp for breath. "Hurt me. Go on. If that makes you feel like a *man*."

His nostrils flare. I feel the pressure constricting my airway as he grips my throat tighter. His eyes are emotionless, dark, and scary.

"Hurt me, Lyka!"

He yanks down my jeans along with my panties. Before I can react, he picks me up, my legs dangling as he kicks away my discarded clothing. Without delay, he pulls down his jeans and underwear, his erect cock springing free. He grips my thighs, hoisting me up again and pinning me against the tree. The rough bark digs into my back, giving me a sharp pain.

"Pain...You want fucking pain," he hisses.

Before I can respond, he thrusts his hips forward, his cock slamming into my pussy with a force that makes me scream. "Lyka!"

He doesn't listen or give me time to adjust. His hips pound into me, each thrust driving me harder against the bark. I can feel it scraping through my T-shirt, cutting into my skin. There is pain yet pleasure as they blend together.

I let out little whimpers. My hands lock together behind his neck, gripping tightly as if holding on for dear life. He grunts with each thrust. I can hardly see because my eyes are filled with tears.

"Does it hurt?" he asks.

"Mhmm," I whimper.

"Good," he grunts.

The bark cuts deeper into my back, the sting adding to the moment. I move my hand to his shoulders, my nails digging in, scraping against his skin. Tears stream down my face and my body quivers with each thrust.

He suddenly drops me to my feet and I stagger, trying to find my balance. I feel the blood dripping down my back. Before I can react, his hand is firm and commanding at the back of my neck as he turns me around.

"I think you can take more. Now hold the fucking tree," he demands.

The rough bark presses against my skin as I place my arms around the tree. My face is pushed up against the harsh surface, feeling the sting of the bark biting into my cheek. He spreads my legs with his knee, forcing them apart. Without any warning, he thrusts his cock into my pussy again.

His fingers dig into my skin with a bruising force as he begins to fuck me from behind. I try to pull my face away from the tree, but his hand holds my neck firmly.

His cock fills me completely. My hands grip the tree tighter, my fingers digging into the bark as I let out loud moans.

He slams into me with force as he grips my hips, pulling me back to meet each of his thrusts.

“This is what you wanted, right?” he groans.

My legs shake as my body trembles. My knees feel like they are going buckle.

“Fuck, your pussy is stretching so well for me.”

I can't help but moan, the sound escaping my lips despite the pain.

He reaches one of his hands around to my pussy. His fingers find my clit, rubbing it with a roughness. I feel an orgasm building up.

“Does that make you want to come?” he asks.

“Ye—yes,” I stutter, out of breath.

“You don’t get to fucking come.”

He removes his fingers from my swollen clit back to my hips, denying my release. His grip tightens, his thrusts becoming more erratic. His body slaps against my ass as his cock stretches my pussy. I bite down on my lip, making it bleed.

With a final thrust, he drives deep into my pussy and I feel it tighten around him. I cry out, my body trembling. Lyka groans as he climaxes, his cock pulsating inside me as he comes.

We stand there out of breath, our bodies pressed together.

Lyka pulls out of me and his cum drips down my thighs. He releases his grip on my hips and I can’t help but slump against the tree.

Without a word, he pulls up his jeans. My hands shake uncontrollably as I fumble with my clothes.

I look over my shoulder and see my T-shirt is covered in blood. The pain hits me and I let out a little whimper.

I stare at Lyka, trying to look deep into his eyes. He looks at me with no expression on his face, not saying a word. He picks up the ax, walking towards the cabin as I follow behind him.

As we approach the cabin, the door swings open and Dax steps out. He looks at me and the tears in my eyes as his face hardens with concern. Lyka walks straight past him, bumping shoulders as he enters the cabin. Dax's eyes follow him before he rushes up to me, his hand reaching out to touch my shoulder.

“Ouch,” I cry out.

Dax pulls his hand back, his eyes wide with concern. He walks behind me and gently lifts the back of my T-shirt, revealing the deep cuts and scrapes from the tree bark. “What the fuck did he do,” he growls.

I turn my head and see him inhale deeply before looking toward the cabin.

MY BACK AND PUSSY THROB IN PAIN AS I SIT IN THE TUB WITH MY KNEES pressed up against my breasts. The water soothes my cuts. My hair is tied up in a messy bun, loose strands falling around my face.

Dax kneels beside the tub, dips a sponge into the water, and carefully wrings it out before dabbing it over my back. The water washes away the remnants of blood and grime. I feel relief and guilt; my emotions are a tangled mess.

“I’m sorry, Da–” I begin to say, my voice trembling.

“Shh. It was bound to happen. You’re spending three weeks alone in a cabin with two males.”

I can’t help but cry. Dax tends to my cuts with care, keeping his hands steady.

"It just happened so quickly. I'm gonna need emergency contraception..."

Dax pauses for a moment. "Can it wait 'til tomorrow? The stores are closed."

"I think you can take it up to three days now, so yeah."

"I'll go first thing in the morning," he assures me, pouring warm water down my back.

A new worry creeps into my mind. "Hey, Dax, I don't have to be worried about STDs, do I?"

Before Dax can respond, we hear the door open. We both look up and see Lyka standing there.

Lyka's eyes meet mine. "You're the first girl I've fucked without a condom. I'm clean," he says bluntly.

Lyka lingers in the doorway for a moment, his eyes flicking between us. Finally, he turns and walks away, the door creaking shut behind him. I let out a breath I hadn't realized I was holding.

DAX

I leave Flora lying in bed to rest, closing the door behind me. The cabin is silent as I make my way to the living room, finding Lyka sprawled out on the couch. He looks up as I enter, pausing the DVD with a remote. He has guilt and confusion written on his face.

I sink into the armchair opposite him. "This makes things complicated..." I say.

Lyka leans forward, resting his elbows on his knees and burying his face in his hands. "She wanted me to hurt her."

The raw emotion in his words cuts through me. I let out a deep breath, trying to steady myself.

"What are we gonna do?" he asks. He looks up at me, his eyes searching mine for an answer.

"We'll ask her tomorrow."

Lyka nods, his shoulders slumping. He picks up the remote and presses play, the DVD resuming. We sit there in silence. The tension in the room is intense—my mind races, replaying the past few weeks' events.

I want Flora. I know Lyka wants her, too. What the fuck have we done.

LYKA

I lie there in bed, staring up at the ceiling as thoughts swirl all around me. From the very moment that Flora waltzed her way into our lives, I had a sense of determination to break her. It was meant to be a game for me. I don't like getting close to people.

I fucked a lot of girls. They loved the power I had over them, it's never hard to manipulate them into doing what I want. But with Flora, things were different. She wasn't like the rest. With Flora, it was about fucking with her mind—to make her question everything and strip that façade off her, leaving her raw and exposed. I enjoyed watching the confusion in those eyes of hers as I played out my games. Of course, it was simple: keep her off-balance, keep her guessing.

The only people who have claimed her body are me and Dax. I wanted her over and over. The way her pussy gripped my throbbing cock made me groan in bed. There was something about her eyes...no girl has ever looked at me like that before. Something deeper—something I couldn't quite grasp. I know dark thoughts riddle her mind. They riddle my mind, too.

Maybe she was better off dead instead of giving us so much trouble. *Is there a part of me that cares about her? Shit!* This was Dax's idea. I didn't even want her here. We should have left her in the forest. I'm so fucking conflicted and confused.

FIFTEEN

FLORA

My body is hurting and aching as every cut stings. I had to spend the night lying on my stomach so I didn't aggravate the wounds.

Dax left early to go to the pharmacy for emergency contraception.

I feel a sense of unease wash over me as I walk out onto the balcony. Lyka stands there, smoking a cigarette and looking out at the forest. I should be angry at him for hurting me, but I'm not. My fucked up mind and body want him even more.

I walk over to him, wanting to speak about yesterday, but before I can, he suddenly turns me around and lifts my T-shirt. I feel his fingers trace the wounds on my back.

Before I can ask why he did that, he twists me back and lifts me on the balcony banister. He takes a final drag of his cigarette and flicks it over the balcony. I grip his shoulders and balance myself on the narrow banister. He holds me in place, making sure I don't fall back. I don't know why, but we just stare at each other. He moves his face away from mine and goes to say something, but before he can, I speak up. "Lyka, you never answered my question. Why are you so grumpy with me?"

He looks out into the forest and shrugs. “I don’t like getting close to people.”

Before I can reply, a high-pitched cry rings out. I turn my head and see a bear cub that appears injured.

“It’s hurt!” I shout. Seeing the cub pulls at my heartstrings. I jump down from the banister and rush over to the stairs.

“FLORA, STOP!” Lyka yells, panicked. As I’m about to descend the steps. He grips my arm, sending a shot of pain through it.

I look back at the cub and see what Lyka saw. Out of the bushes steps a massive Mama bear. She sniffs the air and tenderly picks up the cub by the scruff of its neck. The moment they are out of sight, I can hear Lyka deeply exhale. In that moment, I see a different side of Lyka. His grip on my arms loosens as he takes my hand and leads me away from the stairs. We silently watch the Mama bear retreat back into the forest with her cub.

“I didn’t think...Thank you,” I say, my voice shaking.

“You gotta be careful. The forests here can be dangerous, Flora.”

We both look out at the forest, taking in the view in silence. We both don't know what to say to each other.

Lyka breaks the silence. “Come on, let's head inside.”

I follow him back inside the cabin.

Dax enters from the living room as we enter the kitchen. He places a couple of paper bags on the counter and pulls out a box labeled *Plan B*, pushing it toward me.

I look up at Lyka. His expression is unreadable, but his eyes flick to the box and back to me.

I grab the box, open it, and pull out the instructions. “Okay, I just have to take one pill,” I mumble to myself.

Dax passes me a glass of water and I take the pill out of the box. I put the pill into my mouth and grab the glass of water.

Before I take a sip, Lyka's hand quickly covers the top of the glass, pushing it down to the counter.

I freeze, looking at Lyka with confusion. His eyes are filled with an emotion I can't figure out.

What are you doing, Lyka?

Dax notices and calls out, "Lyka..."

Lyka turns around hastily, shaking his head as if trying to clear his mind.

I shrug, feeling confused. I lift the glass to my mouth again and take a big gulp, swallowing the pill.

"I can't believe that pill cost nearly fifty dollars," Dax grumbles, glaring at Lyka.

"What? That's pricey...Do you want any money?" I offer.

Dax's gaze softens when he looks back at me. "No, it's okay, flower. Don't worry about it."

"Question. Did you wear a mask when you went into town?" I ask. I didn't want the risk of catching Covid.

"Of course...Also, I picked you up some new underwear and something else." I don't know what the surprise is, but I feel very grateful for the underwear.

Dax reaches into the bag and pulls out a set of watercolors and other supplies. He places them in front of me with a wide smile.

"Wow," I breathe, opening the watercolor tin and seeing the vibrant colors inside.

"The watercolors in the barn were no good, they were too old. I thought you could get back into painting."

"Dax, it's been so long."

"You can do it. I believe in you. I wanna see how beautiful you can paint."

His words are encouraging as old memories flood my mind. I feel grateful that he wants to see my paintings, but I'm nervous. It's a part of me that I neglected for too long now.

Lyka gets up from the stool and gives me a soft look as he leaves the room.

I WALK ONTO THE BALCONY WEARING ONE OF DAX'S OLD T-SHIRTS THAT hangs loosely on my body. I see an easel, a table with paints, brushes, and a jar of water already set up. A speaker plays Fleetwood Mac music.

I take a seat on the wooden stool. I'm nervous as I take a deep breath and pick up a paintbrush. I look at the forest; the breathtaking view is begging to be painted.

My hand hovers over the colors. I go to start with the color black, but I pause and dip the brush into the vibrant green instead.

I feel hope, fear, excitement—all my emotions take over me. The brush glides smoothly across the paper as I begin to paint. I lose myself in my art, each stroke bringing me joy.

Time seems to blur as I am immersed in painting. Being surrounded by natural beauty, two hot brothers, and painting seems therapeutic.

What am I thinking, two hot brothers? I had slept with both of them. I was only a virgin last week. What have I done?

I look over the balcony and see Lyka and Dax chopping wood. They are both topless, a sheen of sweat on their bodies shining in the sun. Their bodies move effortlessly as they swing the ax.

I was tangled in a web—their web. Desire and confusion fill me. I don't know what I want.

Lyka senses my gaze and he looks up at me, his eyes locked

onto mine. I quickly avert my eyes back to the painting, feeling awkward.

Did I want both of them? Could I have both of them? The lockdown will be over soon and they won't want me then. They will throw me back into the real world.

I focus back on my painting and try to steady my thoughts.

I admire my painting as I stand back. I have created something beautiful again. The forest in front of me is now on my canvas. The colors stand out and it feels good to look at it.

After leaving the painting outside to dry, I walk into the kitchen. On the counter are brownies and they look too good to resist. I take one and eat it, savoring the rich chocolate flavor.

Fuck, that tastes good!

I grab another and Lyka walks into the kitchen as I eat it. His eyes are wide with shock.

"Fuck. How many have you had, Flora?" he asks.

"Only two. Why?"

Lyka shakes his head. Before he can respond, Dax walks in and bursts out laughing.

"Please don't tell me they are out of date..." I start.

"They're weed brownies," Lyka replies, biting down on his bottom lip.

I accidentally swallow the last bit of brownie in shock. "Fuck. Shit. *Fuck.* Will I die?"

Panic sets in and I start pacing. I want to make myself sick.

Lyka face palms and Dax just sniggers. "You are not gonna die. However, you're only meant to eat one. You're in for a ride," he explains.

A ride? What? Fuck! I've never done drugs!

Without hesitation, Lyka walks over to the plate, picks up two brownies, and eats them. Dax copies him, grabbing a couple and scarfing them down.

"Nothing to worry about. We'll all be equally high," Lyka says with a smirk.

Dax still looks amused. "Listen, just go with it. You'll be fine," he reassures me.

What he said does very little to ease my worries. I nod, trying to calm myself. "What will I feel? What should I expect?"

"You will feel super chill...Relaxed....You're safe," Lyka says.

I take a deep breath and mumble, "Okay..."

Lyka leans on the counter nonchalantly. "It's gonna take a while to kick in. About one to two hours."

Dax nods his head in agreement. "Don't overthink. Just let it happen." He walks over to the back door and steps out onto the balcony.

I look at Lyka and he just nudges his shoulder with mine, trying to reassure me.

"Fucking hell!" I hear Dax say loudly.

I walk outside on the balcony and see him standing there, admiring my painting.

"Damn. You can paint! This is amazing!" Dax exclaims.

I bite my bottom lip awkwardly and reply, "You think?"

"Yes. It's beautiful. The colors and details. It's something, flower."

I blush, fiddling with my fingers as I bite my cheek. "Thanks..."

My parents come to mind as I look at the painting, standing there and daydreaming.

Lyka approaches from behind, snapping me out of my daydream. His voice is soft as he speaks. "Dax is right. This is incredible, Flora."

"I wasn't sure if I had it in me. It's been so long since I painted with color..." I admit, but pride washes over me as I look at the painting.

Dax places a hand on my shoulder. "This is a gift. You never lost it. Keep doing it."

"It's a powerful gift," Lyka says as his eyes meet mine. He shows emotion in his eyes for a moment.

We all stand there in silence, admiring my painting. However, my thoughts go back to the weed brownie.

"I'm scared," I admit.

"Don't be, you have us. We will never let anything bad happen to you. I promise," Lyka reassures me.

Never let anything bad happen to me.

His words make me feel weak. I hope he will keep his promise.

SIXTEEN

FLORA

The scent of oil and gasoline mingles in the air as we all stand in the garage around the motorcycles. *Jigga What/Faint* by Linkin Park and Jay-Z plays on a stereo in the corner. The moon shines through the open door, casting shadows on the trees.

"It's been an hour. When will these brownies kick in?" I ask.

"Just give it time, flower," Dax replies with a smirk playing on his lips.

Lyka chimes in, "When it hits, you'll know."

I walk over to one of the bikes and run my finger over the metal. The garage starts to feel alive.

"Hey, let's go for a ride while we wait for the brownies to kick in," Dax suggests.

Lyka raises his eyebrow. "Backroads?"

Dax nods. He walks over to a workbench, grabs two helmets, and passes one to me.

Lyka helps me adjust the straps and ensure the helmet securely fits me. As I stand between them, a silent question hangs between us. My eyes dart between them, not knowing whose bike to choose.

I decide to walk over to Lyka's bike. Dax scoffs and shakes his head. I can tell he is a bit annoyed by my choice.

Lyka smirks as he holds my hand, helping me mount the bike. They both start the engines and they roar to life. I feel the bike vibrate underneath me as I straddle it.

"Hold tight," Lyka states.

I wrap my arms around his waist, feeling his muscular body under his T-shirt. He glances back at me, his eyes meeting mine through the visor, and gives a nod.

Dax pulls out of the garage first and Lyka follows closely behind. We speed down the gravel driveway to the backroads.

I can feel the cool air against my skin, the wind rushing past us as we pick up speed. The trees on the side of the road start to blur.

I tighten my grip around Lyka's waist. I start to feel the brownies kicking in and my senses start to heighten.

The back roads are deserted. There isn't a person in sight, only nature and the night sky.

Dax leads the way as the road twists and turns. Lyka handles each corner with ease.

The brownie's effect deepens. When I look up at the sky, the stars sparkle and everything seems more alive. It's breathtaking.

Lyka accelerates, pulling up alongside Dax. They ride in perfect sync, side by side. Silent communication is shared as they look at each other and fist bump.

This makes me shake my head and giggle. My laughter becomes infectious for some reason and I can't stop chuckling to myself. The song playing in the garage continues to play in my mind. The brownies have fully taken hold now.

I close my eyes briefly and let the wind hit my skin. I feel so free, like I'm flying.

Lyka and Dax navigate the roads with ease, their bodies moving perfectly with the bikes.

Dax picks up speed and does an impressive wheelie on his bike. The front wheel lifts off the ground and he lands it perfectly. I watch him in awe and cheer him on.

Fuck. Being high feels good.

We make our way back to the cabin and the ride home is smooth. The rush I feel at the moment is unreal.

We finally pull up to the garage. I jump off the bike and take off my helmet. I can't stop giggling to myself. Dax and Lyka follow suit. They both exchange smug looks and laugh, too. "The brownies have definitely kicked in," Lyka states.

I don't know why, but something compels me as I walk up to Lyka. I wrap my arms around his neck and kiss him deeply. I feel Dax's presence standing behind me. He places his hands on my waist and starts kissing my neck.

I am nestled between them as they kiss me. *I want both of them so bad.*

My rush of desire and breathlessness is interrupted. I pull back from Lyka. "I'm hungry," I state.

"Let's get you something to eat then," Dax chuckles as he takes my hand and leads me towards the cabin. Lyka follows behind us.

We head to the kitchen, opening cupboards and pulling out snacks. We find some chips, cookies, and crackers.

We all sit at the kitchen table. Dax throws a bag of chips towards me and I tear into them.

"Why am I so hungry?" I ask with a mouthful of chips.

"Weed tends to have that effect," Lyka explains, taking a bite of his cookie.

I lean back in the chair, holding the bag of chips. "Man. I feel chilled."

Dax puts a hand on my thigh. “Weed takes the edge off everything. Making you feel just right.”

Everything has brought us closer: the brownies, laughter, late-night ride.

“Thanks, guys,” I say.

Lyka raises his cookie in a mock toast. “To us, the cabin, and the brownies.”

“To us,” Dax says, joining in.

I lift my own chip, giggling. “To us.”

We decided to watch a movie to wind down. After the DVD ended, the room fell silent with us lost in our thoughts. We are super high and feeling mellow.

“They say you have intense orgasms while being high,” Dax comments casually, breaking the silence.

I feel intrigued.

“Oh, really?” I reply, smirking.

Dax moves his hand to my thigh and starts stroking me, our lips and tongues meeting instantly.

I feel another hand slide up my other thigh and I see Lyka joining in from the corner of my eye.

My sensations are heightened by the weed. Both brothers touch me seductively, making me feel weak.

I break the kiss with Dax, pulling back and looking at both of them. They both move their heads to my neck, trailing kisses along my skin.

“Lyka, I thought you didn't share,” I say, my voice shaking. He stops kissing me and lifts my arm as he starts trailing kisses on the back of my hand. "I'll share with my brother," he mumbles between kisses.

Dax kisses harder into my neck. "Is this what you want? Both of us?" he asks.

Desire overtakes my whole body. Lyka moves his mouth against mine as our tongues fight against each other.

"Mhmm," I moan into his mouth.

"That's our girl," Dax breathes as he slips his hand under my shirt and bra. His hand cups my breast for a moment before his fingers make their way to my perky nipples, gently twisting them.

I'm so turned on. I can feel myself getting wet. Fuck.

Lyka's hand moves across my thigh in repeated motions. He quickly traces over my pussy before returning back to my thigh.

I pull away from Lyka. When I see Dax start undressing himself, I help him. My hands explore his abs as he pulls off his shirt. Lyka stands up and starts undressing himself, watching me and Dax kiss.

Dax starts to undress me, pulling items of clothing off me and throwing them behind the couch.

Our breathing is heavy as we are all in our underwear, inspecting each other.

They both rise from the couch and I can see their erections pressing up against their underwear.

I sit there, feeling a mixture of excitement and fear as I look up at them.

"Have you ever had a girl between you before?" I ask.

I bet they have...

They both look at each other and chuckle. "No. You're the first we've shared, flower," Dax says, his eyes are dark.

For some fucked up reason, that makes me feel special.

Lyka pushes my torso back and I lean back against the

couch. He traces his finger from my shoulder down to my stomach, his hungry eyes glancing over my body.

"This untouched body has been craving us for so long," he says, almost sounding primal.

Dax moves close, pulling my panties off. My naked body is on show and exposed.

Lyka kneels between my legs, kissing my thighs as he parts them. I can't help but gulp as I look down at him.

Dax moves and sits beside me. He removes my bra and lets his thumb circle around my nipple.

Lyka's arms move under my thighs, gripping them tightly and prying them open wider. My pussy lips open up for him.

"Such a pretty clit," Lyka says breathlessly.

He spits and I feel his saliva drip down my pussy. His tongue flicks out and makes contact with my clit. I let out a loud whimper, unable to hold it back. He begins to move his tongue in teasing motions. My whole body trembles and I push my head back into the couch.

Dax grabs the back of my head, digging his fingers into my hair and firmly pushing my head forward. "Watch him while he eats you out," he demands.

I do as I'm told. Lyka's eyes meet mine as his tongue works its magic. The desire in his eyes makes me quiver.

Dax holds my head up firmly, not letting me move. Lyka's tongue quickens its pace, flicking and swirling around my clit. I can feel an orgasm building inside me. The sensation is almost too much to bear.

"Look in his eyes. Look how they want you to come, flower," Dax whispers in my ear.

My hands clutch at the cushions on either side of me.

"Does he make you feel good?" Dax whispers again.

I nod, unable to form any words. Lyka's eyes never leave mine. His grip tightens as he pins down my thighs, sucking my clit. I try to throw my head back, but Dax holds me in place.

"Has any other man licked your pussy?" Dax asks.

I shake my head. My eyes gloss over with tears as if the sensation is too much.

Lyka's tongue quickly enters my hole, making me jump. "Fuck, she tastes so damn good," he mutters.

He returns back to my clit, licking it from side to side faster.

"You're ours. *Only ours*," Dax states as he kisses my lips.

Dax pulls away and holds the back of my neck, ensuring I keep eye contact with Lyka.

I am consumed by pleasure, on the brink of an orgasm. "I'm...gonna...uhh," I cry out.

"Cum on my brother's tongue," Dax commands.

Lyka's tongue moves faster, his lips occasionally sucking. I push my body toward him and my eyes flutter.

"Look at him or he'll stop," Dax warns.

Lyka's tongue flicks a final time and I loudly cry. My body convulses as an orgasm crashes over me. My vision blurs and I grip the cushions tightly, holding on as my orgasm rips through me.

Lyka doesn't stop as his tongue continues on my sensitive, swollen clit.

"That's it, flower. Such a good girl for us," Dax hums in my ear.

I manage to climax again. "Fucking hell!" I scream.

Lyka eases his grip on my thighs. He brings his head up and his lips glisten with my juices.

Before I know what I am doing, I reach up and bring Lyka down to my lips, tasting myself on him. I catch my breath and fall back on the couch. I feel like I am floating on a cloud as I lay there, my body feeling weak. Dax kisses me as I ride the after-effects of my orgasm. I sink into the couch, out of breath.

"Being high does make everything more intense," I say, my body tingling all over.

They both sit on either side of me and I see excitement in their eyes.

"Oh...we're not finished yet," Lyka whispers as he leans in close.

"Have you ever sucked a dick before?" Dax asks with a mischievous tone. I can't help but let out a gulp and shake my head. My eyes flitter between them.

Lyka stands up from the couch and pulls down his underwear. His erect cock bounces up, hard and ready. He looks down at me and motions with his finger. "We better teach you then." He smirks.

Without hesitation, I let out a deep breath and kneel on the couch. I can feel my hands tremble as I reach out to touch him. I look up at him for reassurance and he nods.

His cock feels heavy in my hand as I hold the shaft.

"Get it wet..." he instructs.

I spit on the head and my saliva drips off it. Parting my lips, I take him into my mouth, feeling his cock fill me.

Lyka groans as he raises his arms and places his hands on the back of his head. "Fuck, that's it. Take your time, Flora..."

I tighten my lips around his cock, moving up and down. I can see Dax watching as he starts to rub my back. Lyka's breathing becomes heavy and I feel his cock twitching in my mouth.

"You're doing so good," Lyka moans as he thrusts into my mouth.

I look up at him, meeting his eyes. My cheeks are hollow as I continue to suck.

"Just like that..." Dax whispers.

Lyka fists my hair and moans my name repeatedly, making me feel desired.

"I gotta stop or I'll cum," Lyka breathes.

Dax moves closer to me, pulling off his underwear and grabbing my chin. "My turn."

Lyka groans as I remove my mouth from his cock. I turn to Dax and wrap my lips around his cock.

Although the taste and texture are different, they both taste amazing. Dax rests his hand on my head, gently pushing down.

"You're such a fast learner," he praises.

I go to lift off his cock, but he pins my head down. His cock hits the back of my throat and I fight the urge to gag. "Take it... Take it," he growls. He releases his grip and I continue to suck. My mouth makes slurping noises as he thrusts in and out.

Dax removes his cock from my mouth and saliva drips down my chin. He stands up abruptly and walks over to his jeans.

"Watching your lips around my brother's cock turns me on so much," Lyka whispers.

Dax stands there and starts rolling a condom over his thick cock. He walks back to the couch, throws a condom to Lyka, and extends his hand for me to take.

Dax sits back down and motions with his fingers for me to sit on top of him. I position myself over his cock, facing forward. He places the palm of his hand on my back.

I lower myself as his cock pushes past my lips and enters my pussy.

"You're so wet," Dax grunts as he thrusts up. My body arches, making my toes curl as I cry out. Lyka moves forward, holding the base of his cock in front of me as I open my mouth for him.

Dax grips my hips and pounds into me over and over. My moans grow louder, muffled by Lyka's cock. Lyka's hips buck back and forth as he fucks my mouth. "Don't you dare stop," he orders.

I struggle to keep up as both their cocks fill me completely.

Dax's hands reach around and slide up my body. He grabs my bouncing breasts and cups them in his hand.

"Fuck," Lyka groans. I suck on his cock harder and swirl my tongue around his tip.

Lyka suddenly pulls out of my mouth, saliva dripping down my chin. He wipes it away with his thumb.

"I wanna stretch her," he says to Dax.

"Do you think she's ready?" Dax asks.

Desire overcomes me. I wanted them to give me everything they had. I feel the fullness of Dax inside me as I command, "Use me. I want you to both use me."

Dax shifts his body and leans his torso back on the couch. He pulls my hair so my head tilts and my back presses against his chest. His cock thrusts into me, making me gasp.

Lyka opens the condom packet and rolls it down on his cock. He moves between Dax's legs and mine, resting one of his knees on the couch for support. He spits on his cock and rubs the saliva over the condom for extra lubrication.

"Use me!" I cry out as Dax fucks me from below.

Lyka uses the tip of his cock to tease my clit. Dax slows down his movements as if he knows what's about to happen. Lyka grabs the base of his cock and slowly starts inserting the tip into my already-filled pussy. The stretch is so intense it feels like my pussy is going to split open.

"Fuck, FUCK!" I wail.

"You have two cocks in your pussy. How does it feel?" Dax murmurs in my ear as he places his hand around my throat.

I am unable to speak. They fill me completely, pushing me to my limits. My pussy aches and throbs around them. Lyka pushes deeper, stretching me further. His hands grip my hips for leverage. Dax moves his hand from my throat and grips onto my ankles, holding me in place.

"You're taking us so well," Lyka groans as he concentrates, pushing further into me.

They start to move in sync and my moans turn into desperate cries.

"How does it feel having both the Faulkner's cocks inside you?" Dax asks.

"So...good. Don't stop," I beg.

"Oh, we won't, flower. I want you to milk us dry." His grip tightens around my throat.

Fuck, I have two cocks in my pussy! Lyka pounds deeper and faster.

"I want you over and over," I cry as tears fall down my cheeks.

Dax's thrusts become more demanding and quicker. My breasts bounce up and down, nearly hitting my face. "We'll use you until you can't take anymore. Is that what you want?" Dax asks.

I shake my head as Dax's grip restricts my breathing, making my head feel light.

"Say you want to stay here forever," Lyka commands.

"I...I..." I stutter.

"Say it!" Dax growls.

"I want to stay here forever!" I cry as my voice breaks.

Lyka and Dax's eyes darken, something flashing across them before they start thrusting harder. My body feels weak, my pussy taking everything they are giving me.

Their thrusts become erratic as they are close to coming. With a final, deep thrust, Lyka comes, and his body collapses on top of mine. Dax comes straight after. We are all a sweaty mess as I'm nestled between them. Their cocks pulsate and twitch inside me. The room is silent. All you can hear is our heavy breathing. As we lie there, catching our breath, the reality of what happened sinks in.

Laying between them, I feel the warmth of their bodies, providing a soothing presence. All of us are fully naked with our limbs entangled with each other. I've never felt such a sense of belonging before; I feel utterly connected to them. Slowly, I sit up and look at both of them, my eyes tracing their faces. They both squint their eyes open.

"You okay?" Dax croaks.

I shake my head, unable to speak. Lyka reaches out and wraps his fingers around my neck, pulling me back to bed.

"You're ours. Forever..." Lyka mumbles, still half asleep.

"It's not long at all, if you think about it," Dax adds in a sleepy state. His hand moves to my shoulder as he traces patterns on my skin.

I don't ever want to leave them, but I know the lockdown will be ending soon.

I lie there, feeling their steady breaths against my body. My mind races as I think of what we've shared and the intense bond we have formed. I feel a sense of certainty as if this is where I am meant to be.

Dax's arm drapes over my waist, pulling me close to him with Lyka nestled on my other side. I close my eyes as a sense of peace washes over me.

SEVENTEEN

FLORA

DAX WANDERS INTO THE LIVING ROOM WITH A HUGE SMILE ON HIS FACE. I look up from my book and ask, "What are you smiling at?"

He sits beside me on the couch and says, "We were thinking of having a date night with you."

Lyka enters from the basement, his smirk matching Dax's.

"I'll be honest, I've never been on a date before," I confess.

"We plan on getting dressed up and taking you for dinner by the lake this evening. How does that sound?"

Biting my bottom lip, I try to hide the smile. "I'd really love that," I whisper.

Dax leans down to me and plants a kiss on my cheek. "Great!" he exclaims, rubbing his hands together. "Lyka and I are just going to sort some bits out in the barn."

"Okay," I reply as I watch Lyka walk towards me. He leans down and his lips capture mine in a tender kiss.

"We'll be back soon," Lyka murmurs, caressing my cheek. They walk towards the door and leave.

I sit back on the couch, alone in the cabin. My mind races.

What am I doing? Am I in a relationship with two men? Brothers?

I get up and walk over to the window, watching Lyka and Dax head towards the barn.

I turn away from the window and glance over to the basement door. *Lyka left it open.* Curiosity gets the best of me as I walk over towards the door. I push the door and it creaks open as a cool breeze hits me.

I descend the steps. Pausing at the bottom of the stairs, my eyes widen as I see several cannabis plants bathed in artificial light.

I've never seen a cannabis plant before.

A faint light catches my attention and I head towards it.

As I enter the room, I see a computer sitting on a desk at the end of the room. Its screen is on, lighting up the room. I approach the computer and notice several folders on the desktop. One folder captures my attention—*Fake Lockdown.*

My heart feels like a beating drum as I click on the folder. Inside are multiple videos. Clicking on one, I start watching it—it's an identical video to the news report I saw on TV.

It hits me in the gut—everything has been a lie. It was all fake.

Oh my fucking god.

Tears gloss over my eyes. I feel anger and betrayal hit me at once. I look around the room and notice my smashed phone on a table. I pick it up, feeling my hands shake, and it turns on without any problems. Tears fall down my cheek and my mind tries to understand it all.

Suddenly, strong arms wrap around me, pinning my arms to my sides. Panic immediately sets in as I scream out, "Get off me! Get off me!"

Lyka steps out from the dark and reveals himself, his face severe and stern. Before I can react, he snatches my phone from my hand and launches it at the wall.

Dax tightens his grip around my body as I try to kick myself free.

"YOU ASSHOLES! I trusted you! You faked a lockdown?" I wail as my voice breaks.

"Calm down..." Lyka commands.

"You're only gonna hurt yourself. Calm the fuck down!" Dax instructs from behind.

I thrash my legs, desperate to escape, but Dax's grip only gets tighter. My efforts to get out of his grip only make me weaker.

"Flora, listen...We did what we had to. You have to understand," Lyka says.

"Understand?!" I choke out. "You fucking tricked me!"

"Seriously? You should be thanking us. We *saved* you," Dax snaps, his soft, golden eyes now dark. I feel like I don't even know him anymore. I can't help but collapse into his arms.

Dax carries me up the stairs over his shoulder and Lyka follows behind. My body feels limp and lifeless. I struggle to come to terms with reality.

Dax sets me down when we reach the living room and I don't hesitate—I make a break for the door.

"Stop her!" Lyka shouts.

I fling the door open and sprint outside. In haste, I trip on the steps and tumble forward, crashing into the gravel. Pain shoots through me, but I ignore it. *I gotta get out of here.* Before I can get to my feet, Dax pins me to the ground.

"Get off me!" I cry out, punching at his chest. I thrash wildly. "Get off!"

Dax's face is filled with determination as he grabs my wrists and pins them above my head.

"Where do you think you're going, flower? No one can hear you. Scream all you want. We are alone out here," he says in a cold voice.

I struggle beneath him, but he is far stronger than I am.

Choking on my sobs, I feel helpless.

Lyka steps outside and Dax lifts me up. I flail my limbs, trying to break free, but it's useless.

"For god's sake, Flora. You are just gonna wear yourself out," Lyka says flatly.

Dax draws me back inside and my body is filled with exhaustion. I stare helplessly as Lyka locks the cabin door behind us.

"People will know I am missing!" I threaten.

Dax sets me down and I push him away.

"Who, Flora? You have no one apart from us." Lyka's words pierce me like a blade. It's true, I have no one. The last thing I told Nancy was that I was going back to London. Marty and I haven't been in contact since my father's funeral. No one knows I'm here at the cabin and the brothers know that.

I look between them and my heart feels like it is about to burst out of my chest. "The news report, the cable cord, the internet, my phone...all of it. You *lied* to me. You *used* me," I sobbed, choking on my tears.

My knees buckle as I fall to the floor. "I trusted you," I whisper. They trapped me, both emotionally and physically.

Lyka picks me up by the elbow and pushes me towards the kitchen, directing me towards a stool. I refuse to look at him as I stare at the floor. Dax pulls up a stool next to me. He reaches out and clasps my hand in his. His touch feels like a shackle.

"Flora..."

"I let you take my virginity...I trusted you. I fucking *trusted you*," I mumble to myself.

"Flora!" Dax says louder this time.

Anger washes over me as I yank my hand away from his. My head snaps upwards and I look at him. Without thinking, I slap him across the face.

"I hate you!" I scream.

Dax's head snaps to the side from the impact. He doesn't move for a moment. His expression is a mix of shock and hurt. He slowly turns his head towards me as a red mark forms across his cheek.

My eyes dry up. I glare at Dax and his nostrils flare as he clenches his fist. Fear runs through me for a moment, but I hide it. Dax abruptly stands, toppling his stool behind him as he strides to the other side of the kitchen and slams his fist down on the counter.

"Let's all calm down. Flora, have a drink," Lyka says, passing me a glass of water.

My throat is dry from the screaming. I pick up the glass and begin to drink half the glass down, my hands trembling.

I slam the glass down and spring to my feet, screaming at the top of my lungs, "You locked me away! You had no right! I'm leaving!" I grab the glass and launch it at Lyka, but he ducks before it can hit him.

"You aren't leaving this cabin..." Dax states in a menacing tone.

"Watch me!"

Lyka lets out a sinister chuckle as I push past them and exit the kitchen.

"I bet you twenty dollars she won't make it to the front door," Lyka bets. He sounds like pure evil.

The front door is in sight, the key to my freedom just a few feet away. I reach for the lock, but my fingers start shaking. Suddenly, my vision becomes blurred. The edges of my sight begins to darken and my head becomes heavy. Panic sets in once more.

"No... no..." I whisper to myself.

My knees buckle and I collapse to the floor. My vision fades into darkness. I try to fight the darkness, but it completely engulfs me in unconsciousness.

The last thing I hear is the brothers laughing in the distance.

OPENING MY EYES, THEY FEEL HEAVY. MY ARMS ARE NUMB; I TRY TO move my right arm, but it won't budge. I tilt my head up and notice a metal cuff securing my wrist. The cuff is attached to a chain. I shake at the chain and it makes a metallic clicking that echoes throughout the room.

The bedroom door creaks open. Lyka and Dax enter the room, their expressions unreadable.

"You *drugged* me?" I croak.

They stand at the end of the bed with their arms crossed, staring at me with no emotion.

"So you're gonna keep me chained up like this!" I demand.

Lyka's face darkens. He moves towards me, grabbing my cheeks and squeezing them with his painful grip.

"You said you wanted to stay here *forever*," he says maliciously.

Tears begin to spill from my eyes.

"From the moment we brought you to this cabin, you were ours, flower," Dax says with a glint in his eyes.

The room is spinning and I try to focus on their faces. "Fine! Keep me chained up. But I'll never let you touch me again!"

They both laugh darkly. "It's cute that you think you have a choice," Lyka taunts as he releases my cheeks.

"She'll break sooner or later," Dax whispers.

I turn my head away, trying to create a distance without looking at them.

"The closest neighbor is miles away. Don't think you can escape," Dax warns.

Lyka smirks. "If you try escaping...there will be punishment."

"You...You...wouldn't hurt me." I tremble.

"Are you sure about that?" Lyka asks, raising his eyebrow.

Dax tries to swipe his finger under my chin. "Flora, we've been gentle so far. But don't mistake our kindness for weakness."

Lyka's presence looms over me. "We saved you when you had no one. We're offering you something better. But if you don't appreciate it, there will be consequences."

I pull at the chain, but it only tightens the cuffs against my skin. "This isn't better. This is control," I spit out.

"You'll see in time we did this for your own good. If you don't...let's just say we have ways of making you understand," Dax states.

I feel like I am in a nightmare. I look up at them and realize I have no idea who I am talking to anymore; these aren't the same brothers who nursed me back to health, got me back into painting, cared for me during love-making, empathetic in our shared losses. Their true implications are clear now and I'm at their mercy. No one was going to save me, only myself.

"You will come to accept this. It's just a matter of time, flower," Dax leans down and whispers determinedly, brushing the hair out of my face. "You're *ours,* Flora. Now we get to keep you forever." Dax and Lyka look down at me, pride and excitement filling them like they're children looking at their new favorite toy.

They both turn and leave the room, closing and locking the door behind them. The moment the door closes I burst into tears.

I am now captive in their fucked up prison.

EIGHTEEN

FLORA

I glare up at Dax as he unlocks the chain from the bed. All night, I have been thinking of ways to escape.

"All the doors and windows are locked. So don't try anything stupid," he mumbles with his deep morning voice.

He pulls on the chain, leading me to the toilet. I feel like a slave, like a dog. I stand there with my arms crossed while he holds the chain and opens the toilet seat for me. "Go on then..." he gestures.

I scoff and utter, "I'm not pissing in front of you."

"Flower...I've seen your pussy many times. Even cleaned blood from it. Seeing you piss is nothing."

His words cut deep, a reminder of how I once trusted him. How he once looked into my eyes with tenderness. I pull down my panties and sit on the toilet. I'm surprised when Dax turns around and gives me privacy.

"What happens when I need a shit? I am definitely not shitting in front of you."

I can see Dax's body shift up and down as he chuckles. "We'll cross that bridge when we come to it."

I pull on the chain as I reach for the toilet paper. Dax looks over his shoulder to see what I'm doing. I quickly wipe myself and pull up my panties.

"Done," I say in a defiant tone.

Dax turns around. He doesn't say anything as he tugs on the chain out of the bathroom.

How the fuck do some people find this sexy? I feel like a fucking animal!

He leads me to the kitchen, the chain rattling with each step. Lyka stands in the kitchen, plating up food with a calm demeanor. Dax pulls me to a stool and chains me to the island. I glare at him, my eyes filled with hatred and defiance.

"Oh, stop glaring. I know you want me," he says arrogantly.

I refuse to give him a response so I just clench my jaw. Lyka places a plate of pancakes in front of me, but I shove them away.

"Flora. Don't make me feed you," he warns, narrowing his eyes. He picks up the fork, digs it into a pancake, and moves it in front of my mouth. "Fuck you!" I swear.

"You're not going to win this by starving yourself," Dax states, digging into his own breakfast.

"Open," Lyka commands.

I shake my head and press my lips tightly together. I see a flicker of amusement in Lyka's eyes. "We have all day. You can be as stubborn as you want. I can assure you, we're not going anywhere."

I hated them, but if I was going to escape I needed to eat and gain energy. I was still feeling drained from getting drugged last night. Lyka moves the fork closer to my mouth. "Eat."

Feeling defeated, I parted my lips and allowed the fork to enter my mouth. Lyka smirks as he watches me chew.

"That's a good girl," Lyka smirks, looking triumphant.

Dax brushes a strand of my hair from my face. "That wasn't so hard, was it, flower?" he croons.

I swallow the food, wanting to cry. But I won't let them see that they have won. I look away and stare at the kitchen floor. Dax pushes a glass of orange juice along the surface.

"Fuck no. You've probably drugged it again."

"We haven't drugged it," he says as he rolls his eyes.

Yeah, right! I don't trust them at all.

"Don't make me pry your mouth open. Now drink it," Dax commands.

Lyka gives me a warning look. I can tell they are not bluffing.

I'm so tempted to smash this glass over one of their heads.

"You're really making this harder than it needs to be," Dax says, exasperated.

I lift the glass to my lips, watching them closely as I sip. They both look at each other and smirk. They love having this control over me.

Dax finishes the last of his pancake and says, "You're gonna chop some wood with me today."

"No," I reply bluntly.

Lyka looks up at my defiance, pulls on the chain, and pulls my arm toward him. "Don't defy us, you're not the one making decisions here."

I pull back and feel a surge of anger and frustration. His eyes bore into me with amusement.

Feeling like a bratty teenager, I continue to glare at them.

"Your eyes can be so cruel," Dax states quietly.

"I can say the same," I say as I look up, meeting Dax's gaze. There's a flicker of something in his eyes, a brief vulnerability that surprises me. It's gone almost as soon as it appears.

Lyka grips my face, his fingers pressing into my cheeks. I try to pull back, but he turns my head so I have no choice but to look at him.

"You have different colored eyes..." he notes.

"*Wow*, asshole. You've only just noticed?"

There's something unsettling about how he looks at me as if searching for answers. "I've never paid attention before," he says flatly.

His admission cuts more than it should. His hand falls away and I'm left blinking. I rub my cheeks where his fingers had dug into. "Well... Now you know," I say, shaking my head and trying to sound nonchalant.

Lyka leans back in his chair. "Yeah," he murmurs, his eyes still fixed on mine. "Now I know."

I finish my pancakes. Dax helps me off the stool and unchains me from the island.

He leads me to the bedroom. I can't help but feel a sense of dread creep over me.

"Don't expect sex!" I exclaim.

Dax shakes his head. "Don't do anything stupid. I'm going to unlock the cuff."

He removes the metal cuff from my wrist. The sensation of freedom feels fantastic as I flex my fingers.

I watch him rummage in the closet, selecting clothes for me. He turns around and holds out an outfit. I take it without thanking him.

"Arms up."

I comply, lifting my arms up as he removes the oversized T-shirt. I feel his eyes gaze at my breasts and he bites his bottom lip.

"Now...do you want to go braless? Or leave it on?"

"Leave it on."

A smirk plays on his lips. He grabs one of his flannels and helps me into it, buttoning it up.

"These panties need to come off."

He drops to his knees in front of me, his hands pushing my legs apart. His eyes are locked onto mine. I feel a flush of anger and unexpected arousal, my body and mind at war.

His fingers hook into the waistband of my panties and he pulls them down slowly. I bite my lip, trying to suppress any reaction, but my body tingles.

"No panties for you today. I want you to go commando."

I force myself to look away, staring at the wall as he removes my panties completely. My breath catches in my throat as he pauses, his hands lingering on my thighs before he spreads my pussy lips open. He slowly licks once and I can't help but gasp.

I hate him so much. But, fuck, I want him to eat me out.

He looks up at me, his eyes dark and filled with a twisted amusement. "Good girls get rewards."

His hand comes up and he slaps my pussy, a quick sting that makes me flinch. I roll my eyes, trying to mask my arousal. A part of me craves more of his touch despite the fury inside.

Dax chuckles, the sound low and sinister, and he stands up. He grabs a pair of jeans from the bed and kneels again, helping me into my jeans.

Once the jeans are on, he retrieves the metal cuff and snaps it around my wrist. He tugs on the chain, pulling me closer, his eyes locking onto mine with a dark intensity.

"Let's go."

He leads me out of the bedroom to the living room. Lyka stands there, watching me closely. He gives a once-over. "Behaving, are we?" His tone is mocking.

"You wish, asshole."

Dax tugs on the chain and my whole body moves toward him. "Remember, only good girls get rewards. So I wouldn't keep calling us assholes."

His words sound dangerous, yet I can't help but retort, "I'll never be your good girl." I grit my teeth.

I might be chained up now...but I won't be forever.

Dax drops the chain and the metal makes a loud noise as it hits the floor.

I don't waste a second and run. I can hear them laughing behind me.

"Where are you going, Flora?" Lyka calls out.

I run to the front door, but it's locked. I look up at the stairs and race up them.

"For fuck's sake. What is she doing?" Dax asks.

I don't look back, reaching the landing. My breathing becomes heavy. I lean over the railing, force myself to stand tall, and grip it with one hand.

"I'll jump and kill myself!" I scream down.

Lyka and Dax stand at the bottom of the stairs, looking up at me. They burst into laughter, mocking me.

"You'll only break your ankles from that height," Dax shouts up the stairs, shaking his head.

I feel helpless as I struggle to keep my balance.

Lyka slowly makes his way up the stairs. "Come down. If you jump and break any bones, we will not be taking you to a hospital."

He reaches the top step and his face is full of anger. My body trembles as I look at him.

"Your favorite movie is *Misery*...There's a scene where she breaks her ankles with a sledgehammer. If you wanted your ankles broken, you just had to ask, baby," he taunts.

I let out a gulp as I remembered the scene from the movie. "You... you...wouldn't." I tremble.

His eyebrow raises as he gives me a warning. I take a hesitant step forward.

"On your knees," he commands with an evil grin.

"No," I bluntly say, feeling humiliated.

He glares at me and starts walking towards me. He stops as I drop to my knees.

"Now crawl..."

The hard floor presses into my palms and knees as I crawl toward him. The chain drags along the floor behind me, making a scraping noise.

I reach him, looking up and seeing his smug expression as he picks up the chain.

"Next time you're a brat, you will be punished," he explains. He pulls on the chain, forcing me to rise to my feet.

Dax walks up the stairs, shaking his head. His voice is low as he says, "Flower, you need to understand the more you defy us... the worse the punishment gets."

My whole body shakes from fear and anger. Lyka pulls me closer as he grips the chain tightly.

"Accept it," he breathes in my ear.

I hate them! I hate them so much!

Lyka leads me downstairs and Dax follows close behind; he feels like a shadow.

"You're gonna help Dax. Don't think about running. We will outrun you. Don't try to hide. We will find you," Lyka explains while unlocking the front door.

The door opens and the fresh air rushes in. As I look out, it feels like a cruel taste of freedom.

A world beyond my reach.

Dax takes the chain from Lyka and guides me outside. "Come along, flower."

We walk to the log shed and Dax secures the chain around a wooden pillar with a wall-mounted device. "This is called a kindling splitter," he explains.

I examine it, looking at the notches.

"I'll be cutting logs. You must put them on the notches and

pull the lever down," he continues, demonstrating how the device works. Lyka walks past and heads straight to the barn without looking at us.

Dax grabs my hands, making me flinch. He slips a pair of gloves on, saying, "Don't want splinters now...do we?"

The chain is long enough to grant me some freedom to move. I watch Dax place the first log on the chopping block. He brings the ax up above his head and then back down. The log splits cleanly in two. He throws a piece toward my feet. Bending down, I pick it up and look at it.

"Now, your turn."

I carefully place the log on the notch and align it. I grip the lever, pull it down, and the log splits into smaller pieces.

"Good, keep going. We need a lot of kindling."

I focus on the task and keep cutting the wood. Dax continues to chop the larger logs.

As my hands keep doing repeated motions, I start daydreaming. I think about the fake lockdown and the betrayal. Looking back, the red flags were always present. Being naive, I just ignored them.

"Dax...what if I never found out about the fake lockdown? What was your plan?" I ask.

I can sense Dax looking at me, but he says nothing.

"Well...?" I press, turning my head.

"You said you wanted to stay here forever," he says simply.

"That was a heat of the moment thing in sex!" I say, incredulously.

Dax doesn't reply as he continues to chop logs and fling them toward my feet. I narrow my eyes, trying to gauge his thoughts.

"Why me? Because I was a virgin? *Untouched*? Out of all the girls in town, why the fuck me?!"

I start feeling angry as he just looks down and pretends not to listen.

"Well, Dax, I might not be the untouched angel you think I am," I taunt.

He suddenly looks up, his eyes filled with anger. "What do you mean?"

I love getting a rise out of him and I know I've got to him. *Payback time. Asshole!*

"Well...Marty, my father's friend—"

"What the fuck about him?!" he growls.

Haha! You don't like it, do you?

Dax rushes towards me with fury in his eyes. Before I can react, he pins me up against the shed. His body presses against mine as he holds the ax blade to my throat.

"Fucking tell me now!" he seethes.

Fear and defiance overtake my body. We are frozen in the moment as the sharp edge of the ax holds me in place. I take a deep breath, trying to maintain my composure.

The memory of Marty was buried deep in my mind and I hated thinking about it.

However, I know this provokes Dax so I tell him with tears in my eyes.

"We kissed...then he got on top of me. I thought I was going to lose my virginity to him."

Dax's grip on the ax tightens as he grits down on his bottom teeth. "Then what?"

I swallow hard and tremble. "I screamed and he stopped. I felt fearful and helpless."

Dax's eyes search mine for the truth and his breathing becomes harsh.

"Why? Why are you telling me this?"

"Because. I want you to know you can't break me. I'm not afraid of you," I say, looking at him dead in his eyes.

He falters for a moment, then he lets out a growl as he pushes away from me. I stand my ground as he stares at me, trying to intimidate me. He walks back to the wooden block and resumes chopping wood.

I feel shaken up, but I refuse to let him see it. I return to splitting logs, trying to focus on the task.

A few moments passed between us. “You kissed...Did you do anything else?” he asks in a low tone.

I hesitate for a moment, then shake my head. “Nothing else. I backed out when he said I looked like my mother.”

“I wanna kill him for even trying. You’re *mine*.”

With all his anger, he lifts the ax and hits the chopping block. He lets out a loud grunt.

“I wanna kill him...I wanna kill him,” Dax repeats over and over as he continually swings the ax down.

He looks up at me, his eyes searching mine for something. I see a different side to Dax.

And it’s dark.

NINETEEN

FLORA

Days have dragged by, each one blending into the next. I have planned many ways to escape, each of them seeming impossible when I'm chained up like a dog.

We are outside on the balcony. They both smoke their cigarettes while I sit on the bench.

I look down at the chain wrapped around the leg of the bench, a stark reminder of my situation.

"Can I have a shower?" I ask.

"I didn't hear a *please*," Lyka taunts, looking at me pointedly.

"Please."

"That's better. Dax will join you."

I freeze, rolling my eyes in disbelief. "Seriously?"

Dax and Lyka both look at each other and smirk. I hate how they find amusement in keeping me captive.

Without a word, Dax stubs his cigarette out, unwraps the chain from the bench, and leads me back into the cabin.

We enter the bathroom and he gives me a warning look as he uncuffs my wrist.

"Get undressed then..." he says, locking the bathroom door.

I peel my clothes off my body as his eyes watch me. Once, I would have loved this, but now it makes me feel terrified. I turn on the shower and step inside, feeling the water cascade down me.

I try to ignore Dax as I wash my hair and body. His eyes do not leave me. I see I have grown some hair on my legs and pussy. I look around for a razor, but I can't find it.

“Is this what you’re looking for?” Dax's voice breaks through the silence as he holds up the razor. I open the shower door and hold out my hand, expecting him to give it to me.

“You think I’m stupid enough to trust you with a razor?”

I look away as he starts undressing. He steps into the shower, fully naked with his cock semi-erect.

He looks down at his growing hard-on and smirks at me. My stomach churns.

I’m not having sex with him, he can fuck off.

He kneels down, takes my leg, and starts shaving gently.

“You’re tense, flower. Just relax,” Dax observes.

“How can I relax when I’m being held captive?”

He ignores what I just said and carries on shaving me. I close my eyes briefly as he shaves my pussy, getting in all the crevices. He finishes, opening the shower door and placing the razor on the floor.

“All done.”

The water drips off him as he stands up and, surprisingly, exits the shower. He puts his hand out to help me, but I step out without taking it. We both dry off and get dressed.

I notice that Dax hasn't put the cuff and chain back on my wrist. He opens the bathroom door and we exit to the hallway. I see Lyka bringing in logs from outside. The cool breeze shivers up my body as it touches my skin.

“Dax...” I whisper, my voice laced with seduction.

He turns around, but I press my lips against him before he

can react. I push him against the wall, and his hands touch my waist as we kiss.

Out of the corner of my eye, I see Lyka stepping back into the cabin, carrying a heavy load of logs. The cabin door is wide open and I can taste freedom.

Sensing my opportunity, I deepen my kiss and bite down hard on Dax's lip. I knee him in the balls and break away abruptly. He lets out a grunting noise as he drops to the floor. Without a second thought, I sprint towards the door.

"You bitch!" Dax moans out in pain.

My heart races as I burst through the threshold. I feel the ground beneath my bare feet as I continue to run.

I head straight to the trees, each branch that touches me cutting at my arms. I manage to look over my shoulder, expecting to see Dax and Lyka, but there's no sign of them.

As I look around, the forest seems endless. I continue to sprint; my lungs feel like they are bleeding and my feet are getting cut up.

I hear in the distance, "*Flora!*"

My pulse quickens.

Ducking behind a thick oak tree, I have no choice but to try to hide. The forest is dead silent, not even a bird is chirping.

My body shakes with fear and adrenaline. Searching for any signs of them, I look around.

Then, I see Dax running off to my left, but he doesn't notice me. Relief floods through me and I exhale.

I stand up, keeping an eye out for Dax, step backward, and then collide with something hard.

"Going somewhere, baby?" Lyka whispers right behind me.

I don't even have a chance to turn around before his strong arms wrap around me. I let out a piercing scream and thrash out my legs.

"Let me go!" I cry out.

He presses his lips against my ear and I feel his hot breath. "You really thought you could run away? That you could leave *us*?"

Dax appears out of nowhere and grabs my legs. I try to kick out as they carry me towards the cabin. I scream as loud as I can, hoping anyone can hear me.

"No one can hear you, flower. Let's take her to the barn," Dax says, his voice sounding sinister.

"Please. Let me go....please," I sob as they haul me towards the barn.

They throw me down on the hard floor and pain shoots through my body. My feet are stinging from the cuts, and with each movement, I let out a whimper.

"It's time for your punishment," Lyka says coldly.

Dax rushes towards me, grabbing me and positioning me between his legs as he sits on the floor. He completely immobilizes me as his legs wrap around mine.

I feel utterly powerless. "What...What are you gonna do?" I tremble.

"You're going learn your lesson," Lyka hisses.

Dax's fingers dig into my arms, pinning them down.

I scream in terror as Lyka walks over to the workbench and picks up the branding iron and a blow torch. My whole body shakes frantically.

"Shh, it's okay, little flower," Dax whispers in my ear.

"Please...Please! No...No! I'll be good!" I scream.

They don't listen to me. Lyka turns on the blow torch and the flame turns blue.

He holds the branding iron over the flame and the letter *F* starts turning red.

"Please! I'll do anything. Please, don't do this!" I beg.

Lyka looks at me with predatory eyes and I try to struggle

against Dax's hold. With each passing second, the branding iron glows brighter.

Dax manages to pull my shirt up and push my jeans down. Lyka walks over, holding the branding iron steady. His demeanor is so calm that it's frightening, like this is just another afternoon for him. "I'd stay still, if I were you," he suggests.

My vision glosses over with my tears as I brace myself.

I'm trapped in a nightmare. I blink hard a couple of times, hoping to wake up.

"It's only going to hurt more if you move," Dax whispers in my ear.

Lyka closes the gap between us. I grit my teeth together and force myself to stay still.

The branding iron hovers above me and I can feel the heat radiate off it. Tears stream down my face and I can't help but squeal.

Lyka positions the branding iron on the right side of my pelvic area. He presses down on my skin and I let out an ear-splitting scream. The pain is excruciating as the branding iron sears through my flesh.

My body convulses against Dax's grip, but he pins me down. Every second feels like an eternity as I sit there in searing pain.

Lyka ensures the mark is seared deep into my skin. The scent of burnt skin and blood lingers in the air. Lyka grunts and removes the branding iron from my skin.

I can't help but slump in Dax's arms. He kisses my cheek. "You're a Faulkner now," he says with pride in his voice.

I force myself to lift up my head and glance down. The letter *F* stares back at me. I am no longer me. I am theirs, a possession under their ownership.

I close my eyes, shake uncontrollably, and lay there, broken.

There is no escape. I am in hell.

LYKA

I watch Flora as she is fast asleep. I don't know how she looks so peaceful, considering the pain she must be in. Her dark blond hair frames her face, she almost looks angelic.

I gave her some strong pain medication and sleeping tablets. I lift the cover and pull it to the side, hoping I won't wake her up. I carefully inspect the brand, looking as it stands out against her pale skin. A slow smile spreads across my lips at the physical sight of our ownership over her. She stirs, moving her head slightly. With her eyes still closed, she furrows her brows.

I reach, moving a strand of hair away from her face, and place the cover back over her. Walking over to the other side of the room, I settle back down in the chair.

I admire Flora; she is very strong-willed. I've never seen someone as strong as her. This world was too cruel for her, leaving her alone with no one but Dax and me.

Dax insisted, telling me we were saving her and giving her a chance. Part of me didn't care if she killed herself in that forest. But the other part wanted to keep her. Claim her.

Now, she's marked and bound to us. I wouldn't have it any other way. I didn't give a shit if we went about it in a fucked up way.

I lean back in the chair and sigh, thinking about everything.

She was so lost and broken when we found her. I knew Dax was going to take her virginity; it was only a matter of time. The night it happened, I could see it in his eyes. He claimed her in the most intimate way. Of course, I wanted to be her first, but I was not worthy and never will be.

I've seen the other side of Dax, the side that he keeps hidden very well. He's very good at putting on a fake mask, it helps lure people to us. But his darkness lurks beneath the surface. We're equally as fucked up as the other. He manages to handle his emotions better than I do. However, despite this, we are brothers. We are Faulkners. And now, Flora is one of us, too.

She is ours.

I hear the door creak open and Dax enters the room.

"She's still asleep then..." Dax says in a low voice.

"Yeah. The medication has knocked her out, thankfully."

Dax gives a closed-lipped smile as he walks and stands beside me. We both watch her in silence. Flora makes a little whimpering sound, like she's having a bad dream. Too bad she won't escape it when she wakes up. I sigh. It may take some time, but she will eventually come to terms with things. She doesn't have another choice. When she gave her virginity, her trust, her art, her laughs, her broken heart, her shared desire to stay here forever with us...we knew that we would never let her go. A sick part of me loves watching her break in the process.

As much as I admire Flora's strength, I admire her broken more.

We can only watch, wait, and hope she'll understand in time.

The things we would do to keep this girl here. She has no idea.

TWENTY

FLORA

I HOLD UP MY SHIRT FOR DAX AS HE KNEELS IN FRONT OF ME, HOLDING a tube of cream. I let out a whimper as I look down at the raw *F* mark on my skin. My eyes gloss over tears. "Ouch," I sob.

Dax applies a small amount of cream on his finger and gently dabs it onto the burn. I can't help but flinch at his touch.

"It's okay. I know it hurts. This cream is antiseptic and numbing, it will help soothe it," Dax explains as he applies more cream.

Dax pauses, looking up at me. There is a flicker of emotion in his eyes. *Is that regret?*

"We need you to learn, but I don't want you to suffer in pain."

He seems almost human for a moment; the darkness I've seen before is gone. He applies the last bit of cream and his fingers linger above my skin for a moment. He starts tracing the brand with his fingertip, a small smile tugging on his lips.

"You need to understand that we are in control at all times. You're ours, Flora," Dax says.

I lower down my shirt. Dax's eyes are still on me as I move away from him and approach the bed.

"You're monsters," I whisper out.

Dax sighs. "We're not monsters, Flora. We're just doing what needs to be done to keep our flower safe."

I don't answer him. Sitting down on the edge of the bed, he joins me.

Dax places a hand on my knee. I sit there paralyzed. I should be angry, hitting him and lashing out. However, the memories of my parents flood my mind. I want them here, making me feel safe.

"I want to die. I don't want to be here anymore," I whisper quietly.

Dax's grip on my knee tightens. "That's why we won't and can't let you go."

Tears fall down my cheek and Dax moves his hand from my knee to my face, wiping away my tears.

"We're all you have now, don't you understand? We're your family, flower," Dax tries to reassure me.

I shake my head and bite down. "*Family*? Family doesn't brand you or hold you captive. My real family is *dead*. This is a prison! I'll never be safe with you two!"

"Flora. It's a different kind of safety. You don't understand yet, but you will," Dax says while gripping my face.

I want to scream and fight him as fury overcomes me. "*One day, I'll understand*...That's all you keep saying! Shut the fuck up!" I scream.

Dax releases my face and stands up, looking back at me frustrated.

Anger overtakes me as I stand, but I do not feel scared, so I step closer to him.

"Calm down..." he warns.

"No. No! I won't. What are you gonna do? Punish me more?!" I shout, finally snapping. "You've *branded* me a Faulkner. Nothing can be worse! Give me all you've got!"

Dax clenches his jaw and his fists.

That's right. I'm fighting back, fucker.

I've shocked him and he doesn't know how to react. He then steps closer, towering over me.

"I'm not your fucking property!" I yell in his face.

He grips both my arms tightly, pinning them to the side. "You need to calm down or things will get worse."

I look at him, really look at him, and I see fear in his eyes for the first time.

So that's it, you hate losing control.

"I'm already in the worst place I could ever be, with the worst people I could ever be with. I'm already in hell! Things can't possibly get worse!"

"You're such a fucking brat, Flora!" Dax shouts, his own anger rising.

Without thinking, I dig my fingernails into his cheeks, drawing thin lines of blood. Caught off guard, he stumbles backward onto the bed.

I jump on top of him and start pounding at his chest. Dax lets out a mocking laugh as I continue to punch him.

Dax manages to flip us over in a quick motion. He pins me beneath his body, his knees pressed into my thighs. He grips my wrist, holding them above my head. The blood from his cut drips onto my face.

The door bursts open and Lyka rushes in. "What the fuck is going on?!"

Dax runs his finger along my face, dragging the blood down to my neck. He slides off me and stands up.

"The little brat attacked me. She thinks we can't make things worse for her..." Dax explains as he leans against the wall with blood dripping down his face.

Lyka charges towards me and pushes me against the wall.

The back of my head hits it, making me feel dizzy. His nostrils flare as he grabs my cheeks with a bruising grip.

"Do your worst!" I say through gritted teeth.

Lyka's stare looks dark and menacing as his fingers dig deeper into my cheeks. "You have no idea what we're capable of. Don't test us, Flora."

I am scared shitless, but I refuse to show them. "Show me! Show me how much worse it can get!"

The room falls silent and they seem dangerously calm. Lyka removes his hand from my face and steps back. "By the time we're done, you'll be begging for mercy," he taunts.

I hold my breath, his words sending a shiver through my body.

"Let's take her to the barn," Lyka says, turning to Dax.

Dax uncrosses his arms, steps forward, and grabs my wrist. I hit his hand, my nails scraping against his skin. With force, he pulls me through the cabin, leaving me stumbling to keep up.

Lyka follows behind and starts whistling an eerie tune.

We reach the barn and Dax hustles me inside with the door closing behind us.

Inside, it feels cool and musty, dimly lit with a skylight. There's a wooden beam in front of us with a thick chain hanging down and two ominous handcuffs. The chain whirls a bit as Lyka grabs it. "Do you like it?" he asks, his voice oozing with satisfaction. "I made it last night."

My mouth drops open. "What the–" I mutter out of shock.

Dax and Lyka charge over to me and start stripping away my clothes. I stand there, fully naked, and feel the weight of their gazes on me.

The only thing left on my flesh is the Faulkner brand.

"You won't do shit!" I spit at their feet, not regretting it.

They won't break me.

Dax looks down at the saliva on his shoe and mumbles, "You brought this on yourself."

I clench my teeth together so I don't show them any fear. Lyka pulls me over to the chain, lifting my arms above my head. He reaches up and snaps the metal cuffs around my wrists. I feel the cold metal digging into my skin.

"Do your fucking worst!" I taunt.

I am on my tiptoes, barely touching the floor. My arms stretch up agonizingly, every inch of my biceps straining to this unnatural position. The metal cuffs rub my wrists raw.

They both circle around me like predators. "One way or another, Flora, we will break you," Lyka sneers. "And we are going to have so much fun doing it."

Dax steps forward and whispers in my ear, "You just keep on being a brat...so ungrateful for all that we've done for you."

They both walk over to the workbench with their backs to me. I refuse to let my tears fall.

I will not break. Not for them.

Dax turns around with a wooden paddle in his hand and an evil grin on his face.

"Look at what Lyka made, flower. Do you like it?" he asks, hitting the paddle against his palm. He walks behind me and I try to turn to keep him within my sight, but the cuffs and chain hold me in place. I feel a knot form in my stomach.

Suddenly, the paddle comes down with brute force and sharp, stinging pain on my bare ass. I jerk violently, feeling my breathing hitch up in my throat. My jaw clenches as my muscles lock tight. I refuse to give in and cry.

"You're gonna take everything we give you." Dax passes the paddle to Lyka. He steps behind me, letting out a sinister laugh. I feel the agony again, the hard whack landing on the same spot. The pain radiates through my body.

"Wow. She's tougher than she looks...Everyone has a

breaking point, though," Dax remarks.

"I wonder how far we can push her," Lyka says, forcing the paddle down again.

I feel my skin burning, but through it all, I remain silent.

Lyka leans close to my face and taunts, "Haha...You think you're strong, huh? You think you can withstand this forever?"

"You won't break me!" I spit out.

Dax stands next to him, a mocking smile playing on his lips. "We shall see about that, flower."

Lyka saunters to the workbench. The wood paddle smacks my body again, sending shooting pain through my already bruised skin. I feel the edges of my vision blur from the pain.

From the corner of my eye, I see Lyka spin around, now holding a long, skinny rattan cane. He taps it lightly against his palm, the ominous swish slicing through the air. Dax lands another brutal strike with the paddle.

Lyka brings the cane down on the front of my thighs. The sharp, stinging sensation is agonizing. Despite my best efforts, a small whimper bursts free from my lips.

"Was that a sound that just escaped those beautiful lips?" Lyka asks, his voice dripping with mockery.

I bite down on my lip, trying to cut off any noises. The sting from the cane burns like fire.

Lyka teases the cane along my skin. Dax steps back, giving Lyka the center stage. His eyes don't waver from mine as he brings the cane down a second time against my legs. The pain feels like a lightning bolt as the cane hits my thighs. I curl my fists into balls, feeling my fingernails digging into my palms.

"Cry for us, Flora...Go on, cry," Lyka taunts with a venomous purr.

My eyes flood with tears, spilling over. Lyka grins leaning forward, his tongue invasive as he licks the tears off my face. I try to jerk my head away, but the chains keep me bound.

"Your tears taste so good, baby."

"You're beautiful to watch break," Dax states, circling around me.

I shake my head, attempting to refute the truth in their statements, but the tears keep falling.

Lyka presses his forehead against mine, his eyes burning into mine. "As much as we love watching your fight break, we love your obedience more. Just be ours. Be our good girl, Flora."

In a fit of defiance, I shove my head against his. He steps back, letting out a grunt. His face shows both surprise and anger. Lyka grits his teeth and strides over to the workbench, determined and pissed off.

"Ha! You think ya tough, huh? You're going to regret that. We're gonna show you real pain," Dax taunts, continuing to circle around me slowly.

In horror, I see Lyka holding a large, smooth, wooden phallus. It's long with some girth, polished, and glows slightly under the faint light in the barn.

My heart races and I swallow hard as my eyes fix upon the intimidating object within his hands, unable to look away.

What the fuck is that? It's over ten inches!

"Open your mouth, flower," Dax demands with excitement in his eyes.

"No! Fuck you!"

"Don't make me pry your fucking mouth open!" Dax threatens me as he smacks the back of my ass with the paddle.

As my jaw shakes, I open my mouth and reluctantly satisfy them.

"I spent all night making sure it's extra smooth for you," Lyka mutters under his breath, a sinister smirk playing on his lips. He places the wooden phallus at the entrance of my mouth. The scent of wood fills my nostrils.

"I'd get it extra wet If I were you..."

The humiliation is overwhelming, yet I fight down any further sounds or protests. With a deep breath, summoning the last threads of courage, I spit on it.

"Good girl," Dax croons.

Lyka begins shoving the wooden phallus into my mouth. My lips strain wide past its girth, stretching painfully at the corners.

"Now suck," Lyka commands.

I start to suck on the phallus and it nearly touches the back of my throat. I involuntarily make gagging noises. My eyes begin to water as the tears mix with my saliva while I fight the degradation that is being forced upon me.

Suddenly, Lyka removes the phallus from my mouth. I take advantage and gasp for breath.

His face contorts into an evil grin as he moves south, the phallus prying my legs apart. Then, he begins to rub on my clit.

I throw my head back as shameful arousal hits me.

"Oh look, Lyka. I think she's enjoying it," Dax says as he watches with amusement.

The wood makes my clit swell as Lyka moves it around. "Not for long," he murmurs.

With a jerk, he moves it from my clit and shoves the phallus into my pussy. The pain is sharp, like a blade. I feel the wood stretch and probe, invading me. I shut my eyes, hurling my head backward. "I wanna see how much she can take. Let's fuck her into submission," Lyka says, pushing the phallus deeper.

My body trembles as my fists involuntarily clench at the chains. Lyka pounds the phallus in and out of me relentlessly. With every thrust, it hits that spot deep inside, sending waves of pleasure through me. "Uhh," I moan, losing control.

The wooden phallus stretches me in ways I never thought imaginable. Lyka's movements are cruel, but the phallus is slick with my own juices. I feel such shame as I enjoy their torment.

"Look at you...taking my wooden toy so well," Lyka compliments mockingly.

Dax's face inches closer; his eyes seem to darken. His lips find my neck and I can't help but tilt my head sideways, giving him more access. I feel him smile against my skin at my reaction. His kisses are fierce, almost bruising, like he's trying to claim every inch of my skin.

My body shakes as the phallus stretches and fills my pussy. Dax's mouth moves from my neck, craning his head back to look at his handiwork.

"I love leaving my marks on you, flower. Although our *F* might be my favorite..."

He kisses me, our tongues fighting each other.

I hate them! Why am I so turned on? I fucking hate them! ASSHOLES!

I feel myself letting go, becoming weaker.

Every thrust, every kiss, every touch blurs together. I taste Dax's blood on my tongue as the coppery tang mingles with the saltiness from my tears.

The phallus is suddenly pulled out of me, leaving me feeling hollow and exposed.

I sob into Dax's mouth, my voice smothered by his kisses.

The sound of a zipper catches my attention. I glance to the side and see Lyka lowering his jeans.

Dax readjusts his hold, picking up one of my legs as Lyka does the same. I'm suspended between them in the air, my pussy opened. Lyka's hand cups my pussy, feeling my wetness with his fingers.

"I hate you," I sob.

"Your pussy is dripping wet. You don't hate us," Lyka growls.

I feel the head of his cock push against my pussy. With a brutal thrust, he's fully seated inside of me.

Gasping, my whole body strains against the chains. They hold my legs firmly, keeping me open and accessible to Lyka's relentless thrusts.

Dax's hands grip onto my thighs, his fingers digging into my flesh. His mouth moves back to my neck, biting and sucking over his marks. Lyka's cock stretches me as he fills me. His balls hit against my skin with every thrust. I shut my eyes, trying to block out the reality of what's happening, but the sensations are too strong. My body betrays me and responds to their touches, their kisses, and Lyka's thrusts.

Then, it dawns on me: *Lyka doesn't have a condom on.* My mind suddenly floods with panic as I pull away from Dax's kisses on my neck, my voice shaking with urgency. "You can't cum inside me. You need to pull out, Lyka," I plead.

He shakes his head and continues to thrust into me.

"Lyka. You can't!"

I feel Dax's grip on me tighten, holding me in place. Lyka's hips start to jerk ruthlessly against mine.

"To..."

Thrust.

"Fucking..."

Thrust.

"Late," he grunts.

Lyka pushes himself deep inside me, his cock pulsating as he cums. A cry escapes my lips as a new wave of panic and terror washes over me.

His body shudders as he finally goes limp. He pulls out and his cum drips from me. Lyka steps back, letting go of my leg and mopping the sweat off his forehead with the back of his hand. I barely have time to catch my breath before Dax takes down his jeans, revealing his throbbing cock. A gulp of fear escapes from me. Dax's cock is thick and ready. He doesn't waste time grabbing my thighs to hold me in place. "My turn," he growls.

With one hard thrust, Dax's cock pries between my swollen lips and plows deep into my pussy. "I love fucking my brother's cum back into you," he grunts.

Lyka now stands behind me, his lips pressing sweet kisses along my neck and down my shoulders. He reaches around, his fingers entering my mouth. Instinctively, I suck on them, my tongue swirling around them. Lyka draws his fingers from my mouth, down my back, and I shiver as he reaches the top of my ass. He keeps going down, his fingers slick and wet, as he lightly circles my asshole.

Dax quickens his pace, each thrust more powerful, driving deeper into me.

Lyka's fingers press more insistently against my asshole and then pushes a finger inside, forcing a scream from my lips. The pain hits me and makes my whole body tighten up. He leans down to my ear. "I'll go slow," he promises.

My asshole clamps around his finger, but Lyka holds it in place. "Fu...Fuck!" I loudly stutter.

"Scream for us," Dax demands, out of breath.

I let out a raw, sexual scream as they use my body, my cries filling the barn. Dax's cock drives into me with undeterred force.

"*Fuck*, Flora. Your asshole is so tight around my finger," Lyka whispers.

He then begins to move his finger, twisting and pushing it in. It's too much penetration. It pushes me beyond the brink of what I thought I could endure.

"Shit...I'm coming," Dax moans, throwing his head back.

Lyka thrust his finger into my asshole one last time. Dax's leg shakes violently. He thrusts deep inside me, emptying himself. His cum oozes out from me, trickling down. Lyka slowly pulls his finger out of my ass. He steps back, looking over the scene.

Dax pulls out of me and his cock slips free. His cum continues to ooze out of me, mingling with my own juices as it drips down my legs onto the floor. They both study me with triumph in their eyes. The air is heavy with the scent of sweat and sex.

My head sags and I shut my eyes. My entire body feels so weak it can hardly hold my weight.

I open my eyes to find Lyka standing in front of me, the phallus in hand.

“Spread your legs.”

“No...Please. No more.”

I don’t know how much more of this torment my body can take.

“That sounds like you're begging...” Dax says with satisfaction.

“Spread your legs now,” Lyka growls.

My legs shake as I spread them apart. Lyka steps forward, and he crouches at my already abused pussy, positioning the phallus at the entrance. “That's a good girl,” he murmurs.

He begins to push the phallus inside of me and I let out a sob. My pussy involuntarily clenches around it. Dax stands behind me, his hands trailing down my back. He reaches my hips, holding me steady as Lyka continues to push the phallus deeper. “You’re taking it so well,” Dax whispers.

Lyka finally stops, the phallus fully embedded inside me. I can feel every inch of it inside me. Dax’s hands roam all over me as one floats down to my clit, rubbing slow and deliberate circles.

“Orgasm, Flora. Let go. Show us who you really belong to,” Lyka says in a low, cruel voice.

I can’t hold back any longer. My body convulses with a scream as the orgasm rips through me. Lyka pulls the phallus out of me as Dax releases me from the chains and I collapse, my legs unable to support me any longer. Dax catches me and holds me.

"Open that pretty mouth," Lyka orders.

My eyes flutter open, heavy with exhaustion and pain. Lyka looms over me. He lifts the phallus, now slick with all of our juices. "Taste the Faulkner brothers' cum," he growls, his voice full of sadistic pleasure.

I taste the saltiness mingling with the hard texture of the wood. I feel ashamed, but I comply, licking weakly.

"Does our cum taste good?" Dax asks, petting my hair.

"Mhmm," I say, my eyes struggling to stay open.

Eventually, Lyka removes the phallus from my mouth and I feel relief just for a moment. He lifts my chin with his hand, making me raise my eyes to meet his.

"No more. Please. I beg of you," I mumble, my voice barely audible.

"Say it again."

"I'm," I gasp, "begging you," I cry.

Dax steps around me until his face is mere inches away from mine. "That's more like it," he says, caressing the side of my face. "*Now* you know your place, flower."

Lyka's grip tightens on my chin, "You're ours, Flora. There is no escape from the Faulkners. No one else can have you. No one else can save you."

His hands trail down my body, fingers brushing over the marks they've left on my skin. "You've been such a good girl. That's what we like..."

I am utterly broken as I hang my head. My spirit is crushed under their ruthless domination. They have taken everything away from me: freedom, dignity, and my body. They've broken me.

I belong to them now.

TWENTY-ONE

FLORA

My thighs sting, my ass is bruised, and my pussy is swollen as I lie in bed. I hear the door open, the sound making me flinch. I glance over and see Dax standing in the doorway.

"When I get out of here...I'm sending you my therapy bill."

Dax walks over to the bed, scoffing. I can feel his stare, but I refuse to look at him.

"You better get me Plan B again," I demand.

"Yeah, that's not going to happen. Lyka seems to like the idea of you pregnant," Dax states with a sinister tone.

I feel a surge of panic wash over me. *I pray to God they have weak sperm.*

"You wanna try painting today?" Dax offers. "That cheers you up."

"Fuck off."

I want to be left alone and disappear into my mind's black hole. Doing anything joyous right now seems impossible.

Dax leaves the bedroom without saying a word. I let out a deep breath and pull the covers tighter around me.

I ABRUPTLY WAKE UP, FEELING DAX SHAKING MY SHOULDER. "DINNER'S ready," he states while uncuffing me from the bed. I follow him to the kitchen; my body throbs and aches with each step. I look around and can't see Lyka.

"Where is Lyka?"

"He's in the barn working on something. He said he'll eat later."

"It better not be any more wooden toys."

I feel too weak to act defiant. I sit on the stool and let out a noise of discomfort as my ass makes contact with the surface.

Dax pushes a bowl towards me. I look down and see a type of stew.

"It's venison stew," he says.

"Did you kill the deer yourself?"

Dax nods, his eyes flicking to mine for a second before he looks away. I take the spoon and start eating. The stew tastes excellent. It is probably the best meal I've eaten in days.

"Don't suppose you have any wine?" I query.

"I'll check the pantry. Stay here."

Dax gets up, walks to the panty, returns with a bottle of red wine, then pours me a glass.

I take a sip, tasting the smooth, rich wine on my tongue. We eat and drink in silence. I begin to feel my muscles relax as the alcohol takes effect.

"So what is Lyka working on then?" I ask, breaking the silence.

"I don't really know. Lyka likes to keep busy."

We continue to chat, a strange normality settling over us. I keep taking sips of my wine. As we finish our meals, Dax seems visibly more relaxed. I'm halfway through the bottle of wine and my head starts feeling a little light.

Dax and I make our way to the living room where he drops down onto the couch with a beer. I settle next to him, clutching my glass of wine.

I set my wine glass on the floor beside my feet, careful not to spill it. As I look around, my eyes land on a stereo with music CDs. I walk over and inspect the music.

Dax takes a sip from his beer. "Ah, that's all my mother's music," he states.

My eyes skim and I recognize many of the artists my own mother loved. A pang of bittersweet memory hits me, but I push it down. I select a CD that stands out to me and insert it into the stereo. As the music starts to play, the familiar melody fills the room. I let myself get lost in the music as my hips sway. I feel a sliver of happiness, something I haven't felt in a while.

Dax watches me with a mixture of curiosity and something deeper, almost tender.

As I dance, it feels almost like a normal evening for just a moment, as if two people are sharing a simple pleasure.

LYKA

I hear music as I start walking toward the cabin. The beat and words of the music are muffled through the walls, but I pop my head in to see Flora dancing around the living room. Dax is on the couch, his beer in hand, watching her with a sort of bemused expression. I enter the cabin, locking the door behind me. Dax looks over to me, shaking his head with a laugh, and walks over.

Dax holds up a beer for me to take. "Yeah...she's drunk," he says.

"Fuck's sake," I mutter, shaking my head.

I see a CD case on the side table and pick it up. The song *Left Outside Alone* by Anastacia blares from the speakers. I show Dax the CD case and ask, "Wasn't this Mom's?"

Nodding, Dax can't help but chuckle and sit back on the couch, his eyes following Flora around the room. Flora holds her glass of wine, swaying to the music with a surprising grace. She starts singing, her powerful and emotional voice filling the room with the poignant words of the song.

"*Left broken, empty, and in despair,*" she sings, dramatically pointing a finger at Dax.

He raises an eyebrow, a smirk playing on his lips. Flora's performance is raw, anger mixed with sadness. Her body moves with the music as her voice cracks with emotion.

She whisks her hair and takes a long sip of her wine. My eyes flicker to the wine bottle on the floor. It's nearly empty.

Dax leans back in his chair and takes another swig of his beer. "Damn, she's really feeling it."

I watch Flora as she becomes more extreme and expressive. When the song's chorus comes around, she yells out the words, her voice echoing through the cabin. Flora sings, directing her words at me and Dax.

I gently pace over to Flora, catching her on the arm as she spins around. She looks at me, her eyes all wide and glassy.

"Flora...Maybe you should sit down?" I suggest.

Her eyes blink several times and her expression changes from defiance to vulnerability.

"No! I want to forget. I want to dance," she slurs and nudges me off her.

Part of me feels a twinge of guilt for just a moment and then I come to my senses. She is singing this song and directing it at us. I can feel the bitterness in her tone. She stumbles toward Dax and straddles his lap as the song ends.

"I hate you so much. Just let me go," she slurs.

She leans forward, her lips brushing his in a sloppy, drunken kiss. Dax doesn't kiss back. His hands hold the tops of her arms, steadying her.

"Flower, you're drunk. Let's get you to bed."

She leans backward, her eyes unfocused as she sways dizzily. I see her falling back and quickly catch her before she tumbles off Dax's lap. I wrap my arms around her, pulling her upright. "Whoa, easy there."

I support her weight as I help her stand. Her legs wobble as she leans heavily on me for support.

"Yup...I'm taking you to bed," I say.

Dax shakes his head and agrees. Together, we guide her towards the bedroom. She drags her feet on the floor and stumbles a couple of times. We reach the bedroom and I lay her down on the bed. She murmurs something and her eyes flutter closed as soon as her head hits the pillow. I pull the covers over her, tucking them around her.

Dax walks over to the door. "You coming, dude?" he asks.

My eyes glance at Flora and then back to him. "I'm gonna stay up and watch her. I don't want her to choke on her own vomit."

I move a strand of hair away from her face and tuck it behind her ear.

Dax nods and heads out, closing the door behind me. I lie on the blanket and position myself to study her closely. She makes an incoherent murmur. Worrying she will be sick, I reach out and gently turning her head to the side. My thoughts are a tangled mess; I feel guilt, concern, and protectiveness. She stirs once more, her brows furrowing as if discomforted.

"You're safe," I whisper.

The night goes on and I lose track of time. I doze off but jerk awake many times, checking that Flora is still breathing.

DAX

I sit in the living room deep in thought, the crackling fire casting a warm glow around the room. It had never been part of the plan to keep her here like this. We'd wanted it to keep her long enough so that, just maybe, over the course of these three weeks, she might come to see things our way on her own. Realize that going back to London wasn't truly what she wanted. Flora is very strong, but yet so fragile. So defiant, but so easily tamed and controlled. We can't help ourselves. She became our obsession. Her laughs, her artistic talents, her pussy, how she fits perfectly between Lyka and me, just everything about her made me want to keep her here forever. Me and Lyka ain't ever letting her go. *We* gave her a second chance in life. She owes us her life now. She needs us. We give her stability and security even if it is in a fucked way. She was adrift in the world and we gave her a place to belong. *Isn't that worth something?* When I first saw her lying in the forest, I thought she was a figment of my imagination. She looked so lost yet angelic. As I cradled her in my arms, she opened her eyes briefly, looking so astray and hurt. In that moment I wanted to make her mine, forever. Deep inside, I know the truth. We crossed a boundary and there's no going back. She's ours now, bound to us by so much more than mere physical ties. I want to fuck her up in so many ways. I want her to depend on us like the air she breathes, needing to survive.

TWENTY-TWO

FLORA

I OPEN MY EYES AND INSTANTLY MY HEAD FEELS HEAVY. I GLANCE AT THE alarm clock on the side table: *1:00 p.m.*

Dammit, I've been asleep all morning.

I turn over and startle when I see Lyka staring at me. I realize I must have passed out last night.

"Did you fuck me while I was sleeping?" I ask, fisting the covers, feeling a surge of panic.

"What the fuck, Flora? What do you think of me?"

"That's a hard one." I press my finger on my chin sarcastically. "Hmm, let's see...You've lied about a lockdown, held me captive, branded me, and used wooden toys on me. Nothing would shock me at this point."

Lyka's face twists in anger. He jumps off the bed, his body uptight. Without a word, he charges out of the room, slamming the door behind him. I flinch involuntarily. I glance down at my wrists to find Lyka has forgotten to chain me to the bed. My heartbeat quickens and I scan around the room. Slowly and carefully, I creep to the door, holding my breath as I peer out. Chatter from Dax and Lyka drifts from the kitchen. I sneak out of the bedroom, creeping through the living room. The front door is locked. *Fuck.* I spot a window open instead, just enough to give me hope. I walk towards it, shooting a nervous glance towards the kitchen. I shove the window open all the way and climb out, landing on the porch with a soft thud.

Shit! Shit! Shit!

I freeze, listening for any indication that they heard me. The house is silent. I take off toward the garage in a barefoot panic. Every step on the rough ground sends shockwaves of pain up my feet, but I press on. Adrenaline fills my body.

Inside the garage, I look around the room and spot the ATV keys. I sprint for them, knowing every second counts. The garage door will be loud, but I have no choice. I yank it open; the metallic sound reverberates across the wind. Panic courses through me as shouting breaks out from the cabin.

"Flora!" I hear Dax shouting with fury.

The cabin door bursts open and I see them charging towards me. I launch onto the first ATV, fumbling with the keys, but it's not the right one. I leap to the other, swearing under my breath. They're getting closer, their faces full with rage. I twist the key, praying it's going to start. The engine sputters and my heart plummets. "Please start, Goddammit!"

I try once more and the engine roars to life this time. I slam the throttle, speeding out of the garage with Lyka and Dax screaming at me. I glance back to see the two of them sprinting with their faces murderous. "You'll never see me again! Assholes!" I shout.

Facing forward, my eyes glue to the path out in front of me, weaving through trees. The wind slaps my face, tears streaming from the corners of my eyes. My heart pounds from fear. For the first time in a long time, I taste freedom.

I'm free. I'm fucking free! I'm free at last!

Suddenly, a huge log appears in my path and there is no time to react. The ATV slams into it and I am hurled through the air. The world spins as I crash to the ground. I lie there, dazed, with my breath knocked out of me. I hear the sound of footsteps closing in. I try to move, but my limbs feel like lead. Pain radiates from my side and my vision blurs. I fight to stay awake, knowing I may not get another opportunity if they catch me. The last thing I see before darkness claims is a furious Dax and Lyka looming over me.

MY HEAD THROBS AS I OPEN MY EYES. MY VISION STARTS TO CLEAR AS I squint. I see Dax and Lyka standing there with sinister smirks. I panic as I try to move and realize my arms are tied up. I'm bound to a tree with ropes cutting into my skin at the elbows. I look down at my body and notice I am covered in...*food*? There are some sort of sticky remnants from a meal all over me.

"Never see you again? Huh?" Lyka taunts.

"What the fuck–"

Dax sings a haunting tune, "*If you go down in the woods today, you'd better go in disguise...*"

The twisted version of the nursery rhyme sends shivers down my spine, chilling me to my core.

"Why the fuck am I tied up?! I'm sorry! I shouldn't have tried running away!"

"We warned you not to run away..." Dax says as he steps closer, tying another rope around my body. He yanks it, pulling me closer and tighter to the tree.

Lyka stands beside him, anger blazing in his eyes. "We tried to make you one of us. A Faulkner. We could have given you everything...but you had to push the limits and break the rules, didn't you? You've brought this on yourself," he says.

"Please. I can't take this anymore," I whisper as I struggle against the ropes.

Dax grips my chin and makes me look into his cold, unforgiving eyes. "If we can't have you...no one can." He releases my chin and I drop my head, crying quietly.

They both step back and admire their handiwork.

Lyka sings the twisted nursery rhyme, "*Today's the day the teddy bears have their picnic.*"

"We will come back later to check on you...that is, if there's any of you left. Bears and wolves can smell food for miles," Dax explains in a sinister tone.

"No...No! You can't do this to me!"

Lyka brings his lips to mine and whispers, "*Every teddy bear who's been good is sure of a treat today.*"

They turn around and start walking off, their laughter echoing between the trees.

"Please! Dax...Lyka!"

I am alone, strapped to the tree, and covered in food. The forest turns silent and I can no longer hear Lyka or Dax. Panic sets in the situation I am in suddenly hits me. I try and struggle, twisting myself to the ropes binding me. I feel exposed, like prey waiting for predators to strike. The food smeared over my body attracts insects that buzz around me.

My breathing quickens, shallow and uneven. I start trying to work my way out of the ropes again.

I'm going to die. This is how they want to kill me. Too coward to kill me with their hands so they get a bear to eat me!

The minutes drag on, feeling like hours. I close my eyes and my parents come to my mind. I wish they were here at this moment.

Suddenly, pulling me out of my thoughts I hear a low growl. I open my eyes, looking around the forest in fear, yet I see nothing. No shape or form that matches the menacing sound.

The growling gets louder. My heart races and I dare not move. I hold my breath, fearing any sudden noise will bring whatever creature is out there closer. I clamp my mouth shut and shake involuntarily. I yank at the ropes, but they don't budge. I am paralyzed when I realize they are the sounds of bears.

Please let my death be quick. Please let my death be quick!

I look toward the sound of a twig snapping, expecting to see a bear. My hair raises on my neck as the noises reverberate through the trees. I brace myself for the wild animal to pounce.

Instead, what I see freezes me with another kind of horror. Dax and Lyka stand there with evil smirks, holding phones that play recordings of bear growls. They start laughing wickedly.

A scream rises from deep inside me. I let out all of my anger and fear in that scream.

I'd rather have wooden toys inside me again than have this mental torture. I drop my head in defeat. My body shakes uncontrollably with relief that it isn't a real bear, but quickly reminded that I'm still surrounded by monsters. Monsters that will never let me go. I slump against the tree. My vision blurs with tears as my eyes fix on Dax and Lyka.

Dax walks up to me slowly, with an amused, smug satisfaction on his face. He lifts my chin, forcing me to look at him.

"I'm yours. I won't defy you anymore. I promise," I say, my voice breaking. Lyka watches with a twisted grin as I admit my defeat. "Say it again," he demands.

"I'm yours! Okay? I'm yours!" I scream.

TWENTY-THREE

FLORA

It's been three weeks and I haven't done anything to aggravate Dax or Lyka. Every command has been followed and every punishment has been avoided. I have earned some of their trust with my submission. They no longer cuff me and I can now move around the cabin with ease. But the doors and windows are still locked, of course.

I sit on a wooden stool in the living room. My eyes are focused on the paper in front of me with my palette only holding black paint. It's the only color I can bear to use. The fact I can paint at all is a miracle in itself. I paint an abyss, a reflection of my soul, without hope, without color.

Taking the brush, I sink into the black paint. The bristles slide across the paper, leaving dark trials like shadows in my mind. "All of this is temporary," I whisper to myself. These words I hold on to like a lifeline. I am better off dead than being stuck in this hell. I hear footsteps behind me, but I don't turn.

"How's the painting?" Dax asks, his voice casual. He leans over my shoulder.

"It's coming along," I say quietly, my eyes glued to the paper.

"Good, stick at it. Maybe one day you'll paint something more cheerful."

I don't say anything in response. Dax sighs as he turns and leaves.

"It's all temporary," I repeat to myself in a whisper.

Lyka walks into the room and stands behind me, looking at the painting. He bends down and puts his finger under my chin, guiding my gaze towards him. I lay down my paintbrush. He kneels down beside me, making our faces level. I look into his eyes and see nothing, except I'm pretty sure when he looks into my eyes, he sees the same.

"You don't have to fight this...you don't have to fight *us*..." he says, pushing my hair behind my shoulder.

"I'm too weak, mentally and physically, to fight you anymore," I mumble as my eyes gloss over. "What do you want from me, Lyka? Why are you still keeping me here?"

"Me and Dax would be fools to let you go. You're ours now, Flora. Plus, who do you have apart from us?"

"I might not have anyone, but I would have freedom."

"You have everything you could ever want here. We just want to take care of you."

If I had the energy, I might have scoffed.

"Take care of me? You've tortured and tormented me. You lied about a Covid lockdown. My mother *died* from Covid. How can you be so cruel?" I whisper.

I see guilt in his eyes for a moment, but he quickly looks away.

"Me and Dax are all you have, and it's staying that way. Yes, we did some fucked up things, but you were ours the moment we brought you back to the cabin. I didn't want to bring you back here. But–" he stops talking and swallows. I try to look down at the floor, but he holds my chin in place. "I had to keep you here. I'm just as tainted as you. The dark thoughts that trouble you...Well, they trouble me, too," he whispers.

For a moment, I feel a connection to the man who holds me captive. We just look at each other, a silent conversation passing between us. His eyes search mine, but I don't have anything else to say. The numbness has taken over any other emotion in me.

His forehead presses against mine and I feel his breath against my lips. Despite everything, in this moment, I want to kiss and hold him. I want to feel something.

Dax strides back into the living room, his voice breaking the fragile tension between me and Lyka. "Flower, we have a treat for you since you've been a good girl," Dax coaxes, holding up a backpack. I turn to look at him and my eyebrows flicker, confused. Lyka stands up, his demeanor still soft. "We're gonna take you to the lake and have a picnic, go fishing. What do you think?"

"Uhh...I would like that," I stutter, caught off guard by the offer to leave the cabin.

Dax steps closer, his voice lower and stern, almost threatening. "You've been so good for us, flower. Don't give us any reason to punish you." His eyes bore into mine.

What they don't know is that I don't have anything left to give. The last of my fight bled out of my body three weeks ago. I nod and stand up from the stool. The thought of heading out into the open to see the lake sends me waves of both thrill and terror. I haven't been outside since being tied up like a sacrifice. Lyka helps me gather my things while Dax just watches us. His eyes still locked on me, reminding me of the boundaries that are still present.

We walk toward the door; some outside light filtering into the cabin. My heart pounds in my chest. Stepping outside, I fill my lungs with the fresh air, and for a moment, I feel a flicker of something I haven't felt in weeks—hope. But their presence behind me reminds me how imaginary that feeling is.

We walk toward the garage as Dax takes my hand; his grip is firm but tender. It's like we are boyfriend and girlfriend. I can't find it in myself to care; I'm just happy to be outside. The breeze feels amazing against my skin and the view of the forest is something else. It's as if I haven't seen the outdoors before; everything is so vivid.

"You'll be getting on the back of my ATV," Dax says, pulling me along.

Lyka drops the backpack on his ATV and opens a container filled with weed brownies. "Let's have these before we leave," he says, holding out the container. They both take a brownie and eat it, enjoying the treat. I reach for one of the brownies and scarf it down, letting the rich chocolate dissolve in my mouth.

Dax guides me toward the four-wheeler, boosts me to the seat, and then holds my hand steady. He starts the engine and I feel the strong vibrations traveling up the seat into my body. "Hold tight," he says over his shoulder.

I wrap my arms around his waist, feeling his solid muscles beneath his shirt. We speed off into the forest, the wind whipping past us. Lyka follows behind us.

We come to an open area beside the lake. The water glistens in the midday sun. Dax parks the ATV and helps me off.

Lyka pulls off the backpack and spreads a blanket on the grass as we sit down to eat. The scene is idyllic. I slide all the way back, leaning on my elbows, feeling the sun's warmth soaking into my skin. Lyka and Dax sit on either side of me. Though their proximity reminds me of my captivity, I let myself appreciate this moment in the sun for now. I look around, seeing mushrooms spread across the grass, ducks zip across the lake's surface, and butterflies flutter by.

So beautiful. I may be noticing more because I am high.

Dax pulls out containers of food and lays it out. There are sandwiches, fruits, chips, and nuts. Lyka hands me a bottle of water and I take it gratefully; my throat is parched. It almost feels like three ordinary people are picnicking in beautiful weather beside the lake. The darkness of our reality was pushed out of my mind.

"Oh, shit. We forgot the fucking fishing rods!" Dax states, breaking the moment. I can't help but chuckle and shake my head.

"I'll see if there is anything in the fishing cabin," Lyka says, rolling his eyes and standing up from the blanket.

Dax pulls out his pack of cigarettes and gets one out, putting it to his lips. He tosses me the lighter and it lands on my lap. He nudges his head for me to come over. "Light it for me," he mumbles from the side of his mouth, the cigarette dangling between his lips. I flick the lighter a couple of times, but my fingers feel a little unsteady. Finally, a small flame appears and I hold it to the end of his cigarette. Dax takes a long drag and then breathes it out. He then places an arm around me, pulling me back to his side. For a quick second, something like comfort washes over me, like I'm not captive, but just sitting beside a lake with someone who cares.

Dax drags on his cigarette once more and I watch the smoke drift away into the air. Part of me hates him, but another part is desperate for human connection.

Even if it comes from a person who has caused me so much pain.

Dax holds out the cigarette in his hand, the tip still glowing faintly. "Oh, I don't smoke." I shake my head.

"You're so innocent, aren't you, flower?" he says, smirking down at me.

His tone has a hint of condescension and it vexes me. I don't know why, but I take the cigarette between two fingers, determined to wipe that smirk off his face.

"Inhale..." he instructs.

I lift the cigarette to my lips and take a cautious drag. The acrid taste of smoke invades my mouth. I pull the cigarette from my lips. The unfamiliar taste and sensation make my eyes water a little.

"Inhale again so it goes here," he explains, tapping my chest.

I do, and the smoke goes down my throat. It slightly burns as it hits my lungs. I hold it for a moment before exhaling. The taste is coarse and unpleasant on my tongue. I start coughing.

Dax watches me, a small smile playing at the corners of his mouth. "Not bad for a first-timer," he says with a hint of approval.

I pass the cigarette back to him and wipe my mouth with the back of my hand. "It's disgusting," I mutter under my breath as I can feel the taste of smoke still on my tongue.

"You'll get used to it..." he says, leaning back and looking at the sky. "Just like everything else."

I feel a flicker of something resurface in my chest. "Please," I mumble softly. "Let me go."

Dax looks up at me; his face is completely emotionless as his hand reaches out and twirls a strand of my hair, mindlessly. "Never," he whispers.

His words are heavy like a hammer. I turn back to the lake, trying to soothe myself.

Lyka comes back, holding two fishing rods and a tackle box. "Found some things," he announces.

Dax stands up, stretching his arms. "Well, we better get to it, then."

The weed brownie starts kicking in more. The world grows softer and colors get brighter. Every sensation becomes heightened. A little giggle slips out from my mouth. We pack up the picnic items and walk to a good fishing spot. The walk feels surreal as if I'm gliding rather than walking.

Oh, I'm high. Yup! I'm high.

I follow Dax and Lyka along the rim of the lake. We settle beside a large fallen log right at the water's edge, perfect for sitting and watching. I plop down on the log. They set up the fishing gear with ease. I watch them, feeling detached yet aware. Lyka's muscles flex as he casts the fishing rod, arching the line and it cleanly enters the water.

"Stay right here," Dax reminds me.

"I will..."

They stand at the edge of the lake. I tilt my head back and breathe in the sweet, earthy smell of the forest. The warm sunshine falls on my face and I close my eyes to soak it in. I feel the full effects of the brownie, my mind drifting like a cloud of euphoria. I enjoy the moment.

I open my eyes and look around. Lyka glances back at me, nods, and goes back to fishing.

"Enjoying yourself?" Dax calls out across the quiet lake.

"Yeah," I respond honestly. "I am."

Dax's fishing line begins to twitch and his rod bends. "Gotcha!" he hisses, reeling in the line. The fish gives him a pretty good fight. His muscles strain, but he is determined. Finally, he draws it out of the water, holding it up proudly.

"Look," he grins, holding up the little fish.

I can't help but give a little round of applause. "Nice catch," I say.

Lyka takes one look at the fish and chuckles. "Ahh, dude, it's pretty small. Throw it back. We'll get bigger."

Dax sighs, rolling his eyes. "Fine," he says, taking the hook from the fish's mouth.

He bends down and gently places the fish into the water. It

swims off really fast and out of sight deep into the lake. Dax wipes his hands on his jeans and casts again.

I feel myself basking in the sun again. Dax's voice cuts through the tranquility. "You feeling the brownie yet, dude?" he asks Lyka.

"Yeah. It's hitting just right," he replies.

I hear the sounds of Dax and Lyka gathering up the fishing gear. They walk over and sit beside me on the log. "You've been such a good girl today," Dax murmurs. His lips touch my neck, making me quiver.

Lyka's hands travel up and down my thighs, applying firm pressure. His strokes are slow and soothing against my skin. Everything feels amplified because I'm high. Dax's kisses move up my neck to my jawline, each one teasing me.

"You like this, don't you, flower?"

"Mhmm," I groan.

Lyka's hand glides higher. "Why don't we have a little fun?" he whispers. He looks at Dax as silent communication passes between them.

They suddenly rise from the log, looming over me with their smirks, unsettling and ominous. "Me and Dax are gonna give you just *one* chance for freedom," he says, holding up a single finger as if to punctuate the heft of the opportunity.

This has to be a cruel joke. A twisted, evil prank? Humiliate me further? Or could it be a genuine chance to escape this nightmare?

"If you can run to the other side of the lake to the fishing cabin, without us catching you–" Dax explains.

"Yeah?!" I interrupt loudly. A surge of disbelief washes over me.

They share a knowing look and cross their arms. "We will let you go," Lyka declares.

I glance around. Behind them, the cabin looms, promising

freedom. *Would it be possible to make it...without them catching me?*

"You said you'd never let me go...If this is some sinister game, you've won already," I state with a concerned look on my face.

"Hey, flower, if you wanna stay, just say so..." Dax says with sarcasm.

"No, no. Just pinky swear this isn't some cruel trick?"

Dax extends his pinky toward me, his face serious. "Pinky swear," he mouths silently. I twist my pinky finger with his.

"What happens if you catch me?" I manage to ask, swallowing hard against the lump in my throat.

"You'll see..." Lyka replies with a chilling smile. "We will give you a head start. As soon as you pass that boulder, that's when we start chasing you," he says, motioning to the massive boulder at the lake's edge. I take quick breaths while my chest heaves up and down. The lake stretches out before me. Every instinct urges me to run, to take this slim chance at freedom.

I stand there and a thousand thoughts cross my mind.

Can I trust them? Is this really my way out? Or will it lead to more pain and punishment?

I feel a rush of adrenaline course through me. I decide. I take a deep breath and brace myself. My eyes flicker from Dax to Lyka, then over their shoulders to the cabin.

Without a word, I start sprinting. My feet pound against the earth as I race past that looming boulder. I push myself towards the distant sanctuary, the fishing cabin, and pray that this time, maybe, I'll make my way back to freedom. I don't look back to see if Dax and Lyka are on my trail. My heart is thumping with fear and desperate hope. I don't hear anything else around me. My tears blur my vision, but I push forward with all my might. In front of me, the cabin looms closer and closer. I can taste freedom. Just as victory seems within my grasp, I feel a weight come crashing down hard on me from behind. I am knocked forward and my body thumps sickeningly onto the ground.

"Nooo! Nooo!" I cry out.

I'm flipped over and Dax hovers over me. his chest is heaving. My eyes blur with tears and I can hardly understand the cruel reality unfolding in front of me. A mocking laughter comes from Dax and all my hopes of freedom are shattered. I am too out of breath to fight. I lie there defeated.

"What happened, flower? I thought you wanted freedom," Dax taunts, out of breath.

I look over Dax's shoulder and see Lyka standing there, catching his breath. "You really thought you could outrun the Faulkner brothers..."

"I hate you!" I scream, feeling the first rise of any emotion besides numbness in three weeks.

Dax moves one of his hands to my waistband and slips it under my panties. "Your pussy says differently. Hate us? Then why are you so wet..." Dax asks, rubbing his fingers down the slit of my pussy.

My one chance of freedom is gone. I was a fool even to think I could outrun two muscular men.

Dax removes his hand from my pussy and gets off me.

Lyka holds his hand out to me. I nudge it away, but he grabs my wrist and pulls me into this body. I pound my fists into his chest and cry. His hands move to the back of my thighs and he picks me up. I wrap my legs around him and I cry into his shoulder.

"We caught you. You lost, Flora. Now you're ours forever," he murmurs as he carries me towards the cabin. I look behind me and see Dax standing by the door, holding it open with a sinister grin.

We enter the cabin and I bury my face against Lyka's shoulder, trying to shield myself from the reality of my situation. He sets me down and Dax moves behind me, cocooning me in their presence. I feel Dax's arm come around my body as he begins to rub my pussy over my jeans. Despite everything, my body accepts him easily. *I should hate them. What am I doing?* I raise my hand and place it on the back of his head as it rests on my shoulder.

Lyka's lips find mine, kissing me passionately like he owns me. I melt into his embrace, our mouths moving together. I moan into his mouth as Dax continues to rub me. His fingers trace over the top of my jeans. I feel myself seeking more. Their bodies press against mine. Dax's hand works on pushing my jeans down my legs. My breath catches in my throat as he pulls my panties down, his fingers delicately parting my lips.

"Fucking hell. She's so wet, Lyka," Dax groans.

Lyka steps back and begins to undo his belt. His eyes are fixed on mine with intensity.

"Is your pussy excited for us?" he asks with a smirk. I shake my head in defiance.

Dax's fingers move faster on my clit and my body seems to lean into his touch. Lyka's belt comes undone and he slides it off. He pulls down his pants and underwear, kicking them to the side. Dax's fingers leave my pussy as Lyka walks over with his hard erection. He places his hands behind my ass and lifts me. I wrap my arms and legs around him on instinct. His body radiates heat against mine and I feel his cock press against my sensitive pussy. He pins me against the wall with his cock at my wet entrance, ready to plunge into me.

His hips thrust forward and I gasp as his cock slides deep into me. The rough texture of the wall against my back adds to the sensation. I hold onto him tight as he thrusts deeper inside me. I hear the slick sounds of our bodies moving together, the wetness between my legs. His fingers dig into my skin while he fucks me with force against the wall. I glance over Lyka's shoulder to find Dax standing there, eyes locked on us. He doesn't waste any time, pulling his jeans and underwear down. His cock springs free, already hard as he begins stroking himself.

I watch Dax, his movement as fast as Lyka's thrusts. I arch my back into his thrusts, my fingers digging into his shoulders. My moans grow louder at the feeling of being filled by him and the exhibitionist thrill of Dax watching us.

Lyka grunts and suddenly pulls out of me. I remove and unwrap my legs from his hips as he places me down.

He guides me to the bed, his eyes silently demanding. Dax follows us, his gaze heavy behind mine. Lyka nods toward Dax, giving him a silent cue. Without a second thought, Dax lies on the bed as his cock twitches. Lyka's grip on my hand tightens and he stands behind the bed. "Get on top of him," he commands.

I straddle Dax's lap, feeling his cock directly below me. Dax reaches up, gripping my waist and guiding me into position. I line myself up with him and the tip of his cock pries my pussy lips open. Slowly, I lower myself onto him, gasping as he fills me. His hand grasps onto my hips and I start grinding on him. Our bodies move together and I feel Lyka looming over us as he watches. "There's a good girl," Lyka says, full of satisfaction. He reaches out his hand and moves my hair out of my face. Dax's cock stirs inside me, making me gasp. Lyka's hand moves from my hair to my cheek, his touch possessive. "Do you like how he stretches your pussy?"

I bite my lip and struggle to find my voice. "I...I love it," I force myself to stutter.

Lyka leans closer, his breath warm against my ear. "Ride him...Show us how much you love a Faulkner's cock."

His words make me feel weak as I roll my hips and grind against Dax's cock. I feel Lyka's strong presence move behind me as he gets onto the bed, his hand pushing down on my back. Lyka's voice cuts with a commanding undertone. "Dax may have been the first one in your tight pussy, but I'm gonna be the first one in your ass."

I let out a loud gulp and stop breathing for a second. A mixture of nervous excitement and arousal swirls within me. Lyka prepares himself to claim what he wants. His hand gropes around my ass followed by a resounding smack, making me let out a little whimper. The sound of his spit hitting my skin makes me stiffen as the warm moisture lands just right above my exposed asshole. I can feel Lyka's cock pressing on my tight entrance as he starts to rub his cock against my hole.

Dax guides my head down to his neck. His grip on my neck gets a little tighter, urging me closer.

Lyka grabs the sides of my ass cheeks and I feel a sharp, jabbing pain in my asshole, a burning sensation running through me like wildfire. I'm being stretched to the limit as I cry into Dax's neck.

"I can't! Fuck!" I sob.

"It's okay, it's okay. Just breathe," Dax repeats, soothing me.

He holds me against him as he continues to thrust beneath me. I grit my teeth through the searing pain in my ass.

Lyka's grip on my ass tightens, his fingers digging into my flesh as he pushes further into me. My body quakes. I feel myself ready to collapse as the pain becomes too much to handle. Tears stream down my face as he bottoms out.

"Fucking look at them dimples above your ass," Lyka says out of breath.

Dax and Lyka move inside me together. I feel every inch of them stretching and filling me. I relax and let the sensations ride over as hands move all over my skin.

"She's taking our cocks so well. I think she can take more,"

Lyka says as he thrusts deeper into my asshole, his balls slapping against my skin.

Dax moans loudly as he continues thrusting. I feel Lyka's firm grip as he fists my hair, grasping at me like he's claiming me. He pulls my head up and I turn my face to the side. "Open your mouth," he demands.

I open wide, sticking out my tongue as he spits in my mouth. It tastes slightly bitter and I swallow hesitantly.

"You're one of us, *a Faulkner*. Do you understand?" His words resound inside me. Pride washes over me, mixed with a twinge of submission. Lyka grips my throat and squeezes. "Do you fucking understand, Flora?" he asks again.

I meet his gaze with desire, my defiance crumbling as my eyes lock onto his. Dax pounds into me from below, making it hard to think coherent sentences.

"I...I..." I stutter.

"Use your words, baby."

"I understand," I breathe out.

Lyka's grip tightens around my neck. The pressure is tight, a forceful reminder of his hold on me.

"Ly...Lyka... Dax," I manage to shriek.

"Scream our names, flower. We want everyone to know we are inside you," Dax says. I obey and scream out their names.

Their bodies pump deeper and faster inside me with each thrust.

"Fuck. I'm gonna fill you with my cum," Dax says, moaning.

"You...You...can't," I stutter.

Dax kisses me to silence me, his moans mingling with mine as our lips meet. I can feel the tension building within him.

I feel his cock twitch and pulse inside me as his orgasm washes over him. Lyka growls, his nails digging into my skin as Dax pulls out.

“My turn. I can’t wait to fucking breed you,” he grunts, pulling out of my ass as he starts to thrust in my pussy.

Dax clings to me and holds me in place so I can’t move. Lyka pounds into me harder and harder. “I'm coming. I'm coming,” he chants as he holds my hips. “Don’t move, I want my cum to work its magic,” he says as he finally releases in me.

Out of breath, we all collapse on top of each other. “That’s our girl,” Dax whispers.

The Faulkner brothers both claim me as theirs. *Was there now a part of me that enjoyed it?*

Lyka lets out a deep, rumbling chuckle, like a purr—self-satisfied and possessive.

We all fall silent; I don't want them to leave my body. I want to savor this moment for as long as possible. I should fucking hate them. I do.

Right?

My body's weak, still aching as we exit the cabin while Lyka adjusts his belt outside. I get that sharp twinge in my asshole, reminding me of what had just gone down. My mind's in a haze and I feel like I'm floating from my high; both from the weed and orgasms.

“Well, well, well,” a voice cuts through my daze. I look up to see Jonny standing there with one of his friends.

Jonny saunters toward us with a mocking smile. “The British girl taking more than one guy? She didn't strike me as a whore, but do I get to take her for a ride?”

Dax flushes red with anger, storming up to Jonny. “Fucking say that again!” he growls, their faces inches apart.

Jonny's friend steps forward, but Lyka cuts in front of him. The atmosphere is tense as they face each other. Jonny and Dax put their foreheads together. I rush toward them and grasp Dax's arm, trying to pull him back. “Dax, don't,” I plead hastily as my voice shakes.

Jonny's eyes dance with sadistic pleasure. “Hit me, Faulkner. I know you want to,” he says, egging Dax on a little more.

“DAX, PLEASE!” I scream again, my voice shattering. I tug really hard on his arm, trying with all my heart to prevent impending violence.

“Go on, Dax, be a good boy and listen to your whore,” Jonny hisses, his voice dripping with venom.

I force my way past and step between them. I'm trembling as I reach up and grab Dax's face, my fingers pressing against his cheeks.

“Dax, look at me,” I cry, my voice shaking. “Leave it.” Dax's enraged stare falters as he looks down at me. Slowly, he steps back from Jonny, his muscles still tight but his demeanor weakening. I don’t want to see him or Lyka get hurt.

Lyka steps back from Jonny's friend, who sneers, “Who knew that Faulkner brothers were such pussies?”

Dax holds my hand tight as we turn away, his breathing heavy. My heart is racing as we walk off. The tension in the air is still thick around us. Jonny's voice pierces the air again.

“Hey, British, how's your father?”

The mention of my father sends a shock wave of pain through me. Dax stiffens beside me, anger reigniting. He starts to turn back, but I give a hard yank on his hand, my eyes begging him not to react. Swallowing the lump in my throat, I refuse to let Jonny see how his words cut so deep.

We finally reach the ATVs and I can feel my composure slipping.

Dax and Lyka don't waste another second. We ride off into the forest at lightning speed and I hold on tight as the wind whips my hair in my face. The forest seems to blur around us, the trees a rush of green and brown. I can't shake the memory of Jonny's mean comment. It lingers in my mind—a reminder of the outside world. How cruel it was.

We pull into the garage and the tension is still high. Dax hops off the ATV, pacing back and forth. He picks up a helmet off of a nearby table and sends it flying across the room. It hits the wall with a loud thud. I instinctively step back as fear rises at the sight of his uncontrolled anger.

"I need to go back there and kill them! *No one* speaks to you like that!" Dax roars, turning around to face me, his face inches from mine. His eyes are wild. He's furious. I can feel the heat of his breath and I'm trembling.

Before I can even react, Lyka slides between us. "Calm the fuck down, dude!" he orders.

Dax's fists clench, his eyes darting wildly around the room as he storms over to the wall, beginning to punch into it. I can see his knuckles start bleeding, leaving smears of red on the wall. Lyka runs toward him and snatches Dax's hand before he can punch the wall again. "Enough, Dax!" Lyka demands as he locks onto Dax's wrist.

I've never seen this side of Dax before.

Dark. Feral. Utterly terrifying.

I look at him and once again he's a stranger to me. I step back and my back hits the cold metal of the ATV behind me. Fear must be written across my face because Lyka looks over his shoulder at me, his expression softening.

"You're fucking scaring her," Lyka says more softly. His grip on Dax's wrist loosens, but still firm enough to constrain him.

Dax looks over at me. The rage is replaced with regret,

perhaps even shame. He unfurls his fists slowly and Lyka lets go.

Dax takes a step back, running a hand through his hair. His knuckles are raw and bleeding. “I'm sorry...” he finally mutters, perhaps more to himself than us. “I just, I can't stand that asshole.”

Dax inhales deeply again; his shoulders slumping as the adrenaline rush dies down. He turns toward me and his expression softens. “You shouldn't have seen that,” he says, looking down.

Still in shock, I nod. “It's okay,” I say, though I don't even believe myself. *I'm not okay.*

Lyka steps closer and places a reassuring hand on my shoulder. “Let's get you inside,” he says, guiding me gently toward the door.

I look back as we move away. Dax hasn't budged an inch, still standing by the wall, staring down at his bloodied hands. The darkness I saw in him stays with me.

TWENTY-FOUR

FLORA

I SLIDE INTO THE HOT WATER, THE WARMTH CURLING AROUND ME, seeping into my stiff muscles. The events of the day swirl through my mind.

Is this my life now, being a captive to two biker brothers?

So very different from five years ago. My parents were alive and I was living in London. Life seemed so much easier. Predictable. But how happy was I really? I had nobody but my parents. Now, trapped in this cabin, my captors are as close as it gets to human connection. I dunk my head in the water, letting it rise well over my ears, closing off the world. I shut my eyes, letting my thoughts go wild. I think of Dax and Lyka, their touches, words, anger, protectiveness, and shocking tenderness.

Am I falling for them? Do I care about them? Or is it just the result of being held captive, a psychological trick in my mind?

The Faulkner brothers haunt my mind, making me feel scared yet strangely safe.

I forget I'm underwater. Panic surges and my lungs start to ache for air. I lift my head upwards and break the surface with a gasp, the water cascading down my face. I draw a deep breath, feeling the heart pound against my chest. I lean backward on the rim of the tub, wiping at the water on my face. The sound of footsteps outside the bathroom door pulls me back to reality. I tense up, wondering which brother it is. The door opens a crack and Dax peers through, his face a picture of concern. "All good in here?" he asks.

I nod, not trusting myself to speak. He steps inside, his gaze scanning the room until it finally rests on me. Something in his expression when he looks at me makes my heart flutter to life despite everything.

"You've been in here a while," he says, leaning against the doorframe. "Just wanted to make sure you're alright."

"Yeah, just thinking..."

Dax just nods, his expression impossible to read. "Well, don't stay in too long. We need you downstairs soon."

As he turns to leave, I call out to him, my voice shaking. "Dax?"

He stops, turning to face me. "Yeah?"

"Today, I saw a darker side of you."

"Really? So, keeping you chained up, the branding, wooden toys, you didn't see the dark side then?"

"Today...felt different."

"Everyone has a dark side, flower. Some people just don't show it."

I bite the inside of my cheek and look away. Before he leaves the bathroom, I tremble, "Thank you."

I don't know why I am thanking him. He gives me the smallest, most tentative smile. "Get dressed and come on down when you're ready." He closes the door.

No! What the fuck am I thinking?! They lied about a lockdown! They have branded me! They tied me up and used wooden toys on me! What the fuck am I feeling?

I get out of the tub and glimpse myself in the mirror. My eyes instantly go to the *F* branded into my skin. I can't help feeling this strange connection to it. I run my finger over the scar and let out a sigh. I dry my body and get dressed.

I make my way into the living room and my breath catches in my throat as I enter. Dax and Lyka look immensely hot in their skin-tight, white shirts and black trousers that seem to further accentuate their bodies, already so rugged in appearance.

Lyka walks toward me as he approaches me with a smile, takes my hand, and gently presses his lips against my knuckles. "Because you have been such a good girl, we want you to experience a proper date," he says softly, in such an inviting way.

Dax approaches, his shirt unbuttoned at the top, revealing a glimpse of his chiseled chest. His eyes smolder, gazing straight into mine. It makes me feel weak.

Fuck! They look like gods! They are so fucking hot!

Dax leans in close, his breath hot in my ear. "We want to dress you up, cook you dinner, and then get down on our knees and fuck you with our tongues." My whole body quivers.

I swallow and my brain shifts into overdrive. Lyka lets go of my hand and steps back.

"We're gonna take you to a store so that you can pick out a dress."

My eyes fly open and I'm genuinely shocked. Feeling my surprise, Dax clamps down at the back of my neck with his hand. His fingers glide into my skin, reminding me of their dominance and control.

"Don't get your hopes up," Dax growls, his voice low, rumbling, and full of threat. "You pull any shit and we'll punish you."

Lyka steps closer; his eyes pierce into mine. He holds my

cheeks in his strong hand, squeezing them tight. "Do you understand?" Lyka asks firmly.

I nod as much as I can against the tight hold. "Yes," I force out.

Lyka's eyes search mine for a hint of rebellion or deceit. Detecting none, he releases my cheeks.

"Good girl," Dax says, stepping back and crossing his arms over his chest. "We're putting trust in you, flower. Don't make us regret it." His eyes never leave mine, a silent warning. I breathe in deep, trying to still my racing heart.

Lyka takes my hand, his grip firm yet reassuring, and we leave the cabin. The moon is bright in the sky, tangling everything with its silvery light. The forest falls silent around us—nothing except the crunch of our footsteps on the gravel path and the echo of an owl's call.

Dax walks to the garage, pulling out the dark green Land Rover. The headlights cut through the darkness and a path is illuminated. Lyka walks me to the passenger side, his hand never leaving mine. He opens the door and I climb into the front seat, feeling the soft leather beneath. It has three seats, enough for us all to sit together in front.

Lyka comes in behind me, shutting the door. Dax looks at me briefly before shifting the car back into drive.

As we drive, the silence in the car grows so thick that my heart thrashes around my chest with a mix of fear and anticipation. It feels like it has been forever since I saw stores, people, or anything resembling the normal world.

We finally reach the fringes of the small town. Streetlights flicker to life as we pass by, casting their glow across quaint stores and silent streets.

We pull up in front of a twenty-four hour store, the neon sign above the door pulses softly. Dax kills the engine and there is a deafening silence. He turns to study me, his eyes hard and unreadable.

Lyka opens the glove box. My heart skips a beat when I see the glint of metal inside. He reaches in and retrieves a pistol, passing it to Dax. He takes the pistol, his fingers curling around it with a familiarity that terrifies me. He catches my eye, his gaze cold and unyielding. "Just a reminder that we expect you to behave," he says, his voice dangerous.

I nod, my throat too tight to speak. Their gun is a constant reminder of the hold they have over me. Lyka opens the door, helping me out with his grip tight.

Dax has pulled the Land Rover into a dark corner of the parking lot. I look at Dax, searching for the shape of a gun, but it's hidden somewhere.

They walk beside me as we enter the store. I look like a tramp compared to them in their sleek attire.

The automatic doors slide open and we step inside the brightly lit store. My heart pounds in my chest with every beat echoing in my ears. We move through the aisles as shoppers engrossed in their own personal lives go around us, ignorant of the silent drama unfolding amidst them.

I feel a strange mix of fear and longing when I see other people going about their daily, mundane tasks. Lyka steers me into the area for clothes. "Look around and pick something you like," he says. Dax stands slightly behind us, his gaze sweeping the area, being vigilant.

I weave in and out of the racks, my fingers trailing across fabrics alien to my skin after so long. A deep red dress catches my eye. Elegant with a modest neckline, it flows down in a full skirt. I touch it, feeling the smooth texture under my fingers. Lyka nods in approval. "Very sexy. Try it on."

He steers me toward the fitting rooms with Dax following

close behind. As we approach the fitting rooms, I hear a voice rising behind me. "Flora!" My body halts and I can feel the heart jumping up to my throat. Turning around, I see Marty walking towards me with a young lady. Lyka's grip tightens around my hand. He bends close to me, whispering, "Stay calm. Don't want anyone getting hurt." Marty saunters over, his expression curious. "What are you doing here? Nancy said you went to London."

I fumble for an excuse, trying to put on a light smile. "Marty, ahh, yes," I reply quickly. "I did, but I'm just back sorting the house out for the week."

He nods, seemingly satisfied that my explanation is good enough for him. He shoves the woman toward me and I take a second to look her over. "Ah, cool. Well, guys, this is my girlfriend, Summer."

Summer could be in her late twenties, a feature that makes her quite distinct from Marty. Given his known preferences in the past, I cannot help but note the irony.

Lyka tugs on my hand, signaling it's time to leave. "Well, Marty, it's good seeing you," I respond, trying as hard as I can to slip away with Lyka.

We turn around, but Marty calls out after us again, stopping us. "Wait, aren't you one of the Faulkner brothers?" he asks, his voice wary.

Lyka takes a step closer to Marty, his tone dangerously soft. "Do we have a problem?"

Dax rushes to his side and places himself beside Lyka. I can see Dax balling a fist.

Just fuck off, Marty.

Marty's eyes flicker between us, then finally land on Summer. "No, no. Well, anyway, Flora, nice seeing you," he says, then turns quickly and walks away with Summer.

We walk to the fitting rooms and I'm tempted with a narrow window of escape.

Lyka's hand on my wrist reminds me of my precarious situation. We reach the fitting rooms and he ushers me inside, his eyes scanning the area for any lingering threats. "We will be just outside the fitting room."

I go inside an available stall, take off my clothes, and slip into the dress. I stand in front of the mirror and see that the red dress hangs on me so beautifully. The dress embraces my body in all the right places. I allow myself to be beautiful in that moment.

I reluctantly take off the dress and put on my own clothes again. While preparing to leave the fitting room, I bump into Jenna and her friend. Her shoulder connects with mine as she eyes me up and down with a face full of loathing, muttering, "Whore."

The word slaps me in the face. Part of me wants to attack her for an explanation, to defend myself. Another part of me knows it could easily spiral into a confrontation, drawing unwanted attention—especially with Dax and Lyka waiting outside.

I act as if I didn't hear her. There is no way I can afford to fight with her and not attract everyone's eyes in this public place. With my head held high, I pass Jenna and her friend, never looking at them while keeping my inside turmoil intact.

Shit! I forgot the clothes hanger.

As I walk back to pick up the hanger I had left in the stall, I can't help but hear Jenna and her friend in the next stall over. Their voices ring out, packing a punch through the thin walls.

"I still can't believe Jonny ran her father off the road," Jenna whispers with an unsettling chuckle from her friend.

My heart sinks, my eyes well up with tears, and there is a

lump in my throat. The words echo again in my mind, confirming what I just heard.

Jonny killed my father.

I burst out from the fitting room in fright, the red dress forgotten. I stumble past racks of clothes, trying to escape the painful truth hammering in my mind.

"Flora!" Dax shouts out. I can hear their heavy footsteps behind me. I get outside the store.

Dax catches my arm, spinning me around with force in his tight hold. "We warned—" Dax's voice drops as soon as he looks at my expression and tear-stained face.

I collapse into Dax's arms and he stalls for a second. He lifts me and carries me toward the Land Rover. Lyka quickly opens the door, and together, they settle me into the passenger seat. They look me up and down, their faces a mix of worry and determination.

Dax's voice is calm, yet fierce as he asks, "What happened, flower? Who do we need to kill?"

I take a shaking breath, attempting to steady myself enough so that I will have the ability to talk.

Tears stream down my cheeks as I recount what I had overheard Jenna say in the fitting room. My words shake with emotion as I tell them how Jonny ran my father off the road, killing him. Dax's jaw visibly grinds as his eyes glint sharply. Lyka's expression darkens, his gaze turning hard with a silent promise of protection. "Flora," Lyka says softly. "Look at me." I meet his eyes, feeling unsafe and vulnerable. Lyka's eyes search mine for a moment before he nods to himself as if reaching a decision. "We'll take care of it," he says finally, his tone full of authority. "You're a Faulkner. No one fucks with a Faulkner."

I nod and my eyes fill with tears, breaking out in a flood of emotion as the weight of Jenna's words hits me again, followed by haunting memories rushing into my head of Dad's passing.

Suddenly, amidst my turmoil, Marty's voice pierces through the haze. "Hey, hey, Flora," he calls out, jogging over towards us. His brows furrow with concern.

"Marty, please, not now," I rasp, trying to hold my tone steady as my emotions threaten to break down further. Dax and Lyka cross their arms in a protective stance.

"Why are you crying, Flora? What's going on? Do I need to call the police?" Marty asks.

Dax steps out, moves forward, and asks in a dangerously low voice, "Where is your girlfriend, Marty?"

"Waiting in the car, why?"

In one quick, unexpected motion, Dax grabs Marty's head and slams it hard onto the side of the vehicle. There is a sickening thud of impact, a sharp crack, and blood instantly pouring out of Marty's nose. His body sags against the car, dazed and shocked from the sudden attack.

I gasp, instinctively reaching out to him, but Lyka holds me back.

Dax releases Marty, stepping back. "You stay away and don't ever think about her again. Do you fucking understand?" he growls, the clear warning in his deep voice.

Marty staggers back, clutching his bleeding nose. His eyes are wide with disbelief and pain.

"Ok, ok, I'm...I'm sorry," Marty mumbles.

"Go!" Lyka interjects with a firm voice as he points toward Marty's car. "Get out of here before we do more than break your nose. Next time, it'll be your fucking skull."

Marty stumbles backward, then turns around and makes a hasty retreat to his car.

"I think we should go and see Jonny," Lyka says, his voice hushed and full of suppressed anger. I can't help but let out a nervous gulp.

Dax grins, then flexes his jaw. He reaches inside his waistband and recovers the gun. "Oh, I agree."

They both hop into the Land Rover quickly. Dax speeds out of the parking lot, his hands grasping the wheel firmly. The vehicle falls uncomfortably silent as we speed away. My heart pounds in my chest as the adrenaline surges with Dax focusing on the road.

What are they going to do?

TWENTY-FIVE

FLORA

Dax and Lyka work on what consists of the plan, their faces stern and concentrated as they talk in muffled voices. I feel the weight in the air of their determination, grateful and afraid for what they are about to do.

"You can't do this for me," I manage to whisper, my voice trembling with anxiety.

"You're one of us. It's the least we can do. He ain't getting away with what he did," Lyka says.

Dax pulls out the gun, tightening his jaw. He cocks it resolutely, the sound loud in the car. He then opens the door and steps onto the gravel driveway leading up to the house with Lyka staying close behind him.

I watch them from the safety of the car, feeling a knot tighten in my stomach. Dax and Lyka take their positions, their bodies hidden in the dark shadows. Summoning every ounce of my courage, I step out of the car and walk toward Jonny's front door. I raise my hand and knock, the sound echoing through the silent neighborhood.

It is almost as if seconds are stretched out into hours until Jonny finally opens the door, his figure filling in the doorway.

He leans back casually on the frame, a smirk playing on his lips as he sizes me up with some combination of amusement and arrogance.

"Look who it is..." he drawls, oozing self-assurance.

I am flanked by the invisible Faulkner brothers, their presence lurking just out of view. Dax and Lyka are hanging back, their silent presence adding in on the weight of what is starting to feel more and more like a stand-off. I take a deep breath and raise my eyes to Jonny's, trying to keep open the pathway between us despite my fear.

"I've been thinking about you, Jonny," I say, trying to sound seductive as I step closer to him. The smirk on his face widens further as he pushes off the door to let me through. There's a gleam in his eyes, like a predator. I move across the threshold, scared shit-less.

Jonny slams the door behind me, his voice oozing with smug confidence. "Knew you'd be wanting me eventually, doll."

Jonny leans his face down and starts kissing my neck. A revulsion comes over me for a moment and I immediately push him back hard. He steps back, his face going from arrogance to confusion as I pull myself up right.

"I just have one question," I manage to say seductively, my voice not wavering.

"Can't you ask later? I want to fuck you so bad. My little British doll," he says, grabbing his crotch. His actions make me want to puke, but I keep the fake smile.

I saunter over to him and place my palm on his chest, going in for a kiss.

"Why did you run my father off the road?" I whisper, catching him off guard and cutting through the tension with unwavering directness.

Jonny's face twists in shock and anger. Before he can react, the front door unexpectedly bursts open with a tremendous crash as Dax and Lyka rush in, slamming the door behind them.

Dax holds the gun at Jonny's head, his expression grim. Jonny's eyes widen with alarm, his bravado quickly fleeting. He takes a step back with his hands up in a weak gesture of defense. His face flashes between fear and fury.

Jonny looks at me and hisses, "I said I would get back at you one way or another."

I reel from Jonny's words. My vision blurs with tears as the memories of his threats at the concert flood back, their sinister undertones now fully clear.

"You killed my father over *that*? Because I hurt your tiny ego! You fucking child!" I scream at him. The weight of my loss and anger surges through me, driving my words with a fierce intensity. Before Jonny can respond, the front door crashes open with a violent force. Jonny's friend storms into the room, adding to the chaos already unfolding. Lyka moves fast, attacking Jonny's friend and entering an ugly brawl.

Fists fly, grunts of exertion punctuating the air as they fight for dominance. Meanwhile, Jonny, with fury in his eyes, charges at Dax. Dax sees him coming and quickly raises his gun. Jonny's too quick and grabs Dax's arm, wrestling the gun clear out of his grip as it discharges with a deafening bang, the bullet ripping through the ceiling. The gun drops to the floor with a thud.

Suddenly, chaos erupts with adrenaline-rushed tension. My heart races as the scene unfolds—the feeling of being helpless against violence that threatens at any moment to engulf me.

Lyka's fight intensifies; his opponent does not take a break. I cannot draw my eyes away, torn by the fear that he might be hurt as the confrontation between Dax and Jonny is only rising.

Jonny gets the better of him, catching Dax and pinning him down. Blood spurts from Dax's nose as he wrestles with Jonny.

Standing there, I'm paralyzed by the scene of brutality. I feel like a deer caught in the blinding headlights of violence and revenge.

Jonny's hand darts to his side, fingers closing around the cold metal of the nearby fire poker. He raises the poker, poised to strike with deadly intent.

Jonny's friend suddenly collapses to the floor, his struggles now silent under Lyka's vice-grip.

My eyes flicker back and forth between the brutal struggle in front of me. Jonny holds the fire poker dangerously close to Dax's face, the metal inches from his eye. Dax's tense muscles struggle against Jonny's relenting assault, his hands locked in a desperate struggle to keep the weapon at bay.

My eyes lock onto the gun lying on the floor, its metal glinting ominously in the dim light of the room. Dax's voice cuts through the chaos. "Shoot him, Flora! Shoot him!"

My hands shake as I reach for the weapon; my fingers close around it with a desperate urgency.

Jonny sneers, "She hasn't got the guts! She won't do it."

Suddenly, the adrenaline gushes in me. I pull the trigger, the gun going off with its deafening roar.

A bullet smacks into Jonny square in the shoulder. He stumbles back, his grip on the poker loosening as pain shoots through him. Dax takes the opportunity and wrenches the weapon from Jonny's grasp. He raises the poker above his head, bringing it down on Jonny brutally. The fire poker impales Jonny in the face with a sickening crunch, blood spurting from the wound.

He's dead. I just shot a man.

I recoil at the sight before me, at the brutality. I meet Dax's stare. Our eyes lock in wordless acknowledgment of the horrors witnessed.

The violence and bloodshed.

"Fucking die!" Lyka rages. He gives the death blow to Jonny's friend.

My nerves shout at me to run amidst the chaos. The front door feels like a lifeline; it's my way of escaping from what is happening as I leave the nightmarish scene behind me. I catapult towards the exit, my feet not pausing to think.

Outside, the street just stretches on, blurring motion and uncertainty. Tears trickle down my face and ragged breaths burn deep in my lungs with each gulp as I keep running from the nightmare.

I don't know where I'm going, only that I must put as much distance as possible between me and thc horrors I have seen. Fear propels me forward, adrenaline whipping through my veins like a crazed heartbeat.

My legs start to throb and my chest burns from exhaustion. I spot an abandoned warehouse and run inside. The air inside is stale, heavy with the scent of decay.

I walk over to a wall and slump against it, my body landing on the unforgiving, freezing concrete. I shiver uncontrollably. Both my shoulders and arms throb, feeling as though something has punctured inside me, causing an ever-intensifying sharp, jabbing pain with each movement.

The warehouse around me seems to close in. A wave of nausea washes over me, my stomach churning violently. I double over, clasping my stomach as a sharp cramp seizes me. I puke uncontrollably, the bitter taste of bile filling my mouth as my body convulses with each heave.

I lie curled on the cold ground as time seems to blur into a hazy fog.

The pain in my stomach tightens and my insides are ridden by waves of nausea. I involuntarily scream, my voice echoing in the warehouse. Everything around me blurs and dizziness takes over my senses. The pain in my womb seems to radiate fiercely outwards, spreading like fire through my body.

Fighting for breath, I keep hold of my stomach and curl into a ball on the cold concrete floor.

What's happening to me? Am I dying? Is it just the shock from tonight?

I'm having an out-of-body experience, floating on the edge of consciousness. The pain is so sharp and continual in my abdomen. I open my eyes and see Lyka and Dax rushing to my side, their expressions filled with fear and urgency. "Flora! Why did you run? We heard you scream!" Dax exclaims.

The ache causes me to cry out involuntarily, "Help me," I tremble, lying on the floor.

I manage to look down and see Lyka kneeling on the floor beside me, his hands covered in blood. "Dax, she's bleeding down there!" he shouts, sending sudden panic through me as I struggle to make out what's happening.

"Fuck. Fuck. Fuck! We've gotta get her to a hospital," Dax declares.

My eyelids are heavy and want to shut again. I am trying hard to focus, but everything seems slow.

Lyka and Dax jump into action, moving fast and decisive. Lyka supports my head with a gentle hand as Dax carefully picks me up, cradling me in his arms. Everything they do is urgent, hurrying me toward the vehicle. I'm still clinging to consciousness as much as possible.

My eyes manage to crack open to a blur of bright lights overhead; the sterile scent of a hospital overwhelms my senses.

I am being wheeled really fast through corridors on a hospital bed.

"Is there any chance she could be pregnant?" a woman's voice rings out abruptly.

Dax and Lyka flank me, their faces a picture of concern and determination. They keep pace with the bed. Dax extends his hand and finds mine for a silent promise of emotional support. I glance over to Lyka and his eyes are filled with tears.

The pain grows, a steady throbbing that courses through my body. I shut my eyes again.

TWENTY-SIX

FLORA

My eyes flutter open. I hear a faint yet constant beeping—machines are around me. My surroundings come into focus. I'm in a bright, sterile hospital room. My eyes shift to the machines beside me, showing vital signs that I try to understand. I turn my head to see Lyka and Dax both asleep in armchairs beside my bed, each covered by a blanket. They seemed peaceful in their sleep. It touches me to know they've stayed by my side, never mind everything else.

The door creaks open and a nurse comes in. She fiddles with some monitors, expressing relief at my own awakening. "Oh, good. You're awake. I can let the doctor know."

I clear my throat. "What happened?"

"The doctor will come and answer all your questions. For now, you need to rest," her voice is kind but firm as she fiddles with the IV to ensure my maintained comfort.

She turns to look at Lyka and Dax, still asleep, as she walks towards the door.

"We've had to bring them food. They have refused to leave your side," she says with a smile, admiring their dedication.

As the nurse leaves, the door closes with a click that wakes

Lyka. He blinks wearily, rubbing his eyes as he sits stiffly in the chair. He mumbles, “Flora?”

Dax wakes up, yawning himself into cognition. His eyes find mine, suddenly open and alert, as he sits up. “You are awake,” he says, exhaling a breath of relief. He unconsciously reaches for my hand.

I suddenly remember everything and jolt up from the hospital bed.

“Oh my God! Jonny–”

“Shhh. It's all been taken care of,” Lyka whispers, reaching for my other hand. I look at them both; their white shirts are stained with blood. Dax notices and looks down. “Don’t worry, we said we were at a spooky party last night.”

“You didn’t have to kill him for me...”

“We would kill anyone for you, Flora,” Lyka says with determination as Dax nods.

I wince in pain as I slowly lower my torso back down. Lyka raises my hand to his lips, leaving a lingering kiss on my knuckles.

“How are you feeling?” he asks.

“I'm okay...”

“You scared the hell out of us, flower,” Dax says, his voice laced with a bit of...fear?

Lyka leans closer and kisses my forehead. “I'm so sorry,” he says quietly.

His eyes are shimmering wet as they look down at me.

“I’m sorry...I’m sorry,” his voice quivers, repeating apologies again and again.

“Lyka...” I whisper softly, feeling confused.

His grip on my hand tightens as though seeking solace through the connection. “I just...” he starts, his throat tightening. Dax places a hand on Lyka's shoulders, trying to reassure him.

"Please, please forgive us," Lyka sobs.

I've never seen him cry, so I don't know how to react. Before anything else can be said, a doctor enters.

Lyka grips my hand really tight as the doctor explains the news. He tells me I suffered from an ectopic pregnancy and a ruptured fallopian tube that needed to be removed. I sit silently with my mouth half open in astonishment.

The doctor finishes and assures me that I still have one functioning fallopian tube and can conceive in the future. *I was pregnant?* I'm still in shock and don't know what to say. The doctor leaves and Dax draws me into a tight, desperate embrace. I lean upon him and let his warmth and strength comfort me.

"We're so sorry," Dax whispers, his voice husky with emotion.

I nod against his chest as the tears finally spill down my cheeks. Lyka joins us, his own tears mingling with mine as we share a moment of silent solidarity.

I WALK OUT OF THE HOSPITAL EMPTY. I DID NOT KNOW WHAT TO THINK or do as we walk to the car.

"Ouch," I mumble as I enter the passenger seat.

The weight of everything that has happened recently presses down on me, along with the discomfort I have from the surgery.

We drive off through the town. Every scene that passes by triggers painful and poignant memories of my past, of loss, and of the unexpected turn my life took with Dax and Lyka.

Lyka places a hand on my thigh as we reach a crossroads, spread out before me like a metaphor for my own choices.

Turning right is the way to my house. Left will bring us back to the cabin.

"Where do you want to go? It's your choice. We'll set you free, flower. We swear. Go on with your life and blossom. Move on and don't look back," Dax's voice cuts into my reverie. His eyes are filled with tears. Lyka nods in agreement, his expression a mix of understanding and fear.

"We don't want to let you go, baby. It will kill us. But we will understand," Lyka says, choking on his words.

For the first time, I actually believe that they mean what they say. That they are willing to let me go.

"I want to go home."

Lyka shakes his head as tears spill down his cheeks.

Dax indicates the car right. "No," I say firmly, letting a slight smile curl on my lips. "I want to go home...back to the cabin." They both look at me with shock. "After all, I'm a Faulkner, right?" I add softly, reassuring my decision and acknowledging the bond now formed between us. Tears fill their eyes. They say no words as they sob quietly.

I lean back in my seat. Dax flicks on his left indicator, nudging us further down the twisting road toward our cabin. Although the future holds no certainties, I strangely feel at peace.

I am not alone anymore. With Dax and Lyka by my side, I have found my home, refuge, and family. It's complex, a bond that comes from a web of feelings and experiences that has us wound together. They are, undoubtedly, the worst thing to have happened to me. However, they are also the best thing: an anchor that keeps me on the ground, a fire that keeps me warm. I am a Faulkner. This identity, this belonging, is something I wear with pride and acceptance. I am theirs. I can go home and be myself, totally without fear or hesitation.

If someone asks where my home is. I would say a cabin in the deep forest made of cedarwood.

It's where I belong, with Dax and Lyka.

It's who I am, Flora Faulkner.

ONE MONTH LATER

LYKA

Dax and I stand in the barn, our bare chests exposed. The blow torch fires up, alive with its blue flames as it heats the iron to a glowing red. Flora's eyes glint with amusement. A smirk plays across her lips as she speaks. "It's *my turn* to claim you. Who's first?"

Dax and I quickly glance at each other. His eyes are determined, but mine betray a flicker of fear. I can feel my heart pounding in my chest. I let out a gulp, the sound barely audible over the hiss of the blow torch. I nod slightly to Dax—that I am ready, or as ready as I could be. Taking a deep breath, I step forward, gritting my teeth. Flora wastes no time and presses the branding iron against my lower stomach. The searing pain is white-hot and immediate. It takes all my strength to keep my jaw clamped shut, to not allow myself to scream out loud.

Dax is watching me, knowing he's next. He sucks in quick, shallow breaths, chest expanding and contracting.

"Hold still," Flora taunts. "You don't want to move," she parrots the words we used with her back to us.

Every second feels like forever; each second is spent in agony. I hold myself perfectly still and clench my fists.

Flora rips the brand clear from my skin, leaving a blistering, raw mark behind. I did it for her. I survived. Dax's hand moves out to catch me as I sway.

"Your turn, Dax."

She sets the brand under the nozzle of the blow torch again. The flames ignite a menacing red.

Dax steps forward, his eyes fixing on the red-hot iron. He slaps his own face, the sound rebounding throughout the barn. "I'm ready! Let's fucking go!" he announces.

Flora steps forward and sets the branding iron to Dax's flesh. Again, the air is filled with the pungent stench of searing skin. His face contorts in pain, baring his teeth in a grimace as he fights not to scream. Flora lifts the branding iron off to show the blistering, raw mark scorched into Dax's skin. The pain is apparent in his eyes, but there is now some relief and pride in them, too. We look at each other and see the *F* branded into us.

Flora steps back, her job completed. But the look in her eye says it all—she loved every moment of our suffering. I don't blame her, after what we did.

Flora reaches a hand out toward me and kisses me without a word. She leaves my lips and turns toward Dax. Their eyes meet, an unspoken understanding passing between them, and she kisses him. It is a kiss of solidarity, shared pain, and triumph—reaffirming our bond.

"You're Faulkner property now," she taunts. She went from broken to something real. Flora made us a family. But it was up to us to be something more. We needed her just as much as she needed us. She had become the center of our world. If she wanted to hurt us, if she needed to release her pain upon us, we would welcome it with open arms. We deserve it. For her, we would endure anything and that weight of truth washed over us. We could never let her go. We were Faulkners—bound by a darkness that could never truly fade.

BONUS CHAPTER

FLORA

Nothing ever came of Jonny and his friend 'disappearing.' Rumor around town is they went on a hunting trip that went wrong. No bodies were ever found.

My vibrant, nature-themed paintings have been selling like hotcakes around town; there's even a waiting list for them. Three of my works are proudly displayed inside the local art gallery.

After the ectopic pregnancy, I decided to go on contraception. Lyka was hesitant, but agreed.

Dax and Lyka let me work part-time with Nancy at the bar. Of course, there are rules, including me being picked up after each shift.

I never told Nancy the truth about Dax and Lyka. She took my word for it—that I went home to London for some time, then changed my mind about staying, and so on. She didn't know that the truth was far from that—much more sinister—that Dax and Lyka held me captive. She thought Dax and Lyka were my saviors, who welcomed me back open-armed from my *trip*.

I wipe down the last of the tables, making sure everything shines under the bar's dim lighting. It has been a long night. Finally, there is just an empty bar with the faint smell of beer and polished wood. Finishing up, I glance to my right at Nancy. She retrieves the bar keys from their hook behind the counter.

"Sure you don't need a ride back to the cabin?" she asks.

"It's fine. Dax and Lyka will be picking me up."

"Ahh, they are so good to you. picking you up each evening," she replies as we leave the bar.

We step out into the fresh, cool night air. I tug my jacket closer around me.

Nancy locks the door behind us. She turns to me, the soft glow from the streetlamp bathing her face. "I'm so glad you decided to come back. Your father would be proud of you having a life here and working with me," she says, a touch of wistfulness in her voice.

"I know he would."

I shuffle my feet and clear my throat.

"Nancy, I don't think I thanked you enough for being there with me when my father passed away. Thank you," I say softly but sincerely.

Nancy's eyes soften and then she gives me a warm, quick hug. "You don't need to thank me, Flora. I'm just glad I could be there for you. I'll always be there for you. Please don't take this the wrong way, Flora. I know I could never replace your mother. I'm too old to have a child, now. But...I see you like a daughter."

Nancy's words melt my heart and nearly bring tears to my eyes. I give her a big hug and don't say a word. She's right—no one could ever replace my mother. But I did see her as a mother figure. I know my mother is looking down, proud of Nancy.

Dax and Lyka pull up in the Land Rover, the headlights shining bright on Nancy and me.

"I'll see you next week, Flora," Nancy says, walking to her car.

Dax gets out of the car and holds the door open for me. "Are you ready to go home?" he asks.

I plant a quick kiss on his cheek and jump into the passenger's side, kissing Lyka.

We drive down country roads heading back to the cabin. Dax is behind the wheel and Lyka sits in the passenger seat beside me.

I scoot a little in my seat. "You know," I say, flirting, "it's been a long time since we used the hot tub."

"Hmm." Dax sounds contemplative, keeping his eyes fixed on the road.

I spread my legs apart. The fabric of my skirt moves, giving Dax and Lyka a fleeting glimpse of what I intend to do. I begin to rub myself over my panties gently.

Lyka chews his bottom lip as his gaze stays on me. "You're being very naughty tonight," Lyka groans.

"Maybe..." I whisper.

I move my panties to the side, putting my pussy on display. I start rubbing my clit and let out little moans.

"Fuck," Lyka exhales.

"Don't make me pull over this car and fuck you," Dax warns, gripping the wheel tightly.

Lyka puts his fingers to his mouth and licks them. He then moves them down to my pussy and starts circling my clit.

"I've been thinking about you two all day," I say out of breath as Lyka fingers me.

"Ugh. We're nearly back at the cabin. I'm so fucking hard," Dax complains.

I reach over and feel Dax's erection, rubbing it over his jeans. Lyka continues to rub my clit as it swells under his fingers.

"Lyka..." I moan, biting my bottom lip and pressing my head back into the seat. Two fingers quickly enter my pussy and I can't help but thrust my hips into his hand.

"You look so fucking pretty grinding up against my hand."

He continues to push his fingers in and out. I moan, unable to keep back my sounds. Dax breathes deeply and tries to keep focusing on the road.

Dax suddenly yanks the car off onto the side of the dark road. The headlights cast an eerie light on the trees. "I can't listen to you moan any longer. Get on my fucking lap now," he orders.

Lyka's fingers stop abruptly, leaving me feeling breathless. I turn to him and he nods, giving me the silent encouragement I need.

With my panties still pushed to the side, I straddle Dax, feeling the hardness of his cock pressed against me. I ease over him, my hands bracing on his broad shoulders.

Dax grips my hips as I take out his cock. "That's it, flower," he growls, guiding me down on his cock.

I begin to move, my hips rolling as Dax matches with his thrusts. The sensation of his cock inside me is overwhelming. His hands move down to my ass and grip tight, guiding and encouraging me to move faster and harder.

Lyka's hands move to unbutton his own pants, his eyes

never leaving mine. He pulls down his pants and lets out his rock-hard cock. The mere sight makes my pulse race.

He takes one of my hands and places it on his throbbing shaft. His cock against my palm is so hot and exciting. I start working my hand along his shaft while bouncing up and down on Dax. He throws back his head and lets out a moan. The car's windows quickly steam up. All I can hear is moans, gasps, and slaps of skin against skin.

"You're gonna keep fucking me while I drive to the cabin," Dax says out of breath.

The car surges forward as we climb the road to the cabin. The headlights cut through the blackness and light up the way as the cabin nears. Dax peers his head over my shoulder as I bounce on his cock, taking hold of the steering wheel. Every bump on the road on the way to the cabin makes his cock hit my cervix. The bumps cause my hand to spastically jerk up and down on Lyka's cock, making him moan louder and louder.

The car jerks slightly as Dax pulls up to the cabin, gravel crunching under the tires. Dax pulls his cock out of me and I climb back into the passenger seat.

Dax jumps out of the car and runs toward the hot tub to get it ready for us.

Lyka pulls me from the car and pushes me against the side. He nudges my legs open and drops to his knees, his fingers finding their way back into me quickly. The sudden, quick rhythm makes my head fall back against the car, a moan escaping my lips. Lyka's tongue flicks out onto my clit as his fingers pulsate inside me. The feelings are too much, I can't keep quiet. My hands instinctively go down to hold his head in place, my fingers tangling in his hair.

I can only glance down enough to see him as his eyes are closed with concentration, his tongue and fingers working masterfully to maximize the pleasure he renders. His touch is intense—my legs tremble and I press harder against the car for support.

"Fucking...hell," I moan out.

He lets out a deep chuckle against my clit and stops licking. He stands from his knees, his fingers pulling out of me, leaving me aching for more.

Dax comes bounding over, overly excited. He grips my hand and leads me over to the hot tub. The three of us stand there, and without hesitation, we undress.

As the last piece of clothing drops away, we stand together in our naked forms, shimmering in the moonlight.

We pause for a moment to examine each other as our eyes trace the branding scars on our bodies, our testimony to the past and the unbreakable union between us. Dax stalks toward me, laying a firm hand behind my neck, forcing me closer. "Who owns you?" he asks.

I don't say anything and smirk.

"Don't make us get the wooden toys out," Lyka warns.

Fear and submission mix within me, causing my heart to race. "You do. You both do," I reply, my voice no louder than a whisper.

"That's our girl," Lyka says, the approval and satisfaction evident in his tone. He walks forward and gives my ass a sharp slap.

We step into the hot tub and I feel the warm water on my skin.

"Sit on the edge," Dax demands.

I perch on the edge and watch Dax and Lyka stand in the water. They look like gods, their muscles tightening, their presence oozing dominance.

"Now, spread your legs," Lyka orders.

I immediately obey, spreading my legs wide as my pussy lips part from them.

"We're so lucky...Look at that beautiful pussy," Dax says.

Their mouths almost salivate as they kneel in the water, hunger written into their eyes as they move towards me. As they approach, I can feel their breaths along the inside of my thighs.

They both open their mouths, tongues darting each side of my clit, working in perfect synchronization. My legs start to tremble underneath me, barely capable of holding me up as their tongues work against my clit. Now and then, their touches overlap, but neither of them care, completely focused on making me orgasm.

Finally, I set the palms of my hands on the tops of their heads, my fingers threading through their hair, holding them to me.

"I'm gonna..." I moan.

Their tongues quicken, their tempo increasing with every passing second. They tease and flick my clit. It gets nearly unbearable as my clit aches. I feel my climax building like a big wave of pleasure rising inside me. I orgasm and yell, my voice traveling through the forest. I clench my hand on their heads, pulling their hair. My whole body tenses and jerks.

I let go of the hold on their heads, and as I do, I see their lips glisten with my juices and each other's saliva.

Lyka comes between my legs; his eyes have turned dark with lust. He quickly picks me up and places his cock at the entrance of my pussy.

One strong push and he's inside me. My hands clutch at his shoulders as I try to steady myself, still trembling from my orgasm.

Suddenly, it starts pouring down rain. The raindrops are cool against our heated skin. Lyka pulls me in close as his lips touch mine. There's something romantic about being kissed in the rain.

Dax looks at us with hunger and admiration on his face. "Let's take this inside," he says suggestively.

As the rain pours down on us, Lyka somehow manages to climb out of the hot tub with himself still inside me. His strong arms wrap tight around me as he carries me toward the cabin. Dax quickly opens the door for us as we walk through the cabin. I can feel Lyka's cock thrusting in me as he walks.

We come to the bedroom and he drops me onto the bed. I look up at their wet, towering bodies above me. Their faces show desire, but mainly dominance.

"Do you want both of us in your pussy, flower?" Dax asks.

I bite my bottom lip and nod my head.

Lyka spits into his palm and begins to rub his cock. The wet, sliding sound of his hand moving up and down his length fills the room. He slides down on the bed.

I straddle him, my legs sliding to either side of his hips. I position myself over his cock, and as I start to sink into him, the head settles at my entrance. I lean down to press my bare breasts into his chest. My nipples brush against his skin, shooting tiny shocks of pleasure through me.

I hear Dax shuffling on the bed. I hear him spit and I get excited. I look over my shoulder back to him and see him preparing himself, his eyes glued to the sight of Lyka's cock buried inside me. Dax's breath grows heavy as he prepares himself. His cock is hard and ready. He gets into position at my entrance.

He flattens his body against my back, clasps my hands over my shoulders, and thrusts into me. I let out a loud whine as they both stretch my pussy.

Lyka's cock thrusts inside me from below at the same time as Dax's thrusts inside me from behind. Our moans and wet sounds fill the room as our bodies move together.

They both ram into me hard, over and over. Their motions

are ruthless. My body starts to lose itself in the forcibly intense moment.

"Her pussy is just begging to be filled," Dax groans.

"She's gonna take every drop of our cum," Lyka says, out of breath.

His strong arms hold me close as his hands gently caress my back. They move in perfect harmony with each other, their thrusts timed perfectly. I feel their cocks pulsing inside me, their climaxes building powerful with each of the thrusts.

As they come, I can feel the throbs of their cocks. Pulsing inside me, their cum mingles with my juices.

Dax withdraws his cock from me with a satisfied groan. His body moves slowly as if it doesn't want to leave my pussy, and then falls beside us on the bed.

I'm on top of Lyka and my body feels like jelly, but oh so good. His strong arms surround me, holding me close as I rest against his chest.

"The power we have over you. You'll always belong to us, Flora Faulkner," Dax whispers.

"Always," Lyka adds.

In their embrace, I feel a safety and belonging that no other men could ever offer. Despite everything that happened, I belong to them. I wasn't Flora Lockley anymore, I am Flora Faulkner. Their ownership of me is not a shackle, but a source of security and meaning. My dark thoughts and loneliness disappear when I'm with them.

And I finally feel peace.

ACKNOWLEDGMENTS

Readers

I appreciate you dedicating your time to reading my book. Thank you for your continued support and for allowing me to share my passion for writing with you. I hope you enjoyed the read as much as I enjoyed writing it.

I cried writing the ending. Did you?

English Proper Editing & Disturbed Valkyrie Designs

The women, the myths, the legends. I can't thank you two enough for putting up with me. You go above and beyond each time. Your professionalism and expertise are impressive, and I couldn't have accomplished this without your support. I feel fortunate to have had the opportunity to work with both of you. I am looking forward to collaborating with you again in the future.

My dream team!

P.S. Please never leave me. Thanks.

SAV & YANA

Thank you so much for reading the book chapter by chapter as I wrote it.

Your unwavering support has been incredible.

Beta & ARC Readers

My loves!

I couldn't have done it without your encouragement and motivation.
I feel so fortunate to have you on my team. Thank you from the bottom of my heart.
You mean the world to me.

Callum & Maddie
Thank both of you for being my constant support and helping me.
I feel so fortunate to have you on my team.
You're both such strong people.

Rachel
I'm sorry for accidentally spitting Cola on you.
You're stuck with me for life. I love you. Blah, blah, blah.

Daisy
I love you.

GET IN CONTACT

Jade always enjoys hearing from her readers. If you would like to get in touch with her, you can find her on social media platforms. Alternatively, you can also reach out to her through email at jadewauthor@gmail.com

tiktok.com/@jadewbook
instrgram.com/jadewbook
www.jadewilkesauthor.com

Made in the USA
Monee, IL
16 October 2024

68080928R00192